The Thing
About Jane Spring

This Large Print Book carries the
Seal of Approval of N.A.V.H.

The Thing About About Jane Spring

Sharon Krum

WHEELER
PUBLISHING

Published in 2005 by arrangement with Viking Penguin, a member of Penguin Group (USA) Inc.

Wheeler Large Print Hardcover.

The text of this Large Print edition is unabridged.
Other aspects of the book may vary from the original edition.

Set in 16 pt. Plantin.

Printed in the United States on permanent paper.

Library of Congress Cataloging-in-Publication Data

Krum, Sharon.
    The thing about Jane Spring / by Sharon Krum.
       p. cm. — (Wheeler Publishing large print Wheeler hardcover)
    ISBN 1-59722-085-X (lg. print : hc : alk. paper) ✔
    1. Single women — Fiction. 2. Self-realization — Fiction. 3. New York (N.Y.) — Fiction 4. Large type books. I. Title. II. Wheeler large print hardcover series.
PR9619.3.K78T48 2005b
  823′.92—dc22   2005016647

In memory of Joseph Krum

As the Founder/CEO of NAVH, the only national health agency solely devoted to those who, although not totally blind, have an eye disease which could lead to serious visual impairment, I am pleased to recognize Thorndike Press* as one of the leading publishers in the large print field.

Founded in 1954 in San Francisco to prepare large print textbooks for partially seeing children, NAVH became the pioneer and standard setting agency in the preparation of large type.

Today, those publishers who meet our standards carry the prestigious "Seal of Approval" indicating high quality large print. We are delighted that Thorndike Press is one of the publishers whose titles meet these standards. We are also pleased to recognize the significant contribution Thorndike Press is making in this important and growing field.

Lorraine H. Marchi, L.H.D.
Founder/CEO
NAVH

* Thorndike Press encompasses the following imprints: Thorndike, Wheeler, Walker and Large Print Press.

Acknowledgments

Deepest thanks to Jane Von Mehren and Brett Kelly for their brilliant editing, insights and support in bringing the book to life.

Gratitude to my agent Barbara J. Zitwer for her unstinting belief in my stories and patience in waiting for them to come to fruition.

Thanks to my family, Paula Krum, Henry Krum, Lauren Berkowitz, Joshua and Emily, for the love and encouragement.

For their friendship and cheering from the sidelines, thanks to Cindy Berg, Pamela Haber, John Romais, Suzanne Miller-Farrell, Denise Sadique, Sandra Lee, Roslyn Harari, Jo McKenna, Kim Huey-Steiner, Norman Steiner, Lesley Jackson, Daria McGauran, Lynne Cossar, Patrice Murphy, Stephen Petri, Clare Longrigg, Lambeth Hochwald and Susan Oren.

And last but not least, thanks to Robert Schuette for the legal advice.

Prologue

When you have a certain name, and you look a certain way, people are going to assume certain things about you. If this sounds unfair, it is, this presuming to know what makes a person tick from one glance across a crowded room, one nervous introduction. But that's how we are — all of us, prisoners of human nature, labeling strangers at first sight, boxing them up with ribbon — all so we can keep the element of surprise in check. I already know who you are. You can try, but you can't fool me.

So when people met Jane Spring for the first time, it never took long for their imaginations to take wing. Just hearing her name conjured up blooming flowers and rolling lawns, woodland nymphs and sweet lambs frolicking. Spring was a nice name, soft and comforting, the sound of someone you would like to meet. And then there was Jane herself. The package that came with that feel-good name.

Men saw a tall dirty blonde with the legs of a racehorse and a button nose they imagined stroking after sex. They saw the somber black suit that all but hid her figure, the hair gathered in a tight ponytail at the nape of her neck, the piercing eyes framed by thick black glasses, and the face that barely smiled, but hardly worried.

They had watched enough old movies where the boss's plain, dependable secretary pulls the pins out of her hair and the glasses off her nose to reveal a bombshell underneath to know who they were dealing with. They were sure, because men are always sure about these things, that she was that very sort of creature, the kitten with the tiger inside. They were also sure it would take a special kind of man to unleash the tiger, a man, not incidentally, just like them. And so men loved the idea of Jane Spring.

Women too. Amazingly. Sitting across from her in a subway car, standing behind her at the supermarket checkout, they knew Jane Spring the minute they laid eyes on her. They had all gone to school with her, hadn't they? The lanky girl already so tall in eighth grade that she stooped around everyone, especially boys; the girl who didn't smoke or drink, who read at recess and took first place at the science fair. And they knew that women like her never really outgrew their awkwardness, that she was probably still deeply shy and insecure, and clearly hadn't any fashion sense. And so they still pitied her, even though now she was no longer a child.

But there was something else. At school they had ignored her, but now they embraced her. The shapeless black pantsuit, that face without a stitch of makeup, the flat shoes and that big ugly diver's watch on her left hand — they saw it all and thought, hell, no competition here. I could be friends with you, Jane.

But the thing about Jane Spring was that she was nothing like the fantasies anyone built around her. She was neither the playful sex kitten men presumed her to be nor the pathologically shy and unsure girl women needed her to be. Being neither of these people was a circumstance that was at once her finest asset and greatest curse.

At close range it always marked her undoing. The consequences hurt. At long range, it was a beautiful thing. If people didn't get too close, hear too much, they could stay fixed in their fantasies of Jane as long as their hearts desired. It was fascinating how people worked to dissect and distill Jane Spring, given that she never cared to return the favor.

Then again, once you met her, you really couldn't blame them.

1

Jane Spring made a sharp two-inch incision into her steak and smiled broadly as she watched blood pool, then run all over her plate. Perfect. Just the way she liked it. She hacked off a piece and dropped it into her mouth, ignoring the waiter who refilled her wineglass. Her date tried not to stare; he knew the correct thing was to keep the conversation going. But the way she relished each bite, the groans of satisfaction emanating from her throat, he couldn't take his eyes off her.

He wondered what she would be like in bed.

"How's your food?" he asked, knowing full well people in the building next door likely knew the answer. He wished he had brought a video camera. No one would believe him when he recounted the scenario for his colleagues the next day.

"Excellent. I always say you can't beat raw meat," she said, starting in on the bone. She gnawed at it as if she had a car double-parked. "I see you don't have the stomach for it," Jane muttered, pointing her knife at his half-eaten meal. "Are you going to finish that?"

"You want my — ?" he asked, incredulous.

"Well, can't let good food go to waste," she reasoned. "Come on, pass your plate."

He had met her only days before, and then only for a few minutes. He was new in the office, and his electronic keycard was giving him trouble. Jane watched him swipe unsuccessfully, then pushed him aside and did the honors. He thanked her, then apologized for holding her up. First week, he had explained, all the kinks were yet to be ironed out. He would speak to the security office that afternoon. Jane shook her head, her eyes narrowed like slits. "It's a start," she had said dismissively and brushed past him.

She wasn't exactly Welcome Wagon, but there was something about her that transfixed him all the same. Stealing a glance as she had hurried down the hall, he took in the blond hair, the long legs, the icy stare and the button nose, and he, like a slew of suitors before him, wanted her. The glacial facade, he was certain, was just that. Underneath lay another woman altogether, one he was curious to know, and eventually undress.

And so that afternoon he had called to thank her again, and asked her out.

So now here they were. As the waiter cleared their table, Jane leaned back, folded her arms and looked him up and down.

"That's a very smart suit. Nice line on the shoulder," she declared. "Frankly, I see so few men today who understand the connection between appearance and integrity. It's nice to see. Well done."

He raised his hand to his lapel. His chest puffed out. The first point was on the board. He beamed at Jane, then made a mental note to buy more suits just like it.

"Well, thank you, Jane. And might I also say you, too, look most lovely this evening." Though, to be honest, he was surprised she hadn't dressed for dinner. When she'd entered the restaurant, she looked exactly as she had the day they'd met — somewhat morbid black suit pants and matching blazer, white shirt, flat clunky shoes, diver's watch, no makeup and her hair tied back in a ponytail. He scanned the room, taking note of the other women there, all painted faces and tight dresses, tottering to the bathroom on six-inch heels. Not Jane. She was all business.

It almost made him want her more.

Jane took a sip of wine; he followed her lead. The waiter appeared and handed them dessert menus. Relieved, he opened his and pretended to read, buying time to consider his next move.

Their conversation up until that point had consisted of the usual first-date fail-safes — weather, college, hometown — now it was time to move into second gear. Should he bring up work? Past experience had taught him it was unwise to talk shop with a fellow attorney on a date. The potential for the conversation to disintegrate into gossip, or worse, bring out professional rivalries, was too great. And if Jane Spring's courtroom tactics were only half as bloody as her steak, he'd rather not go there just now.

Jane Spring also buried herself in her menu, but she was hardly worried about what she might say next. She knew. Jane firmly believed that without planning there is no success. Whether you were prosecuting a murder trial or having dinner à deux, you couldn't leave a thing to chance. In fact when it came to the latter, it was imperative you didn't. Although the male species was hardly a complicated beast, thoughtful preparation never hurt.

Casually slipping her right hand into her pants pocket, Jane pulled out a small piece of paper and rested it on her knee. On it was a handwritten list of topics in neat cursive.

Conversation Topics for Dinner:

- Assault weapons ban. Time to repeal?
- President's new tax plan. Good or bad?
- Current state of the military
- Decline in public morality
- Movies

Jane scanned the list surreptitiously and then silently congratulated herself on preparing such fun talking points. There was something here for everybody, from the serious to the slight. Jane kept one eye on the menu and the other on her knee. It's probably better to start with something simple and move up to the good stuff, she thought. The last time she'd started with a call for more guns on the street, the date had ended rather abruptly. Pacifists. They're so volatile.

Jane put down her menu and rested her hands on the table. Better to be safe than sorry, she thought. Tax reform it is. But before she could bring it up he started his own conversation.

17

"Don't you just love this time of year? I just can't wait for Christmas." He beamed.

"Really?" she said, feigning interest.

"I love the holidays. Everything about them," he said wide-eyed. "All those street vendors roasting chestnuts on an open fire, the decorations lighting up the city, the kids ice-skating at Wollman Rink and caroling in the streets. I used to carol, actually. When I was small. I had a little red cape with a white collar and everything."

He sat back and smiled. Women love that story. Gets them every time.

Jane raised her eyebrows. "So . . . you would dress up like a little girl and sing to strangers?" she said, perplexed.

"Well, I —"

"Are you like some kind of sentimental new-age man who takes yoga and bakes bread and cries after sex?"

"You sound like you don't approve of such men," he kidded her. She was joking, right?

"I don't approve or disapprove. I was just making an observation. My father taught me it's important to study all the strengths and weaknesses of your opponent before you go into battle. So I was just making my assessment," she said earnestly. Jane leaned forward. "And to answer your question, no, I don't love this time of year. I loathe this time of year. It's two months of blatant commercialism and sickly sweet, manufactured goodwill; canned music; gaudy lighting; tinsel — the whole world seems to become some enormous shopping mall mobbed with rude people exhibiting total lack of self-control. It's absolutely disgraceful."

Unbelievable. She had to be kidding.

"I agree to some extent, but I guess what I hold on to was how magical it was for me as a child. Please tell me that you at least believed in Santa Claus at least when you were young?"

Again, Jane shook her head. A few strands of hair fell across her face. "Please. Didn't you find it strange there was one on every street corner? I knew he was a fraud."

His eyes dilated. "The tooth fairy?"

Jane snorted. "Absolutely not. Nothing but a creation by coddling parents to placate children too undisciplined to deal with losing a tooth. When my teeth fell out, I threw them in the trash and just got on with it. I mean really, hiding them under your pillow for some flying leprechaun to collect in the dead of night? It's preposterous."

Whoa! She was something. Like a monster.

A monster with great legs. He needed air.

He excused himself to the bathroom; in his absence Jane sat back and surveyed the room. There were a number of other women there pushing thirty, or just past it, all about her age and also clearly on dates. It was par for the course; the place was known for its alleged romantic ambiance. It had that deliberately shabby furniture that was all the rage: chipping paint and deflated, threadbare velvet seat cushions. The food was served on china that didn't match. The theme was a decaying country house, a notion men seemed to think conducive to intimacy. Jane thought the place looked like some circa 1862 tavern after the Union Army had sacked it.

Her eyes narrowed, her frown lines knitting in disgust. The women in question had all ordered salads, and Jane watched as they pushed lettuce leaves around their plates with mismatched utensils, never taking a bite. This rudeness, however, was a minor infraction compared to the ridiculous way they cocked their heads, flipped their hair, laughed at every silly joke — all the while dressed like hookers on the West Side Highway. When will they learn that men are not turned on by such transparent, disingenuous behavior?

Her date returned to their table. Jane glanced down at her list again. *Decline in public morality* or *Movies?* Well, she chortled to herself, same thing, really.

"So, tell me," Jane announced, startling him. He was starting to see now how she wanted this to play out. Not so much a conversation as a cross-examination with a side of steak. "Seen any good movies lately?" Men liked to talk about movies; she had once read it made them feel culturally sophisticated.

His eyes sailed to the ceiling and he thought for a minute. Does he answer truthfully and risk another slap on the wrist? What might she call him now? No, he would play it safe. Try to sound sophisticated but still stick with the herd.

"Switching jobs lately, I haven't had time. But one movie I do want to see is *L'amour Rouge.* You know, the French film that won at Cannes."

"Oh yes. The one with all the sex." Jane groaned. "Trust the French."

"Don't tell me you don't approve of sex either."

Jane laughed. "Hardly. But I have zero tolerance for the way it's portrayed on screen. I assume you've noticed that whenever a couple go at it in the movies, ten minutes

21

later *she* is *soooo* satisfied." Jane rolled her head around her neck like a bobble doll. "Just once I'd like to see a movie where the woman doesn't climax. Wouldn't you?"

Oy vey.

"You know, when a man doesn't do it for me, I tell him," she said proudly.

"What?"

"I tell him. Right there on the pillow. And you know something? He appreciates it. They all do. How else are they going to improve? Say we go back to my place later and it turns out you're a total disaster in bed. Wouldn't you value some feedback to correct your game?"

"Feedback? In bed? From you?"

He had to get out of here. This was now officially the date from hell.

The waiter appeared ringside. "Well, what have we decided?"

"Just the che—"

"I'd like a piece of your Death-by-Chocolate Cake," Jane said.

The waiter brought her a piece from the nearby dessert cart, and they watched with astonishment as she tore into three layers of chocolate pastry cemented with chocolate ganache and shaved truffles. They weren't alone. Every female in the room suddenly turned to observe Jane Spring. Such a rarity in New York: a woman partaking of cake. It was like watching a moon landing. Jane spooned cake into her mouth while eyeing her list one last time. She would bring up the tax code, or maybe the military, when he walked her home. Yes, definitely the tax code.

He maniacally pulled out his credit card and slipped it into the billfold. Plate cleaned, Jane leaned over the table and grinned broadly at him.

"Well, I had a great time. Thank you. So when should we do this again?" She pulled her diary out of her bag and opened it. "How about Monday?"

"Monday?"

His head nearly snapped off his neck. It was almost surreal. Had they even been on the same date?

"You're busy?"

"No. Yes. I mean no. I . . . to be honest, I don't think it would be a good idea. For us to do this again."

"You're . . . breaking up with me?" she said, her face frozen in confusion.

"Breaking up? We can't break up, Jane. This is our first date."

"I don't understand," she said, puzzled. "Frankly, I thought we were getting along so well."

He tried desperately to hide his disbelief. "Jane. My God. Please. In the space of an hour you have done nothing but rant and rave, attack my manhood, infer that I might be bad in bed — which I'm not, by the way —"

"I did not attack you. I would never do that," she said stunned by the accusation. "I was just making conversation. I thought we were having an open and honest discussion."

"Jane, I'm not going to see you Monday," he said firmly.

"Is it the film? That French film? If you really have your heart set on it, fine, I'll go. Even though I'm warning you, all the women are faking —"

"Jane, this has nothing to do with the film!" he said, now lowering his voice, aware they might be being watched.

"Fine. Not a problem," she said, waving her hand. "I have to go the bathroom. Excuse me," she said rising from her chair. He watched as she walked across the room — head high, eyes forward, stride as confident as they come.

In the bathroom Jane Spring stepped into a stall and closed the door. She pulled down the toilet lid and sat. She tried to stop them coming, taking deep breaths to hold them at bay, but nothing worked. The tears. First little sobs, which she mopped up with toilet paper, then bigger sobs, then, finally, the flood.

She slapped the wall with one hand while wiping her running nose with the other.

Why does this keep happening to me?

"Jane, I'm not going to see you Monday." Or ever again, actually. Because that's what he meant. Because that's what they all mean.

She didn't understand it. She was a good person, wasn't she? Honest, moral, efficient. She had thought herself highly conversational that night. She had acted interested, asked highly topical, well-prepared questions, gave scrupulously honest answers to everything he'd asked. What was it then?

She just wanted one man to stick around. To want her. Why was this such an impossible task? And she really quite liked this one.

Jane emerged from the stall and stared at herself in the bathroom mirror. "Good God, Jane," she shouted, slapping her face. "Pull yourself together, girl."

Jane Spring felt disgusted with herself for crying, for giving in to her emotions. It was, as her father would say, weak, disobedient, conduct unbecoming to a soldier.

A good soldier never cries, he'd always drilled her. God knows that if General Edward Spring had witnessed that little breakdown, Jane would be facedown on the cold tiles doing push-ups right then.

Chin up, woman, he echoed inside her head. *Get back out there this instant and show them you are not afraid.*

Jane lengthened her neck, straightened her back and walked briskly back to her table. She wouldn't give her date the satisfaction of thinking anything was wrong.

"Ready?" he asked.

He looked at Jane and his stomach sank. Her eyes were red; her face had lost all of its steel.

"You don't find me attractive, do you?" she said softly. She knew men considered looks very high on their lists.

"What?" he squealed, incredulous. He looked around, hoping no one had heard.

"That's why you don't want to see me again."

"No, Jane . . ."

"No?"

"I meant, no, that's not it. You're very attractive."

"So what is it then?"

"Jane, you're . . ."

"What?"

"You don't know?"

And that, in a nutshell was Jane Spring's biggest problem.

That she didn't know.

2

Jane Spring rose from behind the prosecution table and pursed her lips in an effort to conceal a smile. In her entire career as an assistant district attorney for the City of New York, she could remember few cases as easy as this one. And hadn't it been? A child could prosecute it, she had boasted to colleagues. Who couldn't miss how eagerly the bank manager had testified that more than one million dollars had disappeared from the account of his customer, one Gloria Markham?

Who didn't believe beyond a reasonable doubt the fine upstanding lawyer who had detailed preparing documents giving the defendant, one James Markham, access to Mrs. Markham's finances following their, ahem, curious marriage. (His words.) And those witnesses had merely functioned as Jane's soup and her salad. Now the mouthwatering entrée had arrived at the table, more than eager, Jane knew, to give the jury a meal they would never forget.

"Mrs. Markham, you met the defendant

at a charity ball, correct?" Jane said, rising from behind the prosecution table and moving toward the witness box.

Gloria Markham was what the French called a woman of a certain age, what Americans called a Park Avenue matron and what Jane privately thought a first-class fool. She was wearing a floral wool suit with huge gold buttons, looking less as if she'd dressed that morning than been upholstered. The old lady's silver hair had been sprayed into crash-helmet formation, and a bad hip caused her to lean to the left, forcing her to use a cane carved like a swan for support.

"I did," Mrs. Markham responded, looking directly at the jury.

"And would it also be correct to say that your subsequent marriage a mere three months later raised eyebrows among your peers? Let the record show the witness is — well, discretion forbids me to reveal her age — thirty-five years older than her husband. True?"

The jury tittered.

"But —"

"But you loved him. And he loved you. And what's the problem marrying someone as young as your son when you're in love, you want to say?"

"Precisely."

Excellent, she thought. Things were going much as they'd rehearsed the week before. Jane noted that Mrs. Markham had some trouble looking her in the eye, but she put this down to nerves. The jury, however, had no such trouble. They found themselves becoming fixated on the blond prosecutor in the black suit and diver's watch; actually, she interested them more than the trial. The case to them was already clear: the young man at the defense table had fleeced the older woman dressed like a sofa. But that prosecutor — who and what really lie behind those rectangular glasses and inscrutable stare? — now that was a mystery worth unraveling.

Jane walked toward the jury box and leaned against the railing. A frisson buzzed through the jurors. This was the closest they had ever come to her.

"Mrs. Markham, is it true that the day before your wedding you gave the defendant full access to your bank accounts?"

"Yes, so he could help me with my finances."

Jane flashed the jury a broad grin. "And how did he 'help' her, ladies and gentlemen? Three days after they married he withdrew all her money and vanished. Correct, Mrs. Markham?"

"No," the matron said firmly, tapping her cane on the floor. "That's not correct."

"Excuse me?" Jane barked. "What did you say?" Then, out of the corner of her eye she saw the defendant blow Mrs. Markham a kiss.

"I said no, James didn't steal anything from me. He loves me. This is all a mistake. I allowed him to withdraw the money for a business deal. I knew all about it."

Jane Spring's eyes narrowed. She cocked her head and thrust out her lower jaw in disbelief. How dare this deceitful matron cross her? Jane knew she should not have been surprised. This was her perennial complaint about working among civilians: their complete lack of honor. Commitment meant nothing if a better offer came along. This insubordination must be punished.

"Permission to treat as hostile?" Jane asked the judge.

"Permission granted."

"Mrs. Markham, you just testified that your thirty-five-year-old husband married you purely for love. Tell me, I'm curious. Do you also believe Elvis is alive?"

The jurors exchanged glances.

"Objection, badgering," came a voice from the defense table.

"Withdrawn," said Jane.

"This is all a terrible mistake. He never . . ."

"Mrs. Markham, you do understand you are under oath?"

"What?"

"Don't 'What?' me," Jane snapped, lunging into the witness box. She placed a thumb and bent forefinger under Mrs. Markham's chin, a favored technique of drill instructors keeping recruits in line.

"Objection!" came a cry from the defense table.

"An oath is a promise to tell the truth," she declared, boring into the matron's eyes while holding her head in position. "Breaking that oath will put you in jail."

"Ms. Spring, step away from the witness," instructed the judge. "Now."

Jane released her hand and moved back. A petrified Mrs. Markham rubbed her chin. "If you think I am afraid of putting a sick elderly woman behind bars, think again, madam. It will be my pleasure. I just hope you brought your toothbrush," she said, staring the old crow dead in the eye.

Jane then spun around to the jury and folded her arms. I'm sure you're all as disgusted as I am, her knowing glance said. She could just about see in their eyes when suddenly they all seemed distracted by something going on behind her on the witness stand. It seemed Mrs. Markham had started whimpering. The judge passed her a tissue. The faces of the jury puckered with concern. Jane groaned.

"Bailiff, a violin please," she jested, but there were no accordant snickers. Instead, Gloria Markham started to hyperventilate. The court officers rushed to her side, but before they could reach her, she closed her eyes and fell back in her chair. Her cane hit the floor. The jury let out a collective gasp.

Jane Spring would have none of it.

"Oh, well done, Mrs. Markham. Bravo. I do love the theater, although normally I prefer Broadway. Fine, you've made your point; the jury has your sympathy, and you can open your eyes now."

But Gloria Markham did not open her eyes. The judge banged his gavel to quiet the growing banter.

"Can somebody please call a doctor."

Later in the deliberation room, the six men and six women chosen to decide the fate of the defendant were outraged. Not by Mrs. Markham's perjury, but by their own lack of judgment. How could they have been so wrong about Jane Spring? The prosecutor had fooled them all with her black-rimmed glasses and her opaque stare. But there was no sexy secretary or shy schoolgirl there, just a heartless woman in a bad suit who didn't know how to accessorize and who had bullied an elderly woman because she chose to protect the man she loves. But instead of taking the high road, she had threatened her until she fainted.

Just terrible.

And how dare she? How dare she suggest to be one person and turn out to be another?

Sitting in her office waiting for the Markham verdict, Jane Spring smiled and hummed to herself while returning e-mail that had piled up in her absence. She knew the jury was impressed by her challenging that reprehensible, mendacious matron. Of course they realized Mrs. Markham's faint was quite plainly an admission she was guilty of perjury. And the paramedics reviving her on the courtroom floor like that, well, it only made Mrs. Markham seem even *less* dignified. She had it in the bag.

Or so she thought. When the jury came back after three hours of deliberation and delivered an acquittal, Jane Spring didn't so much sit down on her chair as fall back into it. The evidence was clear as day. He married her, then disappeared with her money. How could they acquit?

Then Jane understood. They knew he was a con artist but freed him because the old broad loved him. They didn't want her to be alone. Juries sometimes went with their hearts. She had seen it before. Made her sick every time.

Defense lawyer John Gillespie strolled over to Jane, wearing a grin so wide you could see his tonsils. This man, who had no case — none! — had just been declared the victor. Jane almost gagged. She hadn't only lost, she had lost to Gillespie. She loathed him. That obsequious, conniving, hypocritical windbag. For chrissakes the man consorted with so many gangsters and lowlifes he practically was one. Jane gathered up her papers and ignored him.

"Nice work with your star witness, Jane. What's your technique next week? Putting them in the stocks and pelting them with rotten fruit?"

"You know what happened and so do I. They just felt sorry for her. But I know that you know that I am nowhere near finished with your client, Mr. Gillespie. I'll appeal."

But did Jane Spring really know what

had happened? the sitting judge wondered. No question she had presented a strong case. But the judge, who had watched a number of Jane Spring prosecutions — each one masterful, ambitious, scathing — knew the one thing Jane Spring still had yet to learn. Sometimes she could be her own worst enemy.

3

Susan knew her boss had lost even before she laid eyes on her. She could tell just from the sound of Jane's walking from the elevator to her office. Normally, Jane's stride was so fast Susan had to jog alongside to keep up with her. No easy feat when you're wearing stiletto lace-up boots. But now Jane was doing something resembling a slow goose-step, which Susan knew only happened when Miss Spring was really mad, which meant the verdict hadn't gone her way.

Susan listened as the shoes that normally skidded by her now landed with a decided heaviness at one-second intervals. Left. Right. Left. Right. Susan heard them coming closer, and then suddenly they were standing before her.

"We lost."

"Sorry."

"Morons! All of them! I laid out so much evidence a blind man swimming in a dark lake at midnight could have seen it. That matron made a mockery of the judicial system, Susan."

"Yes, Miss Sp-Ring."

Jane kicked open the door to her office and entered. Susan exhaled. That wasn't bad, she thought, compared to what Miss Spring could dole out when she was in one of her moods. Once, after she lost a trial, she had berated Susan for fifteen minutes about how she enunciated, or rather didn't enunciate, the English language.

"We don't *ax* witnesses if they need a police escort to court, Susan. Beheading is illegal, not to mention painful, I believe. We *ask* people, thank you," Jane had snapped.

Susan couldn't believe the six months she had spent in the employ of Jane Spring in the Criminal Trial Division already felt like six years. She wasn't exactly in love with her old boss in the Civil Division — that arrogant shit who had never learned her name, calling her Sally, Cindy or Sandy depending on the day — but at least she could listen to her iPod, read the *National Enquirer*, play online poker and paint her nails, and he didn't seem to care. If he did, he certainly never delivered a lecture about it. Not like Miss Spring. Oh, she loved lectures. And pronouncements. Gave them at the drop of a hat.

Susan, this is not a disco. There will

be no more tight pants, thank you.

I won't have you reading those ridiculous magazines at your desk, Susan.

The blue nail polish? I expect it gone by tomorrow, Susan.

The gum, Susan. Throw out the gum. We don't answer the phone with gum in our mouths.

Susan, I am not running a casino. You will not play that card game on your computer during working hours.

Susan, we chew our food, not our sentences. Please speak clearly.

Put that contraption away, Susan. We don't listen to music while we work.

I'm thrilled you have friends here, Susan, but lingering by their desks when you have typing pending is insubordinate. It will stop now, thank you.

Man, that Spring chick needed to get that stick out of her ass and get a life, thought Susan every time.

Jane Spring searched her desk for a pile of message slips. She didn't see any. Impossible, she thought, I've been gone six hours, yet also completely possible with Lazy Susan working the phones. That's what she had dubbed her secretary, Susan

Bonfiglio. *Lazy Susan.* Privately, of course. She never complained to the other lawyers on her team, Jesse or Graham, or even to that airhead Marcie Blumenthal, about her idiotic, unprofessional, bone-lazy secretaries because she had been through quite a few of them, and it was becoming quite the office joke. Jane made so many secretaries disappear without a trace, you'd think she worked for the mob. Oh, hilarious.

Lazy Susan guessed Jane Spring would sit in her office at least for an hour after losing the case to sulk and steam; she usually did. Knowing she had this window, Lazy Susan decided to break two rules by playing a few hands of Texas Hold'em on the Internet and opening a can of diet Coke. *(No cans on the desk, Susan.)*

"Susan. Any new messages?"

Jane Spring had sneaked up on her, and Lazy Susan let out a squeal of fright, jumping about an inch out of her own skin, knocking the phone off its base, which tipped the soda can, which caused the diet Coke to then run all over her desk. When people do this in sitcoms, they get big laughs.

But Jane Spring wasn't laughing as Lazy Susan grabbed all the paperwork nearby, including a pile of recent depositions, and used it to soak up the mess. Jane narrowed her eyes and folded her arms. "Did I, or did I not, say no cans on the desk, Susan? I think I did, and now I hope you know why. When I give an order, I expect it to be carried out, thank you. I don't want to see this happen again, Susan. Right, Susan?"

Lazy Susan groaned. "Yes Miss Sp-Ring."

Jane stood over her secretary as she cleaned up the mess. My God, today is worse than yesterday, she thought, surveying Lazy Susan's latest fashion incarnation. Something must be in the water in Brooklyn. How else could one explain it? Jane constantly marveled at her secretary's sartorial taste, the predilection for low-slung pants so tight that rolls of fat buckled over when she sat, for shirts where the top four buttons miraculously couldn't close. All accented with a wild mane of hair streaked pink — well, sometimes blue — a tan from a can and a tattoo of roses that ringed her right ankle. Not to mention the pierced navel. A small bell dangled from the hoop inside it, making it sound like somebody ringing for dinner every time her secretary walked by.

"Well, well, what have we here? Looks like we've got ourselves into a little mess," said a male voice Lazy Susan didn't recognize. She glanced up while Jane Spring pivoted to see who was enjoying the floor show. Staring right at her was the smug face of John Gillespie.

"You are having one helluva rough day, Jane. It just seems to be one disaster after the next. First you lose a slam-dunk trial. Then your secretary turns your court filings into papier-mâché. I can't wait to see what happens next."

"Do you have an appointment here, Mr. Gillespie, or did you simply come by to gloat? Because, frankly, I wouldn't bother. If memory serves, your acquittal rate is thirty-four percent, versus my conviction rate of eighty-eight percent. You might be smiling now, but I think you'll find statistics don't lie. I'm way ahead of you, Mr. Gillespie, and today, as disappointing as it might have been for me, doesn't change that." She smiled contentedly.

"Thank you for that lovely reminder, Jane. You are a most gracious loser indeed. Actually, I came to say hello to Graham."

Lazy Susan looked up suddenly with interest. She would have quite enjoyed Mr. Gillespie sticking it to her boss if she wasn't at that moment in so much trouble herself.

"Last door on the right. Now, Susan. Returning to my original question. My messages?"

Lazy Susan pointed to the ball of soggy paper, a mixture of depositions and what Jane could now see were ten or more blue message slips.

"They're in there, Miss Sp-Ring. We could try and get them out, but . . ."

"No, Susan. I think I'll pass. It might be hard, considering they're halfway on the road to becoming a puppet."

"What?"

"You say 'Pardon,' not 'What.' "

"I'm sorry Miss Sp-Ring."

"Yes, well, I hope this is a lesson to you. *Civilians!*" she said, disgusted.

Jane Spring marched back into her office, her ponytail flipping over her shoulder. Lazy Susan surreptitiously leaned forward over her desk to watch Graham greet John Gillespie in the doorway of his office. She threw the rest of the wet papers in the trash and wiped her hands dry on her pants. Then she went back to her game.

4

Graham Van Outen was one of four criminal prosecutors on Jane's team in the Trial Division. He wasn't the brightest lawyer in their group — that honor belonged to her, she knew — but she trusted him the most of all her colleagues. They had tried a number of cases together and were still on speaking terms, which everyone in the division knew to be a statistical impossibility. But Graham was a workhorse — he mirrored Jane's commitment to the job — and this won over her respect. She prized dedication; it was how she was raised. So what was he doing being friends with that oily John Gillespie? Jane guessed their friendship was one of those many things, among many manly things, that she would never understand.

Coffee. I need coffee, she thought. That will calm me down. Only Jane Spring could steady her nerves with a double shot of caffeine. She walked out of her office, pleased to find Lazy Susan actually working, reprinting depositions she had drowned earlier. Jane walked down the corridor to the kitchen, passing Jesse's office, empty because he was out prepping witnesses for their upcoming trial, and Marcie's office, piled high with bridal magazines, and finally Graham's office, where she could see through the crack in the door John Gillespie sitting on a sofa. She looked straight ahead and picked up her pace. Coffee, she told herself over and over. Coffee now. Alcohol when I get home.

But Graham's office shared a wall with the kitchen, so as much as Jane tried to ignore them she couldn't. Or wouldn't. Although their voices were muffled, if you stood close enough to the wall, you could decipher what they were saying. And when you hear your own name mentioned, come on, who's going to leave?

"Yeah, well, you don't mind her because you don't have to appear opposite her," said Gillespie.

"Hey, I never said I was in love with her; I just said she's not Ivan the Terrible, John. Jane can be aggressive, sure, but her conviction rate is the highest in —"

Jane was pleased to hear Graham going to bat for her. They were friends, after all.

"Aggressive? I don't think I'd call what I witnessed today *aggressive.* She sliced

45

open an elderly woman, Graham. Manhandled her, then threatened to incarcerate her. The woman *fainted*."

"Big deal. That's nothing. She once sent a guy to the hospital with chest pains. A thirty-five-year-old man in the prime of life, to the hospital."

"See! I'm telling you, the woman's a psychopath."

I'm a psychopath? thought Jane. That bastard. I was just doing my job.

"But you know something," Gillespie continued. "If you disregard the fact she's a ball-breaker, in a weird way she's totally hot."

"Oh, I know."

Ball-breaker?

"She's got a nice body under that sack of a suit," John Gillespie continued. "I know. I can tell these things. And if she took her hair out of that noose —"

Jane reached behind to grab her ponytail.

"I'd do her."

"Oh, me too. But she'd have to keep her mouth shut, and that, my friend, would never happen," said Graham.

The two buddies laughed harder this time, and Jane was sure she could hear the muffled clap of a high five. She stood stock-still, horrified. How dare Graham

46

talk about her that way? She thought they were friends!

Jane Spring couldn't leave the kitchen and walk past Graham's office, not after what she'd just heard, so she stayed there drinking two more cups of coffee and counting the tiles behind the sink. In addition to the adrenaline reaction from hearing her name spoken and the onset of the caffeine effect, another feeling had risen up and trapped itself inside Jane Spring's chest as she stood trapped in the kitchen. It was hurt.

Jane couldn't stay in the kitchen forever. She had work to finish, as did Lazy Susan, who, if left to her own devices, would spend the workday's fleeting hours either online gambling or huddling with Graham's secretary, Denise. What pressing matters did a fiftysomething mother of four have to discuss with a twenty-four-year-old refugee from MTV with a pierced navel? Civilians. No respect for the chain of command or due deference to a person's age. Pitiful.

Jane leaned into the wall again, relieved to find the conversation now turning to who would make it to the Super Bowl. Holding her head high, she rushed past Graham's office to her own. John Gillespie said his good-byes and made plans with Graham for drinks in a few weeks. As his footsteps neared Jane's office, she fixed her eyes on her computer. Then she heard Marcie cry out, and it startled her. Marcie had been suspiciously quiet in her office for days now. She said she was working on witness statements. Jane suspected it was bridesmaids' dresses.

"John Gillespie! How are you?" Marcie screamed, rushing out of her office. For a woman who was only five feet two and weighed 105 soaking wet, Marcie Blumenthal sure knew how to make her presence known.

"Oh, my God! I didn't see you come in," she squealed.

"I didn't see you either," he lied. Of course you did, Jane thought, but he, like most people who know Marcie, will avoid her if he can. Not that Marcie is mean. Or dumb. Or a bad lawyer. It's more that Marcie is just self-absorbed. After you hear Marcie talk about Marcie's latest diet ("I've lost three pounds already, Jane"), that she was now practicing yoga ("My god, it's sooo changed my life"), not to mention her latest bargain on eBay ("What a steal!"), well, you start hiding. You stop asking how her weekend was. Because you don't care.

Jesse said she was like an aria. Me, Me, Me, Me. And since the engagement thing happened, which bothered Jane more than she knew, Marcie had gone from unbearable to intolerable.

"How are you?" John Gillespie asked, looking at his watch.

"How am I?" said Marcie, coyly. Jane groaned. She had heard this routine a thousand times in the two weeks since Marcie had emerged triumphantly from Tiffany's with a six-carat diamond engagement ring; she knew exactly what was coming next. Marcie's left hand, with the fourth finger extended, would suddenly start waving back and forth as if she were swatting flies, while her right hand remained firmly behind her back. "You're too late Mister, I *got engaged!*" Marcie gushed, shoving her ring hand directly under John Gillespie's nose. "See!"

John Gillespie feigned interest in the ring, as did everybody Marcie showed it to; and believe it, she showed it to everybody. When Marcie had announced that she and her fiancé, Howard, were going to see the Dalai Lama in Central Park, everyone knew it was only so she could show him the ring too.

"Congratulations!" John Gillespie said.

"When's the wedding?"

"March. The Waldorf. I'm wearing Vera Wang."

Vera who? thought Jane, madly typing at her computer. "Well, that's wonderful," he said. "Your fiancé is one lucky guy," he added in a tone where the sarcasm flew just below the radar; but if you were looking, it was there. Jane wondered if John Gillespie loathed Marcie as much as she did. And if so, did that preclude his wanting to sleep with her too? Or was it just Jane he thought worthy of a hit-and-run?

Jane watched John Gillespie hug Marcie good-bye and head for the elevator. She waited five minutes, then still fuming, still hurting, she stormed over to Graham's office, Lazy Susan's eyes following her every step. Jane Spring was not going to let Mr. Van Outen off the hook for those remarks, private conversation or not.

"Disloyalty in the ranks is unacceptable, Jane. It must never go unpunished."

I hear you, sir.

Graham's office was empty.

"Where is he?" she barked at Denise.

"Top floor. Law library."

Jane Spring flew up the stairs, eight flights, to the law library. Elevators were for lazy people. Civilians with no self-discipline. When she emerged from the fire exit, she found Graham sitting at a long mahogany table taking notes from a law book.

"Counselor, I need to ask you something," Jane said, panting.

Graham looked up and his face broke into a huge smile.

"Well, I'm flattered. It's not every day Jane Spring asks me for advice. Shoot."

Jane looked him up and down. "I can't believe you're wearing that shirt. You do know that designer manufactures all his clothes in sweatshops, don't you? It was probably hand-stitched by a six-year-old girl who should be in school."

"She did an excellent job."

"Very amusing, Mr. Van Outen. Now answer this for me," Jane said, folding her arms. "Why is it that you would sleep with me but would never date me?"

Two librarians and three lawyers seated nearby turned around.

"What?" he cried out in astonishment.

"You heard me." Jane Spring sat down opposite him. "I heard you and John Gillespie joking earlier about how you wouldn't mind screwing me, but you'd never ask me out to dinner. That was the gist of it, yes?"

The smile on Graham's face fell onto the carpet.

"Jane, that was a private conversation," he whispered.

"Which I overheard."

"Eavesdropping is a felony."

"Only when it's electronic."

"Jane, I . . ."

The librarians and lawyers tried to look busy but kept a sideways glance on the conversation. This was better than anything you normally heard in the law library.

Jane sat back in her chair, despondent.

"Jane, could we take this somewhere else?"

Jane Spring folded her arms in front of her. "No, we can't. Answer me now, Counselor."

Graham Van Outen couldn't believe it. For a woman so intelligent, she had no insight into her own behavior.

"Jane, look. It was just guys talking. Shooting the shit. It doesn't mean anything."

"Answer me, Counselor, or I'll report you to the bar association for dating a juror from the Wheatley trial."

Graham Van Outen's heart sank. He knew taking out that juror for drinks was a mistake. "What was the question again?"

Jane's face softened. She pursed her lips, and Graham could see that her eyes were about to water. He wondered if he was dreaming. He had never, never seen Spring so . . . wounded. So . . . *human.*

"Why don't men see me as girlfriend material?" she said softly, plaintively. "This has been happening to me forever with men. At first they seem interested, but they never stick around. On Saturday night I got dumped on the first date. The guy before him, two dates. And this was after I'd slept with him! You would think he would stick around for another poke at it after that. I don't understand! *Why do they keep leaving me?*"

Graham took a deep breath. "You don't know?"

Jane Spring shook her head. Her eyes were now clearly on the verge of tears. She willed herself to hold them back. Her breakdown in the bathroom on Saturday night was bad enough. A severe weakness in character. She vowed it would not happen again.

"Jane, men want certain things in a woman that —"

"That I thought I had. *I know I have.*"

Graham knew he had to tread very gingerly here. "Well, okay, what do you consider qualities men want in a woman?"

"Rigorous honesty. Discipline. Punctuality. Intelligence. Duty. Ambition. Professionalism. Good sex. The ability to take, as well as give, orders."

You forgot castrating, combative and insulting, he wanted to say, but there was no way he was about to take on Jane Spring. So all that came out of his mouth was: "Wow."

"Wow what?"

"Wow it's interesting you think men want all those things."

"They don't?"

"Oh no, they do," he said sarcastically. "There is nothing a man wants more than a woman who is punctual, disciplined and can give and receive orders."

"Well, that's why I don't understand what the problem is."

Graham couldn't comprehend how anyone could be so smart and so deeply un-self-aware at the same time. But then, who really does know how others perceive them? "The problem, Jane, is that list you rattled off. They're not the only qualities men look for in a woman. There are other things."

Graham desperately wanted to move the conversation somewhere else. They had quite an audience now, not that Jane appeared to care.

"And so you're suggesting that if I don't add these other *things* to my repertoire, I'm never going to get a man to love me."

"I didn't say that."

"You most certainly did, Counselor. You said as much in your office. That you would never date me the way I am now."

Graham was now desperate to leave. He would leave, he decided. He stood up.

"Sit down, Counselor. You're not going anywhere until I get some answers."

Nor would he. Because the thing about Jane Spring was that inside that exterior of a man still beat the heart of a woman. Jane naturally affirmed her father's ideas that when it came to love, civilians were vapid, selfish and indulgent and yet she seemed to be suffering from that same curse herself. She had always felt intense love, or lust, for men — call it what you will. One in particular had had her pining like an obsessive teenager, but those feelings had never been reciprocated. And though she was disgusted with herself for wanting love, she craved it, badly. And not just any love, but the kind you see in old movies, you know the ones. True Love.

Graham sat down. Jane tore a piece of

paper from his legal pad and swiped the pen out of his hand. She wrote the numbers one through ten down the left side of the page.

"Okay, I'm ready. Hit me. Tell me what else they want."

Graham looked at the paper, stunned.

"Jane, I don't understand why you're so wound up about this."

And he didn't, either. Jane Spring could get angry, sure, but emotional, *never*. A man kisses her off and she's upset? Spring didn't feel any pain when she'd sent a pregnant woman to jail for twenty years last year. But a meltdown in the library over a guy?

"I have my reasons, Mr. Van Outen."

"Whatever you say, Jane. You're the boss."

"I know," Jane said excitedly. "Men like women who can talk basketball. In my house, we only talked football. I don't know anything about basketball. I can see how that might be a problem."

Jane wrote "Talk About Basketball" next to the number one.

"That's not it, Jane," Graham said softly. He was about to come clean. He was about to say, Jane, men don't stay with you because all the things on your list turn them off, not on. We don't care about duty, honor and punctuality. We don't care that you scored higher than us on the bar exam. But we do know that you make us feel inferior. And we do mind that you think making an old woman faint on the witness stand is fine work.

But then he stopped himself. He realized he didn't want to become Jane Spring's Henry Higgins. He had spoken too much already. If she really wanted to become the kind of woman men wanted, she would have to do it by herself.

"I don't understand," she said exasperatedly as she drew a neat line through "Talk About Basketball." "What do they want then? You have to tell me," she pleaded.

Graham looked at his watch, gathered up his pad and his law book and rose from his chair.

"Jesus, it's nearly six. I've got to run. Look, you're the smartest woman I know, Jane. Maybe even the smartest woman in New York. You'll figure it out."

Then for the first time in her life, Jane Spring experienced an emotion she hadn't encountered before.

Confusion.

5

Sigmund Freud spent his entire life trying to answer one question: What do women want? Jane Spring now spent every minute since her tête-à-tête in the library pondering the riddle in reverse: What do men want?

At home Jane opened her fridge and pulled out a bottle of white wine, poured herself a glass and went into the living room, sinking into her black leather sofa. Even though this was her place, even though her father was sixty miles away and hardly about to walk in and bark his disapproval, she still couldn't bring herself to put her feet on the coffee table. And so she sat in front of the television, back straight, one leg crossed politely over the other, exactly the way she sat behind the prosecution table in court.

Jane grabbed the remote and turned on the TV. She turned it off. She turned it on. She turned it off. What a day, she thought. If I never have another one like it in a thousand years, it will be too soon. First I lose a trial to that despicable creep Gillespie, then I had to decode Graham Van Outen's inscrutable advice to the lovelorn. Both were impossible to decipher.

She marched into her bedroom, threw herself down on her bed and reached for the phone. Wait till I tell Alice about Graham and Gillespie's little conversation, she thought, smarting. Wait till she hears about the showdown in the law library. Alice will be as disgusted as I am. Jane's spirits rose, comforted by the thought of Alice. A tried-and-true friend, Alice Carpenter understood loyalty. Even though she was more than a couple of thousand miles away, she had been Jane's best friend since the first grade, and Jane knew she would never let her down.

She checked her watch. San Francisco was three hours behind New York; Alice would still be at work. No matter. This conversation couldn't wait. Jane dialed the nurses' station on the fourth floor of St. Mary's Hospital. "Oh, hi, Jane. No, Alice is tending to a patient; I'll tell her you called," said a voice at the other end.

Damn civilian patients, Jane thought, throwing the receiver down on the bed. They're constantly whining, and they always want something. Oh, Nurse, I'm bleeding! Oh, Nurse, I can't feel my limbs!

Alice was a military brat too, but unlike Jane, she had attended schools on post only as a child. All the high schools she had attended were civilian. As a result, Alice had experienced a lot of things by the time she was seventeen that Jane wouldn't have dreamed of, like smoking marijuana and going to the prom with a civilian boy.

Not only did Alice have a far greater tolerance for civilians, she understood them in a way Jane did not. In fact, Alice had taken her appreciation of civilians as far as one could possibly go in the military. She'd married one.

"Hey, Springie, it's me," Alice sang down the line ten minutes later. "Did you win? You won, didn't you? My best buddy," she said proudly. "Cleaning up the streets of New York one con artist at a time."

"Not exactly."

"What?"

"It's complicated. My star witness turned on me."

"Jesus, Springie. I'm sorry."

"Oh, it gets better."

"What — the trial?"

"No, my day."

Jane poured out the gory details of every

event that had transpired in the last twelve hours, starting with her ritual two-mile morning swim at the Y, through the hellish debacle in court, on to Graham and Gillespie's dissection of her qualities or lack thereof and ending, finally, with her rendezvous with Mr. Van Outen in the library.

"He called me a ball-breaker!"

"Sorry, Springie. That's horrible."

"And this whole business about *me* not being enough of what men want," Jane said, kicking off her shoes. "Have you ever heard anything more ridiculous?"

Alice took a deep breath. Maybe now was finally the time to say something, given that Jane had opened the door. She had thought to speak up before, like when the civil litigation attorney had dumped her because she kept kicking his ass in squash and telling all his friends how bad he was at sports, or when Jane had informed the doctor that he might want to retake a course in female anatomy because he had no clue how to please a woman. But both times she had held her tongue.

She knew civilian men probably found her friend too rigid, too uncensored for their liking, but she hoped over time they would also see Jane's other qualities: her passion for justice, her sense of duty, her unremitting loyalty. Who dropped everything in the middle of a trial last year to fly to San Francisco and sit by Alice's bedside for three days when her appendix had burst? Jane did.

Alice took a deep breath. "You know, Springie, maybe Graham has a point."

There was a deafening silence on the line.

"I'm . . . I'm not saying he does for sure; I'm just saying it's food for thought. Think about it."

"I can't believe you're siding with him."

"I'm not, Springie. But you're the lawyer; look at the evidence."

Alice inhaled again. She loved Jane, and she could hear her hurting. But she had waited long enough for Jane to figure this out on her own; frankly, she needed help. "Springie, they're always breaking up with you. What does this tell you?"

"But I'm amazing." She began to cry.

"I know you are," she said, soothing her. "Okay. Let's look at this another way. In court when your trial strategy doesn't work, you change direction, right?"

"Sure but —"

"But it's not just in court you have to change tack, Springie. It's in life too. It seems to me, whatever you're doing on dates, it's not working. You're going to have to find another way."

"And which way is that?" she cried out.

Jane hated Alice right then. Who was she to dole out dating advice? Alice had married her first boyfriend; she was *still* married to her first boyfriend. She hadn't spent one minute in the dating trenches; Jane had spent nearly twenty years. Thanks, Alice, but I think I know how to go on a date, Jane thought.

"Oh, Jesus. Okay, Springie, I have to go. Bed seven needs morphine. Don't think about this anymore tonight; we'll talk tomorrow."

Jane threw the receiver down for a second time that evening. She rolled off her bed and returned to the living room, picked up her wineglass and put her feet on the coffee table. Immediately she took them off. And then it started. The moaning and groaning from upstairs. Oh, shit. Of course they would start and rub it in. Jane Spring's upstairs neighbors, the Tates (as in "Hi! We're the Tates! You must come up for a drink sometime!"), had been married a little less than a year. They were still in that phase where they had sex every two hours, and, boy, were they audible!

From the sound of the muffled grunts and knocked-over furniture, tonight they had started in the hallway and were now directly overhead, settling in on the sofa in their living room. With any luck, they'd just keep moving through the apartment and finish up in the kitchen, as they had last night.

That way, Jane wouldn't have to listen to his moaning and her faking it in surround sound. In the meantime, she did the only thing a cool, calm, collected lawyer would do under the circumstances. She turned on the TV. Way high. Anyone entering the building would think the people in 5R were shooting a porn, whereas the woman in 4R was probably ninety and stone-cold deaf.

Jane took another sip of wine and replayed the conversation with Alice in her head, trying to ignore the booming TV and the ceiling fan that had begun to tremble with the gyrations of the Tates. "It's not just in court you have to change tack, Springie. It's in life too. It seems to me, whatever you're doing on dates, it's not working. You're going to have to find another way."

But what else do men want that she hadn't given them? Jane was absolutely stumped. Conversation about basketball? Graham had rejected that notion.

Better table manners? Hers were already impeccable. Even when she doesn't like what's offered, she eats everything on her plate.

Sex? Nobody could accuse her of withholding in that department. Jane prided herself on being a liberated, hot-blooded American woman.

Could she be more direct? Jane knew men didn't like women who played games. But she was already kindly pointing out where they fell short. What else could she do to help them improve? Jane just couldn't crack it. What else did men desire beyond candor, punctuality, self-discipline, tenacity, ambition and athletic sex?

She had it all, didn't she?

She did.

But when she considered the evidence as Alice instructed, she had to concede that a change was in order. She had to find what else they wanted.

When the Tates had finished screwing, Jane turned the TV down. It was easier to deliberate her fate in quiet. She thought of Mrs. Markham, so desperate to be loved that she had married a man she knew wanted her only for her money. Although Jane held her in contempt, she also understood. Who doesn't want to belong to somebody?

For years now Jane Spring had despised herself for wanting to be in love. It was undisciplined to give in to human emotions, degrading to want to belong to a man. She knew it was silly, and yet in her heart of hearts she still wanted it all. The entire package: the butterflies, the kisses, the whirlwind romance, the fireworks, the ring. Surely there was one man who would stay beyond one date? Who would stay forever? There had to be.

But if she didn't discover what *he* wanted, she would never find him. Worse, she had no time to waste. Jane Spring was thirty-four years old. Thirty-four years and nine months, to be precise. Everyone knows that after thirty-five a woman has a better chance of being kidnapped by aliens than finding a husband. There was a scientific study that said so. From Harvard! And as a lawyer, Jane Spring took great stock in scientific evidence.

Which meant if she didn't find him soon, now, she would be alone forever. Unless she married that little green man who kidnapped her.

It was at that moment, hearing the theme song from the news, hearing the afterglow laughter filtering down from upstairs — a sure sign the Tates were gearing up for round two — that Jane Spring came to decide upon three things.

One: She would find out what men really wanted in a woman.

Two: She would become that woman.

Three: She would then meet a man who would stay beyond one date, who would love her forever.

There was only one question left.

How?

6

Failure was not a word in Jane Spring's vocabulary, so this defeat at the hands of the male species had not just been incomprehensible; it was devastating. Her father would order her court-martialed if he knew; he had drilled Jane to succeed at everything or die trying. On top of everything else, the shame of letting him down was now too much to bear. It was bad enough she had already failed him once, a mistake for which she dutifully took full responsibility. That mistake was being born the wrong gender.

Brigadier General Edward Spring, West Point graduate, Vietnam vet, career soldier and now the director of the Department of Military Instruction at West Point, wanted only boys. When Jane was born, after Edward Junior and Charlie, he stared at her sweet blond head and tiny hands, said, "Damn," then walked into the corridor of the base hospital and kicked a wall. The nurses who looked on didn't bat an eyelid. They saw this kind of thing at least once a week. At least the little blond girl would have her mother to protect her, the nurses thought.

But she wouldn't. Jane was just three when her mother, Carol, was accidentally run over by a jeep on base. The Pentagon sent their condolences. The military wives sent flowers. But when the general came home, he told his children Mother wouldn't be living with them anymore and, chin up, there would be no talk of it again. And there wasn't.

"You brushed your teeth, miss?"
"Yes, Sir."
"Your homework finished?"
"Completed, Sir. Permission to turn in, Sir."
"Very good. You may turn in."
"Good night, Sir."

Edward Spring always thought his wife was too soft on the children, and now that he was left in charge, life in the household was going to smarten up. First thing, the children would call him Sir. Now that they were older — Jane three, Charlie four and Edward six — the appellation of Father would disappear from their vocabularies.

Bedroom inspection was Saturday morning, and if Sir pulled out a quarter and it didn't bounce, the bed was remade until it did. The Spring children only took cold showers because the general believed hardship built character. At dinner he filled them with tales of great American generals and quizzed them on American history. One wrong answer meant push-ups. Nobody left the table until they could see their reflections in their plates. They did the dishes together to encourage team-work. When one was punished, all were punished to inspire loyalty. Little soldiers they were, right down to the salute they gave him every evening before turning in.

Honor. Duty. Discipline. The general would drill them daily on the values he expected them to exhibit. Civilians, he told them, had none of these qualities and were to be viewed with overt suspicion if not complete contempt. Jane didn't know any, having only lived on bases, but the few she had met seemed rather tame. But no, the general warned. Don't be fooled. Civilians, he insisted, showed no respect for their elders, for authority, even their own parents. He said he knew of civilian children who not only talked back to their parents, but also called them by their first names.

Really? thought Jane. How many push-ups would that be?

To the outside eye Jane Spring was indistinguishable from her siblings. The general taught her to hunt, to fish, to cock a weapon and fire without fear. Little Jane proved a diligent student. She caught her first bass at three, skinned her first rabbit at six, bagged her first deer at eight. The general even said she was a better shot than Eddie Junior, a comment that had sent her older brother outside into the bitter cold for the entire winter to practice his marksmanship.

There was no question the general believed his daughter had all the makings of a fine soldier. But this was not in the cards given that he firmly, intractably believed soldiering to be a single-gender profession. Women in the ranks were a distraction, bad for morale. Although the U.S. Army had long accepted them into the corps ("politically correct claptrap," he fumed), no daughter of his was going to enlist. And that was a direct order.

Naturally, like their father, Charlie and Edward Junior had attended West Point, then received their commissions in the infantry. Jane, as he had long decreed, would go into the civilian world. First university, then work. The general approved of Columbia University for his daughter because

New York was one hour from West Point, close enough for him to keep an eye on her and to bring troops should a situation get out of hand. Which could happen. He had heard that New Yorkers were the lowest. They stole, they cheated and lied to get ahead. Disgraceful. Worse than communists.

"How many hours did you study this week, miss?"

The general called his daughter every Sunday; God help her if she wasn't in her dorm to take the call.

"Every night and all weekend, Sir."

"Very good. And how many hours of exercise?"

"Sixty minutes a day, Sir."

"Insufficient. Raise it thirty minutes. We can never let ourselves get of shape, Jane."

"Yes, Sir."

"I see in the papers there were twelve robberies in New York this week."

"Yes, Sir."

"My God," he growled. "Be on guard, Jane. Remember, you must be wary of even the ones who appear to be harmless. None of them can be trusted."

"Yes, Sir."

The general was certainly entitled to his

opinions, but seven years of school in New York had taught Jane her father was both wrong and right about civilians. In truth, they weren't *all* that bad, though many of them left something to be desired. They put their feet on their dorm furniture, said "Fuck you, lady" when you complained they cut in line and wouldn't get out of their seats for pregnant women on the subway. Their work ethic was delinquent, and their lack of self-discipline appalled her.

And, oh, civilian women! A collective disgrace. Their most pressing question was not "Did I make the dean's list?" but "Do I look fat in this dress?" Quizzed by a professor, they giggled unapologetically when unable to answer. Shameful really.

But there was one class of civilians that against her better judgment, against her father's mandate, Jane came to find fascinating. Civilian *men.* God forbid she would ever admit that to him. But eighteen years of military fathers and sons left those verboten civilian males looking mighty exotic. She even fell in love with one. Not that he returned the favor.

After graduation Jane attended law school, the only civilian profession she wholeheartedly approved of. The justice system had rules and regulations, even a pecking order like the army. It was sort of like enlisting, but without the combat boots.

After a summer internship in the D.A.'s office, Jane Spring knew she had found her calling. Defining the enemy, grilling witnesses, this mode of communication she understood. The art of prosecuting came to her not by practice but osmosis. Intimidation and interrogation she had studied watching the master. There was nothing for her to learn.

So on her first day of work, Jane Spring arrived at the Criminal Trial Division of the District Attorney's office in her new black pantsuit, ready to take on the world. Her father was a great general, but she would be a great prosecutor. She would make him proud. She would enforce the rule of law in the world just as he had on the battlefield. Which wouldn't be too hard. She had already turned into him.

7

"Who? Who am I going to become?"

That night Jane Spring did not sleep well, waking four times — unheard of for such a committed sleeper — to ask herself this question. This self-interrogation continued as she lowered herself into the pool. Normally Jane's seven a.m. swim at the Y was her salvation, the only place her mind went blank and she felt carefree. But not today.

For as long as she could remember, Jane had loved to swim. The general had taught her at the officers' pool at Fort Benning, and lucky for Jane, she was a natural. A real fish. She still remembered him giving Charlie twenty push-ups when he failed to swim ten laps of the pool at Fort Benning in five minutes. Charlie was seven. Now, surging up and down the lanes, she heard the question play in her mind like a broken record. "Who, Jane? Who?"

Her thoughts wandered to the general, a man Jane had never seen exhibit doubt about anything, let alone who he was or what he believed. There was no question that everything she was today she owed to him. How perfectly he had grounded her in the disciplines of honor, duty, family, country. How he had inspired her at the dinner table with the heroics of Grant, MacArthur, Patton and Eisenhower. *"Let these great men be your guides, Jane."*

And they had been. She always recalled their passion for the cause before starting a new trial, their discipline and direction while conducting cross-examination, their fearlessness before a verdict came in.

Oh, my God, thought Jane, that's it! She broke her head up through the surface of the water and kicked over to the wall to float on her back for a second, letting it sink in. She needed a role model — someone who had been victorious in the war of love just as those men had triumphed on the battlefield. Someone to emulate, to guide her into becoming the kind of woman men want. Jane guessed there must be a multitude of candidates for the job. Would not Eisenhower have a romantic equivalent? MacArthur? Patton? Of course they would.

Buoyed, Jane Spring jumped out of the pool and headed for the ladies' locker room. There she showered, changed into a black wool gabardine suit jacket and pants and headed for work, picking up coffee and a banana en route. Her long hair was soaking wet.

At nine a.m., when Jane had already been working for an hour, Lazy Susan turned up, which was, Jane knew, a miracle of biblical proportions. It seemed that after the debacle of the day before, Lazy Susan had resolved to try harder, or at least come in on time, whichever was the least amount of work.

Jane stepped out of her office and into Lazy Susan's cubicle. She looked at her secretary closely. Is this my hero? Is she what men want? she wondered. Ringing navels, zero work ethic and a mountain of excuses? Impossible.

"My schedule, Susan. It's not on my desk."

"I'll print it out now."

"Susan, you should have done it last night before you left. Please don't require me to speak to you about your dereliction of duty again."

"Yeah, Miss Sp-Ring."

Lazy Susan reached under her desk to turn on her hard drive. "Hey, how's the sergeant major this morning?" whispered a voice. Lazy Susan looked up, and a huge smile crawled along her face. She blushed, then ran her fingers through her hair to fluff it. Graham Van Outen was standing before her, grinning. "Has she court-martialed you yet?"

"Practically. Yesterday she was so mad, I thought she was going to give me push-ups."

"Yeah, well, yesterday she *did* give me push-ups," Graham said, groaning. "In the library."

Lazy Susan started to giggle, then turned around nervously to see if Jane had heard them. Graham Van Outen was the one person who made her job tolerable. Actually, more than tolerable. The two minutes he spent every morning en route to his office joking with her about Jane kept her going all day. That and his mop of curly blond hair and the cleft in his chin.

"Well, carry on, Corporal," he whispered, saluting.

Lazy Susan snickered and saluted him in return. Boy, he looked cute this morning; I think that's a new tie, she thought. She watched keenly as Graham bypassed his office and went across the hall to confer with Supervisor Lawrence Park.

Jane's phone rang, and hearing her pick it up, Lazy Susan decided to make a run for it. Now! Go Susie! She rose quietly and crept along the corridor to Graham's office.

"Hey, Denise, what's up?" she casually asked his secretary. Denise was immersed in the *New York Times* crossword.

"Oh, hey, Susie. Do you know a six-letter word for *dictator?*"

"Yeah, I do, actually. *S-p-r-i . . .*"

"Good one." Denise laughed. "But it has to start with a *T.* Any other ideas?"

"*Tyrant.* Hey, can you check Graham's schedule today? Is he in court?"

"Why?"

"Um, it's Miss Sp-Ring. I think she needs to have a meeting with him, or something."

Lazy Susan hoped Denise was buying it.

"Let me look. No, he's in all day."

"Oh, great!" Lazy Susan replied, maybe a little too enthusiastically. "I mean, fine, I'll tell Miss Sp-Ring."

If Graham was in all day, that meant he would eat his lunch in the conference room. He always did if it was empty. He wouldn't mind if she joined him, would he?

Jane Spring was still on the phone when Detective Mike Millbank appeared in her doorway, shaking out a soggy umbrella.

Jane was so startled by the sight of him she pitched forward, practically ramming her head into her computer screen. She quickly composed herself, stood and faced the detective squarely in her sights. For a second it looked like the beginning of the showdown at the OK Corral.

"Detective, how the hell did you get in here?"

"How did I get in here? Front door. Same way as everyone else. I called your secretary to let her know I'd arrived, but there was no answer, so I showed myself in."

Jane stormed past the detective to find that Lazy Susan was MIA. And here she had been thinking the silence outside her office *might* be a sign that the girl was working. Jane caught sight of her secretary gabbing with Denise, and threw her a disapproving stare.

Lazy Susan raced back to her cube, her stiletto heels leaving tiny indented holes in the carpet.

"Miss Sp-Ring, I —"

"Susan, Detective Millbank had to show himself in. Would you like to explain to me just how that happened?"

"I was just axing Denise if —"

"Frankly, I don't want to hear it, Susan."

Lazy Susan hurriedly searched her desk. "Here's your schedule, Miss Sp-Ring." Jane snatched it out of her hands and read: *9:15 a.m.: Conference with Detective Millbank, 32nd Precinct Homicide. Re: Riley Trial.*

"Just sit!" Jane barked, pointing Lazy Susan to her chair. "Detective, please follow me."

In Jane's office the detective peeled off a brown coat, gloves and scarf and took a seat. Jane returned to her desk and folded her arms in front of her.

"I apologize for the insubordination of my assistant, Detective."

"Oh, no worries. Really, Jane, she's a sweet girl. No need to start the Third World War here. I'm a big boy. I can let myself in."

"It's not you I'm concerned about."

But truth be told, it was he she was concerned about. Bad enough being ambushed by anyone first thing in the morning, but Millbank? Shit. The last time they'd met they had not parted on the best of terms.

She hoped he had forgotten that — shall we say — incident.

He hadn't.

81

8

Jane Spring was pleased. Detective Mike Millbank had done a good job of assembling evidence and interviewing witnesses. Not all of them did. Some of them were so sloppy she couldn't understand how they had made detective rank. But Millbank was thorough. And in the case of *People v. Laura Riley*, he had turned over every last stone. Jane knew why: family. The defendant in the case, one Laura Riley, had shot her husband, Police Officer Thomas Riley, after discovering he was having an affair. Jane couldn't believe how she had found out: lipstick on his collar. Just like in the song. From there Mrs. Riley hired a private investigator, from there he furnished her with incriminating photographs of her husband *in flagrante* with one Patty Dunlap, a twenty-eight-year-old clerk at Central Booking.

From there things get rather murky.

Laura Riley admits she went to her rival's apartment to confront her husband. And she concedes she brought a gun. But it fired accidentally, she swears, after her husband tried to prize it from her during a fight. Jane will argue otherwise: that this was a simple case of premeditated murder of a police officer, punishable by life in prison.

Whichever side you believed, there was one thing in the case of *People v. Laura Riley* you couldn't dispute: The tabloids were having a field day. They had a cop cheating on his wife. A girlfriend who left lipstick on his collar. A private dick who snapped photos of the lovers doing the horizontal hula. And a wife turned vigilante defending her marriage vows. It was pulp fiction come to life. What's not to love?

Looking Jane in the eye, Detective Millbank laid out the case for a conviction. He had an NYPD forensic expert who would testify that because of the location of the entry wound and the bullet fragments pulled from the wall, the shooting was no accident. He had a statement from Mistress Patty Dunlap that she overheard Mrs. Riley screaming, "I am so hurt I could fucking kill you." And the private eye was ready to back up Jane's theory on motive.

But Jane knew that all of this still didn't add up to a day at the beach in court.

Hardly. The defense, she knew, could make a strong case for reasonable doubt. There were no eyewitnesses to the crime, statements made in the heat of argument could be discounted as emotion not intent, experts would surely be summoned to refute her experts and attempt to prove that the gun had fired accidentally. Worse, Mrs. Riley had hired Chip Bancroft, one of the city's most wily trial lawyers, to defend her, and Jane knew what that meant. It would be a prizefight all the way to the verdict.

"Word is that Bancroft is going to push for temporary insanity if all else fails; you know, crime of passion," said the detective, looking around Jane's office. He had been there before, but never taken a serious inventory before now. There was a bookcase full of law books, but little else. No plants, no family photos, just a blotter on her desk and a yellow legal pad.

Where were the Christmas cards? That's weird, he thought. What's Spring hiding? As a detective he was trained to notice these things. In particular, a lack of possessions was the first sign that the perp was about to flee the jurisdiction. Then again, maybe Spring just didn't like knickknacks or have any real decorating skills. What did he care anyway? He couldn't stand the woman.

"Crime of passion is only a defense in Italy, Detective. Only motive and incriminating evidence matter to us. And don't worry about Bancroft," Jane said. "I've known the guy since law school. I know all his tricks. Chip's as transparent as a window. You just deliver the witnesses, I'll take care of the rest."

Jane Spring sounded so cocky, so haughty, dismissing Chip Bancroft that Mike Millbank could never have guessed how tense she always became when facing him at trial. Not that she doubted her ability as a prosecutor, but rather, this was Chip Bancroft, *the* Chip Bancroft, the one she had been in love with all through law school like a dumbstruck teenager, the one who had never so much as given her a second look.

Every campus has a golden boy, and at Columbia, Chip Bancroft had been it. He'd even looked golden, with his year-round tan and sun-kissed hair. A walking résumé of achievement — 4.0 GPA, swim team, law review — he was every mother's dream. Daughter's too, with an aura about him that made every female pulse quicken. And Chip had felt plenty of those pulses (along with the rest of the anatomy), though Jane had never had the pleasure.

She had to satisfy herself with lapping alongside him in the college pool and debating him in law review meetings. "Not bad, Spring," he had said once after digesting her notes on a journal submission. "You argued your point well. I disagree, of course."

No matter. That simple comment had kept her going for weeks.

Chip had this way about him, a confidence Jane never even detected in army men. He didn't kowtow to authority, bowling right up to professors and addressing them as equals. Jane thought this audacious, insubordinate and absolutely intoxicating. If one of the general's men spoke to him with such familiarity, heads would roll.

In college, where the uniform of choice for men (men who were going to be lawyers one day, no less) was torn jeans and a Bruce Springsteen T-shirt, Chip sported khaki pants and custom-tailored, monogrammed shirts, prompting more than a few male classmates to joke, "How's the regatta going, Chip old boy? Late for your Young Republicans' meeting, Chip?"

But Jane hardly thought them funny. In fact, his attention to detail, his pride in his appearance made her long for him even more. For three years Chip Bancroft considered Jane nothing more than a pedantic brain; for three years she pined for him anyway. But that had been ten years ago, so she forgave herself this failing. She had been young and impressionable, and hardly the first woman to fall for his big-man-on-campus routine. Now, a decade later, she could see right through him — all that charm was really self-absorption, the endless string of women (which grew exponentially each year) went to feed his sad ego, and yet every time she saw him, she still felt something.

"Well, that's it then," said Detective Millbank, who rose from his chair and reached for his coat. "If there's anything else, you know where to find me."

"That I do," said Jane, staring at him. Tall with dark hair and blue eyes, the detective might even be quite presentable, she thought, if he pulled himself together. Unfortunately, he didn't. His shoes were scuffed, his black pants and blue shirt clashed with his brown jacket. Some people really do need a uniform, Jane thought. Leave them to their own devices and this is what you get.

"Detective, you will dress appropriately for the trial, won't you?" she said pointing to his ensemble. "You know, in the army they say a soldier's appearance is as important as his aim."

"Well, excuse me, Counselor, I never served in the military."

"Yes, I can see that." She forced a smile.

Jane marched the detective to the elevator in silence. This made him feel uncomfortable, but Jane did it as a reflex. Military personnel do not allow guests to depart unattended.

At the elevator Jane and the detective stood silent, watching the numbers light up in descending order. Suddenly Mike Millbank turned to Jane with fire in his eyes. He hadn't planned to say anything, but the dig about his clothes had pushed him over the edge.

"Listen, Jane, pardon my French, but don't fuck this one up, okay? I worked my tail off putting all the pieces of this jigsaw together, and I don't want a repeat of last time."

Jane's face turned scarlet. She pushed her glasses along the bridge of her nose. Detective Millbank stepped back, suddenly fearful the prosecutor would punch him.

"Excuse me?"

"You heard me."

The elevator door opened. Detective

Millbank put one foot in, but Jane pulled him out and instructed the others inside to go on without him.

"Pardon my French, Detective, but I did not *fuck up,* thank you."

Mike Millbank wasn't buying her I-never-make-mistakes defense. He didn't care how indignant she appeared. Ten months before he had killed himself putting together a case of murder-for-hire and Jane Spring had blown it for him. She had insulted the presiding judge so thoroughly throughout the trial, questioning his interpretation of hearsay and making him furious with her vociferous objections to his evidentiary rulings, that when she respectfully asked for a recess until they found a crucial witness who had disappeared, the judge, in his discretionary capacity, refused. He insisted the witness could already be in Brazil, and he had no intention of waiting for him to surface. But Mike Millbank knew what was going on. Everyone did. The judge wanted to stick it to Jane for getting on her legal high horse and trying to ride it over him. Without the witness they were screwed. Mike Millbank didn't say anything at the time because he was too angry. Now he was ready.

"Well, in my experience, you have most

certainly and unequivocally *fucked up.* Just don't do it again."

"You think the judge didn't grant us a continuance because of me?"

"You said it; I didn't."

"I'll have you know that it is my job to question such rulings, and no matter what that judge said, I was also right about the hearsay exceptions. All I was doing was what every good prosecutor does, which is working to exclude all the evidence that might jeopardize our case."

"I heard you told the judge he didn't understand the rules of prior consistent statements and offered to tutor him in recent case studies in his quarters."

"Absolutely not! What I said was, 'With respect, I would like to make sure you have a clear understanding of the rules so we are on the same page.' Not the same thing."

"Oh, right. Listen, Counselor," he said, stepping right into her face. "I know this is just another day in court for you, but for me it isn't, okay? This was a cop, one of my own. In case you didn't get the memo, we in the police department don't like it when one of our own goes down. Somebody has to be held accountable."

"Or what?" said Jane, taking a step back.

"Detective Millbank, in case *you* didn't get the memo, a member of your 'family' was cheating on his wife. You don't think he was a tad responsible for the predicament he found himself in?"

In the army adultery could get you a court-martial. It was considered a serious breach of duty, both public and private. In the civilian world, Jane had learned to her disgust, breaking marriage vows was practically a sport, with no sanctions attached. It was no longer a crime punishable by law, and privately the civilian mantra appeared to be, If it feels good, do it.

"Whatever you think about his cheating from a moral perspective, he didn't deserve to be murdered," Millbank said.

"Plenty of women might disagree with you, Detective."

"Including you?"

The elevator returned, and this time Mike Millbank stepped in all the way. Jane was too incensed to bid him good-bye; she just stared right through him until the doors closed. Then she marched back to her office, holding her head high. She would regain her composure; nobody would see that she had had words with Detective Millbank.

"A good soldier never betrays emotion, Jane."

★ ★ ★

In her office Jane stared at the phone. How dare he? She would call Internal Affairs and cite Detective Millbank for speaking rudely to counsel. She had dialed three digits when Marcie charged into her office and grabbed the receiver out of her hand.

"Jane! Look. It's started! First snow of the season!"

Jane turned to look out the window. Indeed, a light snow was starting to fall outside. She looked at Marcie thoughtfully. Is she my role model? she asked herself. Is this what men want? Non-stop blabber about yourself, your weight and an obsession with eBay? Marcie was always buying junk through the Internet, and Jane often found herself in the embarrassing situation of having to sign for it. It's not for me, she would protest; my colleague ordered this cuckoo clock and boxed set of Abba's greatest hits. Whatever you say, lady.

"Well, I can see this is very exciting for you, but didn't they predict snow for today?"

"Yes, but have you heard the latest? They're now forecasting a blizzard. Could go until Monday."

"There can't be a blizzard; I'm starting a

trial Monday," Jane snarled.

"Well, I'm just glad I'm not getting married this weekend," said Marcie.

Oh, here we go, thought Jane.

"I mean can you imagine, Jane? Your hair would be ruined by the wind and rain, and there's no way you could wear a strapless gown. You'd probably have to walk down the aisle in a blanket."

What a pity, thought Jane, they can't make you walk down the aisle in a muzzle.

9

Mrs. Kearns was still in her apartment when Jane came home that evening, which made her blood boil. It had been quite a day; she wanted to be alone.

Jane's apartment had only one bedroom, and she didn't own anything interesting in the way of furniture, just the usual mix of sofa, coffee table, bed, TV and DVD. It certainly didn't take a day to clean it. My God, you could probably clean Versailles in eight hours and still have time left over for lunch, Jane thought.

But Jane couldn't let her go. Mrs. Kearns, like Lazy Susan, was the end of the line. Four cleaning ladies had come and gone already. The doormen had started to talk.

She didn't have proof, and as a prosecutor Jane knew that without evidence there is no conviction, but she had long suspected that Mrs. Kearns spent a good chunk of her day in Jane's apartment sitting on her sofa watching game shows and soaps. Jane had thought about hiding a camera inside a radio to spy on Mrs. Kearns, but she had avoided doing so for legal reasons. What if she were brought up on criminal charges of emotional distress? Her career would be gone in a minute. No, better to let Mrs. Kearns spend the day watching washed-up celebrities play word games with witless housewives, and with Storm and Thorn, Dr. Dan and Nurse Kate, only stopping to clean the apartment during the commercials.

Which is exactly what Mrs. Kearns did, by the way. Except her lack of discipline, as Jane saw it, wasn't because she just had to see Mary Jo from Alabama win a washing machine or Dr. Dan from *Medical Center* lose it when Thorn told him he was a disappointment as a father. (This had all come as a shock to Dr. Dan, who didn't even know Thorn was his son.)

Truth was, Mrs. Kearns was a really hard worker, and although she certainly liked to catch a quiz show or soap while she labored, she would never let them swallow her day if she had a job to do. Her lack of discipline in this case was particular to Jane Spring, and it all boiled down to this: She hated Jane Spring's furniture.

Mrs. Kearns actually rather enjoyed being a cleaning lady. Sure, you had to dust and mop, but you could also vacuum in the nude if you felt like it (she didn't), or you could try on couture dresses and expensive jewelry that you couldn't own in a million years (she did). And the homes she cleaned! A swirl of elegant draperies and antiques, Persian rugs and white baby grand pianos. She had some pretty rich clients, corporate lawyers and stockbrokers mostly, and walking into their houses was her an entrance to another world. Why waste time watching soaps when you had real palaces to play in?

After cleaning each room — vacuuming the rugs, polishing the silver, changing the six-hundred-thread-count Egyptian cotton linens — she liked to imagine herself the lady of the house. In the dining rooms Colleen Kearns would sit at the head of the table spooning invisible soup and giving orders (politely, of course) to the help. At the pianos she would sit on the stool while an imaginary singer warbled love songs just for her. In the living rooms, dressed in evening gowns and jewels purloined from closets, she would be the charming hostess of the most elegant cocktail parties.

"What a charming house. And so clean."

"Yes, that's our housekeeper, Mrs. Kearns; what a treasure. Widow, you know."

But in Jane Spring's apartment she had no interest in playing Colleen Kearns, lady of the house. None. Jane's furniture, particularly those ghastly black leather sofas, turned her right off. So did that glass-topped coffee table, which, by the way, was a total dust magnet; the cream venetian blinds (dust magnets squared); the black Formica wall unit, black bookcases and the slate kitchen countertops with the dreary gray trim. There was not a plant, not a flower, not a form of life anywhere.

And don't get her started on Miss Spring's bedroom. Mrs. Kearns thought it had been airlifted from a William Holden war movie. Whoever heard of a woman sleeping between khaki sheets and grayish-green wool blankets? Where were the silk lampshades and the wicker furniture? The flowered quilt and dusty-rose curtains like those in other single women's apartments? Oh, the girl had a reading lamp in her bedroom, but it was one bulb encased in steel. Her blinds were gray; there was not one painting or photo on any of her bedroom walls.

My lord, she thought, the POWs in Stalag 17 decorated their cells better.

And so Mrs. Kearns loathed cleaning the Spring apartment because, as she told her cat, Leon, it gave her the creeps. And the place bored her. No possibility of pretending you were anybody other than an undertaker. So to clean each room in Jane's apartment, Mrs. Kearns had to bribe herself with a series of rewards. If you clean the bathroom, Colleen, you can watch half an hour of *Days of Our Nights*. If you dust the bookcase and the wall unit, Colleen, you can have half a glass of wine from the bottle in Miss Spring's fridge and watch an entire episode of *What's My Secret?* Which explains, then, why it took Colleen Kearns eight hours to clean an apartment that should have taken three. The motivation took longer than the actual job.

"You're still here, I see," Jane growled, walking through the door. "One would assume you would have been done by now."

"Just leaving, Miss Spring."

Jane remained at the front door, arms folded.

"How about the snow, Miss Spring? They say it's going to turn really nasty."

"So I hear."

Mrs. Kearns stifled a yawn, picked up her bag and glanced around the room to check that everything was in its place. Not that anything would be out of place; Jane didn't own anything to move around. Christmas was only weeks away, but there wasn't a piece of tinsel, a card, a pretty bauble or decoration anywhere. Something's very wrong here, Colleen Kearns thought to herself every week when she arrived, and again when she left. She was dying to ask what, but thought better of it. No, Colleen, better dust, polish, take the money and run.

Once her housekeeper had decamped, Jane showered, then opened a bottle of wine — drinking was the one civilian habit Jane had come to enjoy, within legal limits, of course — and sat on her sofa staring at her reflection in the TV set. She thought about dinner, then decided against it. She was too angry to eat.

How dare Millbank criticize me after the way I busted my butt for him? Jane had always thought there was something a bit off about the detective, but now she had real cause to dislike him. Before, it had just been the scuffed shoes and ill-matched clothes that always had her shrieking internally. A man who doesn't polish his shoes? Disgraceful. A man in mismatched clothes? No self-respect. Even before their altercation Jane would see him and think that the man wouldn't survive even one week in boot camp. The general would have had him cleaning latrines with a toothbrush for the unpolished shoes alone. But for the way he'd talked back to Jane today? Three nights in the brig, thank you. "Don't fuck this one up for me, Jane." As if she'd wanted to lose the last one? As if it hadn't been her case too?

Jane Spring took a glass of wine with her to bed and rested it on her bedside table. Closing her eyes, she resolved she would show that detective just how well Jane Spring didn't fuck up, and then she'd make him eat his words. Standing at attention.

10

"The forecast for today is snow, more snow, followed by even more snow!" declared a booming voice from the TV set. It was eight a.m., Saturday morning, and Jane had just come in from the pool. She was wearing gray sweatpants with a matching gray fleece sweatshirt, the word army across the chest.

"But seriously, folks, go out and get what you need this morning because the experts at the Bureau of Meteorology are now confirming that a blizzard is coming our way. Should be starting around noon today, and by tomorrow night, we could get up to three feet! Yes, three feet, folks! More than enough for your kids to build a snowman, and for you to bury that pesky mother-in-law without anyone finding out!"

Jane groaned. Weathermen. Are they all failed comedians?

"The mayor says that in all likelihood the subways will close once the snow becomes too dense for the choo-choos to drive through, so like I said, go out and get what you need now because, people, New

York City is shutting down!"

"Choo-choos? My God. Somewhere in America a village is missing its idiot," Jane said, turning off the TV. She reached for her umbrella, put her coat back on, tucked her wet hair into a beret and went back outside. Sure, it was snowing, but it wasn't windy, and the snow felt soft and easy as it fell on her face. Somehow she was expected to believe that the clown on TV was right when he'd said that in less than five hours it was all going to turn into Armageddon. Just in case, however, Jane went out and stocked up on a few staples: bread, milk, eggs, cheese, coffee, cookies, canned soup, pasta, wine, toilet paper. Done. When she walked in the door she could hear the Tates at it upstairs. She looked at her watch: ten a.m.

Jane prayed that that would be it for them until evening. She needed complete quiet if she was to get through all the paperwork she had to read before Monday. Not to mention that she had yet to write her opening statement. Blizzard or no blizzard, the Tates were going to have to go out and leave her in peace. The phone rang; it was Jesse calling to cancel their strategy meeting that evening. Jesse Beauclaire was her cocounsel for the Riley trial. Though officially he'd been appointed because he was younger, less experienced and Supervisor Lawrence Park felt he could learn a lot from Jane, unofficially it was because he was all of the above and black. Supervisor Park knew from the statistics that juries tended to vote with Jane, but this was the kind of headline case where strong odds weren't enough to help him sleep at night. He needed guarantees. Jesse would be his insurance. It didn't take a genius to realize that a handsome, young African American cocounsel standing shoulder to shoulder with his Viking lead counsel could do much to soften the jury if Jane, for any reason, set them off. Jesse standing loyally by her side, said, she might be one ferocious white woman, but you can trust her. I do.

"You've seen the weather report?" he asked.

"I have."

"There's no way I'm coming across town to see you. I'll never get home."

Jesse was sitting in his boxers and a Jets T-shirt in the living room of his studio apartment in Harlem, case files all over the floor. Although it had fallen out of favor with young urban professionals in the nineties, Harlem was now hot again, and

Jesse was paying a small fortune to live there.

"Oh, Mr. Beauclaire, please. Where's your spine? I can't believe you're afraid of a bit of snow."

"This isn't just a bit of fluffy, harmless snow, Jane. They say by tonight every car in the city will be buried."

"Right. This from the geniuses who predicted a meteor the size of Yankee Stadium was going to land in Central Park. I don't think so."

Jane was pissed. She wanted to rehearse her opening statement in front of a live body, and Jesse gave good feedback. He was still a little green as a prosecutor, but there was nothing a few long and complicated trials under his belt couldn't fix. He had all the raw material; at the moment only his youth was a disadvantage. Time would take care of that.

Jane hung up and turned on her laptop. She tied her hair into a ponytail and pushed any loose strands behind her ears. She straightened her glasses on her nose and sat upright in her chair. Okay, she said to herself. Let's do it. Let's put Laura Riley behind bars. She tapped at the keys, but nothing came to her. The question of how to best prosecute Mrs. Riley seemed irrelevant now that she had her own riddle to answer. And so her mind wandered.

Who the hell am I supposed to be? Who will be my hero? Not Laura Riley, that's for sure.

Her mother would have been the perfect choice. By all accounts men had adored her; the general reportedly fought two men for her. But Jane had never really known her, so, sadly, she was not an option. Lazy Susan? Not unless lowering your IQ to your shoe size turned men on. Marcie? Jane shuddered at the thought. She was engaged, but to a tediously boring hypochondriacal accountant. No thanks. Her friend Alice? After all, Alice was smart. Alice had attracted a man who was neither a hypochondriac nor a dullard but an amiable, sports-loving computer technician. But Alice had lassoed only one romantic interest in her entire life, and Jane felt that her hero needed to be a repeat offender. It had to be someone who had gone into battle time and again and emerged victorious. Alice couldn't promise that level of success.

Well, there was Cleopatra and Helen of Troy, Jane thought, recalling a succession of high school history projects. No question men had fallen at their feet, but with both women romance had been all about ambience. Jane had no kingdom, army, barge, lackey to fan her with palm fronds or a wooden horse to make any of it happen.

She glanced out of the window. Still no blizzard. Fingers crossed. She didn't want anything to complicate this trial. She had witnesses who had taken days off work and hired babysitters, and she knew what a nightmare it could be for them to re-schedule. The phone rang again.

"Yes, Mr. Beauclaire?"

"Jane, this is your father."

Jane sat up straight, squared her shoulders and reflexively saluted.

"Good morning, Sir."

"Bad down there yet?"

"Excuse me, Sir?"

"The snow. I'm calling to get a read on the situation down there."

"It's fine right now, Sir. The blizzard hasn't started yet."

"Not here either, but they say it should have us good and trapped on the post for at least a day or two. I think it will be very good for the cadets to be locked down with no chance of escape. Might give them a sense of what it's like in a foxhole."

"Yes, Sir. It would be like that."

"Now, Jane, you will not leave your apartment when it starts to get bad."

"Sir, from what they are saying on TV, nobody will be going —"

"There's something about blackouts and bad weather that make civilians become absolutely lawless. I suspect there will be looting and all kinds of crime. I remember the last blizzard; civilians in New York were mugging other civilians just for their snow boots."

Actually, the last part was true. A woman in the Bronx had been held up at gunpoint and ordered to remove her waterproof boots. But it was one incident in a city of nine million people. Nobody was hauling color TVs and car speakers out of Circuit City.

"Yes, Sir."

"Jane, I am ordering you to stay indoors until calm has been restored by the police. Not that I expect that to happen, frankly." He snorted. "Civilian police officers are about as useful as a bunch of ballerinas at the invasion of Normandy."

"Yes, Sir."

"Good-bye, Jane."

"Thank you for calling, Sir."

Jane Spring was standing in front of her

coffeemaker waiting for the pot to fill when she heard a shrill whistling noise outside. She moved to the window and her eyes dilated an inch. The blizzard. It was starting, and just like that jester on TV had warned, snow was coming down in a fury. Stunned, Jane watched at the window. It looked as if someone were on the roof shaking out a giant box of powdered laundry detergent.

Pouring herself a mug of coffee, Jane planned her morning all over again. She chided herself for having wasted so much time already; there would be no more consideration of possible and viable hero candidates until the trial was completed. Disgusted that she had let her personal life compromise her professionalism, she resolved that if she let her mind wander again, she would get down on the floor and do twenty push-ups. Now, back to work, Jane, and that's an order.

First she would craft her opening statement, then go over her questions for cross of defense witnesses. From the list Chip Bancroft had provided, it looked as if he was putting everyone from Laura Riley's kindergarten teacher to her cat on the stand to testify to what a fine upstanding citizen she was.

Jane Spring knew her job was to show

Laura Riley as a jealous and calculated killer, to essentially villainize this wife, mother and PTA volunteer beyond a reasonable doubt. The entire NYPD was depending on it. Jane also knew they had nothing to worry about. She would carve up Laura Riley with pleasure. Jane Spring never had a problem riding female witnesses or defendants — just ask Gloria Markham. But she had to admit a small part of her was fascinated by Mrs. Riley. Jane would never condone her crime, but she did envy the woman's passion. This is what true love is, she thought. To feel so fiercely you would kill if it was taken from you.

I want to feel that. I want someone to feel that about me.

Just not a man with the morals of Thomas Riley, thank you. Jane's ideal man would view infidelity as a crime, not a birthright. He would be dedicated to his job, honorable, courageous, well mannered and intelligent. He would integrate the best of the military with the finest civilian ethics. (Civilians could be frustrating, but she was thankful to them for devising her beloved judicial system of law and order.)

Jane Spring caught herself daydreaming and was outraged at herself, again. She put down her coffee mug, hit the floor and began doing push-ups. Ten minutes later she was parked in front of her laptop, arms burning, and newly energized to begin her work. Her hands rested on the keyboard. Her mind cleared. And then as sure as the sun's rising in the east, the Tates started rhythmically humping each other overhead. She threw her pen hard against the wall. Newlyweds plus blizzard equals no peace and quiet, period.

Jane went to retrieve her pen and looked again out the window. The snow was sticking fast, and everything was now covered in a thin white blanket of sparkling dust. Nobody was on the street anymore, just a few children playing. It was then that she realized the Tates weren't the only people making love at that moment in New York City. Marcie was probably in bed across town making Howard look at fabric swatches and feeding him strawberries between kisses. Chip Bancroft no doubt was between the sheets with some model du jour. Everyone in the city was in the arms of somebody right then.

Everybody but her.

Jane Spring felt overwhelmingly sad and utterly alone. It felt like a conspiracy, this being surrounded by a city of people in love. And what did she have to look forward to? A murder trial. So romantic.

She headed back to the kitchen and pulled a bottle of white wine out of the refrigerator. The Tates were growing louder in the lead-up to their big finish, so Jane turned on the TV to drown out the crescendo of squeals and groans. Every network was running blizzard coverage, and, sadly, not one had anything original to say about the event. They all agreed it was bad. End of story. Civilians were such sheep.

Jane starting flipping through the channels, searching for a movie. Something to kill time until the Tates finally exhausted themselves and fell asleep. They *would* eventually fall asleep, *wouldn't* they?

Click. No, I've seen that. It was terrible.

Click. *Apocalypse Now.* My favorite! Oh, it's the end.

Click. Oh look. Doris Day and Rock Hudson. How the hell does she walk in those heels? She must have bunions the size of Alaska from those shoes. God, he was cute, wasn't he?

Even though they turned up on TV every week somewhere in America, Jane Spring realized she hadn't seen a Doris Day movie for twenty years. Maybe more.

Her grandma Eleanor had loved Doris Day; she was, unquestionably, her favorite star. (Elizabeth Taylor had too many affairs, too many husbands and therefore was relegated to number two.) Grandma Eleanor constantly broke into bars of "Que Sera, Sera" — Doris's signature tune — whenever the mood struck her, which must have been pretty often because even all these years later, Jane still knew all the words.

Like her daughter, Grandma Eleanor had been a general's wife. Then, it was a role that required her to play consort to her husband and hostess to the other wives. For every occasion there were shoes, bags, gloves and hats. For condolence calls, black; for a formal welcoming tea, it could be a pink woolen shift, white gloves and a cocktail ring. Even if she was just hosting an informal get-together with the girls, a pencil skirt and twinset topped with pearls was the norm. And that was just on base.

When Grandma Eleanor moved to Washington, D.C., with Grandpa William after his appointment to the Pentagon, she brought out the big guns. She was a Pentagon wife now, meaning a double-faced white wool coat with fox-trim collar in winter, the black patent leather slingbacks and red silk fitted-bodice dress with rhine-stone butterfly pins in summer. A general's wife, like her husband, was always on duty.

Every summer when Jane went to stay with Grandma Eleanor, her mother's mother would insist they watch every Doris Day movie that came on TV.

"Come sit by Grandma, Janie. That's a good girl. We're going to watch a movie!"

This meant canceling all planned trips to the library or pool, which didn't sit too well with Jane. Worse, as far as Jane could see, the films weren't what she considered exciting. She couldn't understand what so transfixed her grandmother. It seemed to Jane that all that happened was that Doris and Rock Hudson or Doris and Cary Grant argued a lot, and then Doris pretended to be angry at them and then they with her, and then they kissed. The end. When her grandma died when Jane was ten, it was the end of the movies for Jane too.

She checked her watch. She would give herself half an hour tops and then go back to work. If the Tates were still at it by then, she would go upstairs and thump on their door, demanding quiet. She had a trial starting Monday. This was intolerable.

But soon the half hour had stretched

into one full hour, which then stretched into two, then three, then, unbelievably, five. By eight o'clock in the evening Jane had done no work, drunk two bottles of wine and sat through three Doris Day classics. Just her luck there was a marathon scheduled. What a pity Grandma Eleanor had to miss it.

In *Lover Come Back*, Jane watched Rock Hudson, a hunky advertising executive and serial playboy, meet spunky, polite, oh-so-virginal Doris, who lives in a bright yellow apartment, and fall head over heels in love.

In *Pillow Talk*, Jane watched Rock Hudson, a hunky songwriter and serial playboy, run into sweet-as-honey, I'm-waiting-till-I'm-married Doris the interior decorator, and go so gaga for her, he disguised himself as an innocent farm boy from Texas to win her over.

In *That Touch of Mink*, Jane watched Cary Grant, a hunky mogul and serial playboy, meet the I-sleep-in-a-single-bed-even-though-I'm-thirty-two Doris and find himself totally helpless as her frosted-lipstick smile, breathy voice and adoring gaze bring him completely to his knees.

And then as the final credits rolled, Jane Spring realized something absolutely earth-shattering about Doris Day. Something she never saw as a little girl sitting with Grandma on the couch in Washington, D.C.: Doris *always* got the guy. She was the woman men *wanted.*

Until Doris, neither Cary nor Rock had ever met a woman they could spend more than a night with, but suddenly they wanted to spend the rest of their lives with *her. Cary* and *Rock!* Then the most adorable and adored men in America. They could have had anyone — male or female. But they wanted Doris.

Why?

Now Jane understood — courtesy of one blizzard, two bottles of wine and five hours of classic movie channel — that the woman men *say* they want to marry, and the woman they finally *do* marry, is not the same woman at all. They say they want someone smart, opinionated, self-sufficient and sexually available, someone say, like Jane. But they don't. Not one bit. No wonder they kept leaving her.

What they really want is a platinum blonde virgin who wears frosted lipstick, tight pink pencil skirts, pearls, gloves and a smile. They want women who wear cocktail dresses for evenings, silk pajamas for night and heels to go everywhere. They want women who sleep in single beds and paint their apartments yellow, women whose voices whisper and purr, who widen their eyes and take deep breaths when they're angry. They want women with spunk, who step out of the shower into robes of chiffon and give up everything for them once they get married.

They want kittens (Doris), not tigers (Jane), and my lord, now she had proof. For a woman to make Rock Hudson fall in love with you twice and Cary Grant once in the space of five hours was incredible, yes? Not if you were Doris Day.

And then Jane Spring came to her second major epiphany of the day, even though by then it was evening.

All of a sudden it was crystal clear: Up until now she had been doing everything wrong. She didn't take orders from men, she gave them. She didn't look up to men, she looked down on them. She didn't purr when she talked or wiggle when she walked. She didn't charm them, disarm them, then play hard to get; she dismissed them, she critiqued them, she commanded them, she displeased them. No wonder she was home alone on a Saturday night with her law books. Doris wouldn't be. She would be at the Copacabana dancing up a storm.

Jane jumped off the couch and stood to attention. Completely blotto now, she cleared her throat to make an announcement, even though there was nobody else in the room. She tapped on an empty wine bottle with a pen, then lifted it in front of her and declared that once the Riley trial was over, when she began looking for *him,* the man who would love her forever, she would throw Doris into the mix. Maybe not everything, you understand. She couldn't do the gloves, the high heels, the pearls. But the voice? Sure, she could purr, and the ladylike conversation? Easy!

And giving up sex until she had a ring on her finger? She had to. That, it seemed, was the clincher.

Jane Spring was positively giddy. She had found her hero. Doris Day was the MacArthur, the Patton, the Eisenhower of love. The general would never believe it. She could hardly believe it. But it was true, and it was going to change her life.

11

In bed Jane Spring tossed and turned, too excited to sleep. Her mind was racing with thoughts about her mammoth discovery. She had found it, her tactical advantage.

Doris Day.

She was positively euphoric, the way some women are about a diet that promises you can lose ten pounds in two days or the way men are when someone slips them box seats to the World Series. Lying there in the dark, she even started rehearsing a few lines she might toss into conversation when the time came.

"You're an exterminator? Well, that must be fascinating. Tell me more, Brad!"

Boy, was she drunk.

Jane rolled onto her side. Then onto her stomach. Then she sat up and turned the light on. Jane Spring, you are being insubordinate, she scolded herself. Here you are lying around drunk when there is a job to do. What are you thinking, woman?

"Procrastination is the father of defeat,

Jane." The general was right. There was no time to waste.

Jane slipped out of bed and dressed herself in a pair of black pants, a gray turtleneck and black snow boots. In the bathroom she washed her face and put Vaseline on her lips, hoping it might pass for lipstick, which she didn't own. She brushed her long blond hair, then tucked it under a beret. She grabbed her bag and keys, and headed confidently out the door.

"He who dares, wins," she whispered to herself, repeating her father's mantra.

Jane Spring strolled into the bar inside the Metropolitan Hotel on Madison Avenue and sat down. The Met Bar was known as a prime meat market for singles. It should be, she assumed, full of amorous men. Perfect for test-driving her new, ahem, strategy.

She peeled off her coat and beret, shook off the snow and hung them over the back of her bar stool. Her head was still abuzz from two bottles of wine. The place was packed. Bright young things who had braved the snow had come out to talk about how they had braved the snow.

This was the best civilians could do for conversation? Painful. Jane ordered a screwdriver and looked around. She was the only woman fully clothed; every other female there was wearing a miniskirt and Ugg boots. No matter, thought Jane, throwing back a little more liquid courage. I don't need a short skirt and fluffy boots. I'll dazzle them with my killer Doris-quality conversation.

She took a deep breath, ordered another round, and as she was reaching for her wallet, a deep voice said, "Hey, put that away, I've got it." Jane looked up to find a tall man with a mustache standing over her; he was a young, playful forty. He looked to be alone, and he wasn't half bad.

"Why, thank you," Jane said, as the drink was placed before her.

"Hi, I'm Hank," he said extending a hand. Jane lengthened her neck, widened her eyes and smiled. "I'm Jane. What a pleasure to meet you," she purred.

Well, that wasn't too hard, she thought. She didn't feel half as stupid as she'd anticipated. Actually, if she was being honest, playing Doris was kind of fun.

"May I sit?"

"That would be lovely, Hank," she said, sliding her stool over to make room for him to squeeze in.

"So, do you live around here?" Jane asked, fixing her eyes onto his.

"No, just in town for a sales conference."

"Well then, welcome to New York! What do you sell, Hank?" Jane asked, tilting her head to one side. Remember, Jane, no matter what he does, act interested. Fascinated. Give compliments.

"Office furniture. Desks. Chairs. Filing cabinets. I know it probably doesn't sound all that exciting but —"

"Oh, Hank. You don't have to apologize to me. I think it sounds *very* exciting. And important! If it wasn't for people like you, Hank, how would any of us be able to do our jobs? I know without my filing cabinets I wouldn't survive a day at work."

Good girl, Jane, now you're getting the hang of it.

Boy, he liked her. She wasn't distracted like the woman he'd met earlier who had ditched him for someone with better earning potential once she learned what he did for a living. That hurt. This one gave him her undivided attention. She was polite, sweet, sexy in a *very* down-to-earth sort of way. He guessed there was a killer bod under all those clothes.

"And where do you work, Jane?" he asked leaning in closer. So close she could smell his toothpaste mingling with his aftershave.

"Me? Downtown." Oh, Jane! The minute she said it, she knew it was a mistake. Doris never worked downtown.

"I mean I work in Midtown. Madison Avenue. Look at me, I don't even know what I'm saying this storm has me so mixed up!" Jane cocked her head and chuckled.

"And what does a pretty girl like you do on Madison Avenue?" he asked.

"I'm in advertising," Jane replied, acting coy. Doris always worked in advertising; apparently, the only eligible bachelors in New York in the sixties worked on Madison Avenue. Everyone else in the entire city was either a wanted criminal or married.

"Wow. What do you advertise?"

"Laundry detergent. Floor cleaner. Pretty much anything with bubbles. At work they call me the Bubbles Queen!" She laughed, finishing her drink.

"Well, I can see why. You're one ball of fun."

Hank beamed. Yep, this one was a winner. If things kept going like this, he might even have a place to stay if they closed the airports.

"Listen, Jane. This place is a madhouse. How about we leave here and go somewhere quiet where we can talk."

"Why, Hank, I think that would be a lovely —"

And then she felt it. A forceful shove in her back that knocked her glasses off her face, her butt off her stool. Jane grabbed on to the bar railing to steady herself, then looked around. A man in his late thirties clad in a Yankees warm-up jacket and matching pants had pushed past her on his way to the other end of the bar. He had kept going; there was no apology proffered. Hank helped her back on her stool.

Ordinarily Jane would have given that disrespectful civilian a piece of her mind supplemented with threats of a lawsuit. This time she merely intended to right the wrong and get some more practice in while she could.

"Just give me a minute, Hank, thank you," she said, standing up. "I think somebody needs to know that is no way to treat a lady."

"Of course."

Jane walked to the end of the bar, Hank's eyes following.

"Excuse me?" Jane said, tapping her assailant on the shoulder. Jane was smiling and twirling a lock of hair.

"Yes?"

The man, Jane could see now that she

had her glasses back on, was big. Huge. The kind of meathead whose biceps' circumferences were so big he couldn't easily fold his arms. And now he was checking *her* out trying to decide whether to file her under school librarian or sexy secretary. His lips seemed to move while he thought. Jane kept smiling. She widened her eyes and lowered her voice to a soft whisper.

"Sir, I just have to tell you that I am a little shocked. I can't believe you would push a lady without apologizing."

"What? Who'd I push? You?" he said. He reached into a bowl of peanuts, grabbed a handful and started tossing them into his mouth indignantly, one by one.

"Yes. Me. As you walked past. I fell off my stool over there and nearly broke my hip!" Jane threw him a huge grin. Doris smiled through everything.

The man threw the remaining peanuts into his mouth and reached out with both arms to grab Jane's waist. Then he ran his hands up and down, starting at her pelvis and ending at her thighs. "Those hips feel fine to me, babe, so I don't know what bug's crawled up your ass. But beat it. I didn't knock you down, so I'm not apologizing for nothing I didn't do."

Jane couldn't believe it. The greasy

hands, the poor diction, the rudeness. This was too much. Screw Doris. Suddenly she dropped the act and resumed being Jane Spring, prosecutor. The voice deepened, the eyes narrowed. She moved in closer for the kill.

"Listen, you pathetic overgrown ball boy," she barked, grabbing his collar and pulling her prey up close to her so they were practically nose to nose. His eyes bulged with fear and surprise. Hell hath no fury. "You have no idea whom you're dealing with." The room went quiet. Hank's head nearly snapped off his neck. When the man protested, she cut off his air supply with her thumb and brought her right knee to his testicles to keep him restrained. "I'm a black belt in thirteen different methods of kicking your ass. And I've made men a lot bigger and a lot stronger than you cry, so I don't want to hear your excuses because, quite frankly, I don't like your tone. You knocked me over right then, and if you don't apologize for that within the next four seconds, *and* for having the audacity to lay your filthy, greasy paws on me, I will charge you with assault and send you up to Rikers for a nice long winter holiday. Come Christmas you'll be getting your stocking stuffed by

Bob and Tyrone and whoever else in cell block eight thinks you're pretty."

"Okay, okay, I'm sorry, I'm sorry," he gasped.

Jane Spring let go of the guy, and he slumped back onto his bar stool.

"You undercover?" he said nervously, massaging his throat.

"You don't want to know what I am," she snarled in her best Clint Eastwood as she turned to walk away.

Satisfied, she marched proudly back to Hank's side, sat down and smiled sweetly at him. "Where were we?" she purred, gathering her things.

Hank stared at Jane. Oh, God, she's crazy, he thought. One of those psycho New York feminazis he'd always heard about. He had to get out of there.

Hank began to make a big show of looking at his watch. "My, it's later than I realized, Jane. I better hit the hay. Busy day tomorrow. Leave me your number. I'll call you."

Jane's heart sank. Whether she was Doris or Jane, she knew that "I'll call you" actually meant "I'll never call you. It's over. I don't like you anymore. I'm moving on."

"It was lovely meeting you, Hank," Jane called after him. Hank didn't even turn around to respond in kind. He left so fast he practically left skid marks.

The bartender cleared her glass and asked about another round. Jane shook her head, then dropped it into her hands. Striking out with Hank was not where she thought the night would end. Another drink, maybe a kiss, but this? She had done everything Doris had done, hadn't she, with the minor exception of scaring the living daylights out of some Yankees fan?

She had, she decided. She had been polite and sweet and interested and even said she worked in advertising.

So why did he leave?

12

Jane Spring woke up in terrible shape. Still in her clothes from the night before, she had no recollection of coming home or of how she'd gotten a copy of the *New York Times*, which was now strewn all over her bedroom floor. All she could admit to was that she had a throbbing headache. That she knew.

She brushed her hair off her face and looked at her alarm clock. Ten a.m. Good grief, this was a disaster. She had a trial starting the next day and more work to do than God. No time to get to the pool, which in her state maybe wasn't such a bad thing. Her head felt so heavy she'd probably drown under the weight of it.

She lowered herself out of bed and dug through the newspaper until she found the Sunday Styles section. Jane would now participate in the ritual carried out by all single women in New York — death by marriage announcements. Each Sunday, one is required to read all the wedding notices in full, torturing oneself with every word.

Jane read about one bride who was both an optometrist and collected Hummel figurines. Is that what want men want? A lifetime supply of prescription glasses and tiny porcelain angels on the mantel? Another bride was an accountant who listed taxidermy as a hobby. Was she what men wanted? A woman who can do your taxes and stuff dead cats at the same time? No. They wanted Doris. She was sure of it.

She threw away the paper and crawled back under the covers. The phone rang, and Jane moaned as her arm crept out slowly to grab it.

"Jane Spring," she said in a very low and deeply hungover voice.

"Jane, I know you're not going to like this."

It was Lawrence Park, her supervisor. Calling her at home on a Sunday morning. No, she didn't like this.

"Court is canceled for tomorrow. The mayor has just made an announcement. All city offices, including courts, are closed until Tuesday."

Jane dragged herself up and looked out the window. The blizzard had stopped; all that was left were three feet of snow on the ground.

"Why cancel court? I don't understand."

He knew she wouldn't.

"Listen, Jane. The subway tracks are frozen. People's cars are still buried under snow. Half your witnesses wouldn't be able to make it anyway."

Civilians! Such babies, they can't seem to function through anything, even the slightest change in temperature. After all, winter came every year like clockwork; you'd think with all of its experience over thousands of years, mankind would finally be prepared.

"Fine. Let's hope by Tuesday the good people of New York will have located their cars and the geniuses who run the subway will have figured out how to get it going again. Thank you, Lawrence. I'll see you Tuesday."

Actually, this wasn't so bad. She needed another day to prepare, given that she'd lost Saturday to the movies. And the bar. Oh God, the bar. And now that she had time, she might even allow herself to sleep another hour before going to work on her cross-examination.

Thoughts of the night before, the full Technicolor disaster, hit Jane as she lay there trying to go back to sleep. What happened? It had started off so well with Hank. He seemed to genuinely respond to her as Doris. He'd leaned in, he'd asked her to leave with him, he'd even called her "one ball of fun." That was a definite first. Nobody had *ever* said that about Jane Spring before. The evidence showed she was definitely on the right track.

So why did he run? She cross-examined herself. Why did my case fall apart at the end? Because I had a few words with that thug who assaulted me? Doris always defended herself when she felt her honor had been compromised. Heck, Hank encouraged me! Maybe I got a little angrier than Doris would have, but it still doesn't explain why he vanished.

Jane sat bolt upright in bed. She hadn't seen it then, but now she knew. Hank had called her a ball of fun. Nice compliment, sure, but it hardly defined her as irresistible. That's what Doris was; that's why men wanted her. Being *fun* wouldn't exactly make men lose their reason, their hearts, their appetites over her. Of course he'd left. She wasn't enough to sustain him for the long haul. And suddenly Jane Spring knew why. To put it in the general's terms, she was only fighting a piece of the battle.

What made men crazy for Doris wasn't just her sunny conversation, it was the totality of her. The hair, the clothes, the shoes, the manners, the speech, even the pastel apartment. It was the *package* that made her irresistible, that made her the woman men wanted above all others.

Jane Spring now saw the error of her ways, and also how she could rectify them. The only way landing a man would ever work, the only way it worked for Doris, was to *be* Doris, heart and soul, not just select parts of her.

That was what men wanted. *That* was what Hank had wanted: Doris in full Technicolor.

But how? Talking like her was one thing, but walking, dressing, sitting like her? Living in a yellow apartment? Taking bubble baths instead of showers? Who had that kind of time?

It was impossible, not to mention unprofessional and patently ridiculous. She was an assistant district attorney for the City of New York with a murder trial starting in less than two days. Apart from everything else, the most important thing Jane needed in court was the one thing Doris didn't possess. Venom.

So here she was at an impasse, fully aware of what she needed to do, but convinced beyond a reasonable doubt that the task was impossible. Jane shook her head, thinking, I'll be laughed out of town, not to mention disbarred. She fell back in bed and pulled the blankets over her, one of the general's old axioms echoing in her head: *"To retreat is to guarantee defeat, Jane."* Except when you work in the civilian world, sir. Then retreat is the only option if you still want to have a job. Jane knew her father would be furious if he could hear her proffering one excuse after another.

The doorbell rang. Jane thought this a clear sign she must get out of bed, and as she was already dressed, she could even open the door. She padded her way across the living room and was so distracted by thoughts of Hank and Doris that she turned the knob without checking through the peephole first.

"Hi, Jane!"

Oh, Lord, it was the Tates. Fully clothed. How refreshing. Jane did her best impression of a smile, though her head seared with pain.

"Hi back to the Tates!" she said.

"We're here to check up on you!" they chorused. They were holding hands.

"Excuse me?"

"They said on TV you should check on

your neighbors if they are elderly, infirm or single. You know, people with disabilities," said the male Tate.

"Like, to make sure you didn't freeze to death or anything. Apparently a lot of pipes froze and people didn't have heat or water last night," said the female Tate.

People with disabilities? thought Jane, holding on to the door to stop herself from falling over with shock. Did I just hear right? The Tates, no, actually, the entire world has tagged me as part of a group that includes the elderly and infirm. Because I'm *single?* This is outrageous! Not to mention totally unconstitutional. It's not like I haven't been trying to start a relationship. Look at last night. No, don't look.

"Well, it was very nice of you to stop by, but as you can see, I did not freeze to death overnight."

"Oh, great!" they chirped. "If you need anything, you know where to find us." The Tates smiled and turned to walk to the elevator. Jane shut the door and straightened her spine, then marched into her kitchen like a cadet.

"The *elderly, infirm* and *me!*" she screamed.

She grabbed a paper filter and shoved it

into her coffeemaker, then tore a fresh bag of coffee open with her teeth.

Well. Now it's clear I have no choice, she thought, filling the coffeemaker with water. What is a prosecutor but an actor with a courtroom as his theater? I act every day; surely I can do this too. They might certify me, disbar me, but this absolutely tells me the situation report is dire, that there is only one path to take for a clear shot at victory.

Gentlemen, start your engines.

Doris, here I come.

13

Now that Jane Spring had made her decision, her interest in spending the day working on the Riley trial was less than zero. How could she think about a prosecution strategy when she had so much work to do personally? She perched on the sofa, a mug of coffee in one hand, a yellow legal pad in the other. She replayed in her mind the movies she'd watched the day before, stopping her internal projector every so often to list the specific qualities that had made Doris the woman men wanted.

1. Persona
2. Body language
3. Personal grooming
4. Wardrobe
5. Home decor

Given the degree of difficulty, Jane decided to start easy and work the steps in reverse. She would create an environment conducive to Doris, and then transform herself into Doris. In short, the plan called for renovating the apartment first, Jane Spring second.

Though the odd store was shuttered, 98 percent of them were open, testament to the great American religion of capitalism. Among adherents of this religion, New York is the Holy Land. No people on God's green earth are more devoted to making a buck than New Yorkers, and a blizzard is a serious opportunity not to be squandered. Umbrellas, shovels, rock salt, snowshoes, warm socks, warm soup, hot coffee, books, videos, CDs, blankets — people wanted them all, and they wanted them now. Forget staying home, Starbucks was wall-to-wall people. Diners were packed. Hardware stores swamped. At Bloomingdale's there wasn't a waterproof boot left on the shelves. Jane Spring walked into Gracious Home, a building supplies and decorating store three blocks from her building, and wove her way through a line of people at the register paying for shovels.

She had only been there once before, and that trip had been uneventful. She'd bought a plunger when her toilet had overflowed. This trip she left with five cans of buttercup-yellow paint, one can of bright white, a paint roller and tray, four glass vases, a canary-yellow sofa slipcover, six dozen silk daisies with stems, two sets of powder-blue silk curtains and rails, two white lamp shades trimmed in blue ribbon, a boxed set of white sheets and pillowcases and two yellow flannel blankets with satin trim.

Once Jane was home she dialed a mattress company that advertised day and night on television. She knew the jingle by heart. Were they open? Of course they were. We're open seven days a week, taking orders twenty-four hours a day — rain, hail or snow. If she paid extra, would they deliver a mattress today? Yes, they would, although instead of two hours, it might be more like four, given the fact that not all the roads were plowed. But we'll get there. Very good, Jane said. I'd like to place an order.

Jane Spring dragged her furniture into the middle of her living room, covered it with an old sheet, and went to work. As if in a trance, she painted her walls buttercup yellow and the black wall unit and bookshelves white. Even the chrome and glass coffee table was transformed with her brush.

She fitted the canary-yellow slipcover around the black leather sofa, and even though the walls weren't dry yet, she couldn't wait to see how the blue silk curtains would look, so she carefully hung them too. Just as she finished the living room, the buzzer rang out, and she instructed the delivery men to bring their package up to 4R.

"I see you're doing a little decorating," said one of the delivery men as he and his partner heaved a single twin mattress and frame through the doorway.

"Yes, that's right," said Jane.

"Which way to your kid's room?"

"Oh, I don't have a child," she said, leading them into her bedroom. "You'll take the queen-size with you, yes, gentlemen? Your ad on TV says you remove the old beds for free."

"This is for you?" asked the second delivery man, incredulous. "You want us to take away the queen and leave with you with the single?"

"Yes." Jane raised her eyebrows and summoned her prosecutorial voice. "Is that going to be a problem, gentlemen?"

They quickly dismantled the queen-size mattress and carted it away, leaving Jane to stare at her new single bed, all shrink-wrapped in plastic.

"Must be some new-age thing where you give up all earthly pleasures and concentrate on your spirituality or something," said one, once they were back in their truck.

"Yeah, maybe it's something to do with yoga."

"No way. Those yoga people sleep on mats on the floor and shit like that, man. They wouldn't be buying a bed."

"Maybe she's going to become a nun, and she's test-driving the idea of, you know, sleeping alone before she goes the whole nine."

The delivery men nodded in agreement. That was it. The chick in 4R was preparing for a life of obedience, chastity and poverty. But then what about that new bright yellow room and those expensive blue curtains? What kind of convent was this chick going to anyway?

At five p.m., with every wall in her apartment sunny and bright, her new bed made up with crisp white sheets and pretty yellow blankets, silk daisies in every room, Jane Spring picked up her legal pad and went to work on her next task.

"Step four," she read out loud. "Wardrobe."

Jane took the elevator down to the basement, her heart racing. Was it the paint fumes that made her feel so light-headed or the excitement of finally having seized on a solution? As she turned on the light in the storage room, a mouse scurried under an old ceiling fan left in a corner. She stepped over a rusted bike and made her way toward an old trunk piled high with boxes and the odd lamp shade. The trunk had belonged to her grandma Eleanor. When her grandmother died, she left all her belongings to her only granddaughter, who until this moment never imagined she would have any use for them. Now Jane wanted nothing more. She leaned over and tried to drag the trunk by its handle; clearly, it was heavier than she'd remembered. She raced upstairs to the lobby to pry a doorman away from the front desk. He demurred until Jane offered him five dollars. Fifteen, he said. Fine, ten. Together they carried the trunk out of the basement and into the elevator.

"What have you got in here?" he asked, groaning under the weight.

"All my grandmother's things," said Jane.

"Really? You sure it isn't your grandmother?"

"I'm quite sure. She just liked to shop a lot."

"Shop for what? Bricks?"

Jane laughed, then stared hard at her sweating accomplice. Sooner than you know, she wanted to say, you'll see exactly what's in here.

That night Jane slept in a pair of Grandma Eleanor's freshly laundered Chinese blue silk pajamas. She liked the way they felt cool and soft against her skin. Apart from turning and slamming into the wall a couple of times, Jane thought the night in the single bed under the soft yellow blankets went quite well. She was so tired, even the cold didn't rouse her. To air out the paint fumes she had left every window in the apartment open. When she woke in the morning, her lips were the same blue as her pajamas. No matter. The first-night bed rehearsal had been, she believed, an unqualified success. She was on her way.

Jesse called first thing suggesting that since the roads were plowed, he take a bus down to her apartment so they could go over the case. "I'll be at your place at nine. Good? I'll bring muffins; you're in charge of coffee."

Jane almost agreed before she realized what Jesse would be walking into. How on earth would she explain a renovation in the middle of a blizzard? Besides, she didn't want anyone to see anything, *know* anything, until she had become 100 percent Doris. She had learned from the incident in the bar that half measures don't work.

142

Only when every heading had been crossed off her list would the magic begin: she would become the woman men wanted.

"Um, no. Look, I've been stuck in here for two days, and I am just crazy to get out. Let's meet somewhere halfway between us; it would give me a chance to stretch my legs."

"Have you been out, Jane?"

"Out? No, I told you. I've been in here the whole time preparing."

"Well, I don't know how much stretching you can do out there without breaking a limb. It's pretty damn slippery. I nearly did a split going out to get the *Times* this morning."

"A little exercise never hurt anyone, Counselor. Let's say Patsy's Pastry Shop on 110th Street."

"Perfect. I'll see you there in an hour."

Jane slipped out of Grandma Eleanor's pajamas and dressed herself in jeans, snow boots, a black sweatshirt, black overcoat, gloves and scarf. She tucked her long blond hair under her black beret, gathered up all her case notes, pushed her glasses up on the bridge of her nose and walked out the door.

If everything went according to plan, she would never leave the apartment that way again.

14

In the café Jane read Jesse her opening statement and, given that everyone else present was sitting quietly and reading papers, she developed quite an audience. Some even applauded when she finished. Jesse also gave her a thumbs-up, and after two more hours comparing notes, rehearsing cross-examination and double-checking witness lists, they parted ways.

Jesse went to the gym.

Jane went to Duane Reade. It was time for step three: personal grooming, that is, makeup and hair care.

It took Jane Spring a few minutes to find the cosmetics section; in thirty-four years she had never been there before. She stared in awe at the wall of products, practically a city block of lipstick, foundation, mascara, concealer. God, did women really wear *all* this stuff? Think of it as war paint, she told herself. Soldiers wear it in battle to secure victory; I will dutifully wear it to secure mine.

When they were teenagers, Alice had

once schooled a reluctant Jane in the basics of makeup application, lessons she hadn't forgotten, only dismissed. At the time Jane had been appalled at the civilian influences her best friend had succumbed to; now she blessed her for it.

Jane selected a tube of mascara, liquid eyeliner, a jar of light honey-tan foundation, one frosted-pink lipstick, one bottle of frosted-white nail polish, one compact of blue eye shadow and a translucent-powder compact. She then moved over to the hair-care section and picked up a can of hair spray, a box of platinum-blond hair dye, a pair of barber scissors, a box of rollers and three packets of tiny hair bows: one red, one pink, one blue.

In the personal care section she grabbed a bottle of bubble bath and a jar of Pond's cold cream. In the electronics section she chose a small hair dryer, and then, after double-checking that she had everything on her list, she stood in line for the cashier. Her cell phone rang. It was Alice. Oh, Alice, Jane thought, what great timing, your old makeup lessons were just on my mind.

"Hey, Springie. How are you surviving the blizzard?"

"Oh, it's nothing. Civilians think it's Armageddon."

"What are you doing?"

"Right now, I'm at the pharmacy. Picking up the usual — soap, paper towels, toothpaste." She was, in fact, buying none of the above, and the woman in line behind her glanced at her basket and gave her a knowing stare.

"So, Springie, did you think about what we talked about the other day?"

Sensing her friend's hurt, Alice had not called back immediately to continue raking over Jane's miserable love life. She had said her piece and wanted to leave Jane space to mull things over.

"I did, Alice. In fact, I did more than think. I'm doing something about it just like you said." Jane emptied the entire contents of her basket onto the counter. "I got myself a dating coach," she whispered. The checkout clerk briefly looked up.

"Good for you, Springie. I hear they're all the rage these days. Who is it?"

"A woman who came highly recommended. Her name's Doris."

"Doris. Sounds like someone you can trust. So how does it work?"

"She gives me advice, I follow it. It's simple."

"Just don't let her make you do anything too crazy, Springie."

"Crazy? Alice, this is me you're talking to." Jane laughed as she handed the cashier a credit card.

"I know," Alice replied. Privately, she wished this Doris, whoever she was, lots of luck. Getting her best friend to change would be no walk in the park. Climbing Everest would be more like it.

Cutting her hair was the hardest part for Jane Spring. She stood in the bathroom in front of the mirror, scissors in hand, and steeled herself. She knew it had to come off. Doris sported a cute, short bob — just one of the things men adored her for.

Jane thought of all those new recruits getting their buzz cuts the first day of basic training. She remembered sneaking up to the windows of the base barber shop and watching the strands of hair slowly fall to the floor as their heads were shaved clean. They whimpered too, so she allowed herself a minute before she pressed on.

She secured a chunk of hair and made the first cut. She held up the freshly shorn locks in front of her. It was at least ten inches long. Well, can't stop now.

The rest of it came off easily. She combed her hair up over her head and matched the shorter strands with the longer, then cut them evenly. When she was done, she cut careful bangs across her forehead, then dyed the whole shebang platinum and dried it so the ends curled under.

When everything was finished, her hair still all over the floor, Jane looked at herself in the mirror again. Really looked. A half smile crept along her face. She liked it.

"Jane Spring, you look great if I do say so myself," she said, admiring herself and patting her hair. "Not half bad at all!"

That afternoon Jane devoted herself to total immersion in the final two steps, body language and persona. Though she considered her outing to the bar and subsequent success with Hank (before he'd bolted, that is) a good first run-through, clearly there was still work to do. Jane dressed herself in one of Grandma Eleanor's cocktail dresses and a pair of pumps (ouch), dragged a chair in front of her hallway mirror and sat, crossing her legs at the ankles and cupping her hands in her lap. She straightened her posture, studied the position closely and committed it to memory. Next, she released her legs and crossed one knee over the other. These were Doris's famous seated poses. She repeated each one twice more. Lastly, Jane patted her hair, cocked her head to one side and smiled. Perfect!

Excited, she pushed the chair aside and started to walk up and down in front of the mirror. Slowly, Jane, slowly. Calmly. Small steps. Remember, you're a lady. This is not a military cadet parade. Shoulders loose. And don't forget, head up, and smile. Doris Day never even crossed Madison Avenue in the rain without smiling. Jane Spring walked up and down her hallway for ten more minutes before her feet gave way. Maybe she should sleep in the heels to get used to them? Is that how other women did it?

She kicked off the pumps and sat on her new yellow sofa. Returning again to the seated formation of one ankle crossed over the other, Jane began conversing with a series of imaginary guests. (And Mrs. Kearns thought she was the only one.) Mastering step one, persona, was critical if Jane was to land Mr. Right. Sure, men responded to Doris's happy apartment and bobbed golden hair, the pink pastel suits and the plucky wide-eyed stare, but what made them fall in love with her was that sunny, ebullient personality and the voice of spun sugar. And, Jane reminded herself, the virgin thing. Don't forget that. Doris was modest, moral and totally inaccessible in *that* department. That's what really drove men over the edge.

Well, at least she wouldn't have to practice not having sex, Jane thought.

"Good morning!" she said out loud with all the enthusiasm she could muster. Smile, Jane, smile. "Hello, Susan. I'm so pleased to see you this morning." Jane blanched. Would she really have to tell that bone-lazy excuse for a secretary she was happy to see her? Were there no exceptions to this plan? Apparently not. The one thing about Doris you could count on was that everyone got the same treatment.

"Ladies and gentlemen of the jury," she declared. Smile, Jane, smile. "No doubt you, like me, are shocked by what you have heard during this trial. A man had an affair with a younger woman (purse lips, Jane, look horrified), but does he deserve to be killed over it?"

For the next forty-five minutes Jane inhabited Doris, body and soul. She practiced greeting her colleagues, her opening statement, her constant smile. By the time she was done, her jaw ached like hell. Jane Spring had never smiled so much in her entire life. She hopped off the sofa and marched into the bathroom. No, stop it

Jane, no more marching. Small steps, remember? She stared into the medicine cabinet mirror and told herself to think of times when she had felt mad as hell. Images of Gloria Markham, Lazy Susan and John Gillespie filled her mind. At those times her first response had been to lash out; now she would take a different path. Think how angry they made you, Jane. Now, concentrate. Jane stood up straight, widened her eyes and took three deep breaths, just as Doris did when confronted with the wily shenanigans of Rock Hudson or Cary Grant. In. Out. In. Out. In. Out. Slow and deep, Jane. Good, Jane. You've got it. One more time. In. Out. In. Ou— she was just coming into the next exhale when the phone rang. She ran to answer it, praying it wasn't the general again.

It was worse. Chip Bancroft.

She wondered for a moment what *he* wanted in a woman. Would it be Doris? Did she dare hope? "Well, hello, Mr. Bancroft. Calling me to brag about winning the trial before it's begun?"

"Oh, Jane. Haven't seen you for months. Nice to hear you haven't changed."

You might not say that, Chip, when you see me next.

"Mr. Bancroft, I have a trial tomorrow

that I'm trying to get ready for."

"Oh, and I'm not? You think with a murder trial in twenty-four hours I'm sitting around watching the game?"

"No, I didn't say that. My guess is you're probably lying in bed with, oh, what's her name this week? Bjorgia? Forgive me, is that with or without the umlaut?"

Jane had read in the *New York Post* that Chip had just split with one model so he could hook up with another. God forbid he should date a woman with brains, let alone a last name.

"Oh, nice, Jane."

"But I'm not wrong, am I?"

"Yes, you are wrong."

"Oh? She's already gone home? You forget, Mr. Bancroft, I've known you a long time. And from what I've heard in my office, some lawyers never change their spots."

Chip Bancroft had no comeback at this point, and Jane knew it. It was common knowledge Chip liked to spread his charm around. There weren't too many defense attorneys who could boast losing a trial but bedding an assistant district attorney as a consolation prize. But Chip Bancroft could say it twice, and that was just in the last eight months. He wanted to tell Jane

Spring he thought her problem was that she just needed to get laid, but he kept his mouth shut. He didn't want to antagonize her, lest she become more vengeful in court.

"Do you want to know why I'm calling, or are you just going to make snide comments about my personal life?"

"No, you're right, Mr. Bancroft. I'll be seeing you tomorrow. It will be so much more effective to make them in person. State your business."

"I'm calling to check whether any of your witnesses have given notice they will not be present tomorrow or Wednesday because of the blizzard. A colleague told me one of his witnesses is snowed in, in Chicago. You do understand that if you have to change the order of witnesses, it would necessitate my prepping for a different cross-examination?"

"Yes. And no, no change, Counselor. All my witnesses will be present and accounted for."

"Great."

"Well, thank you for calling, Mr. Bancroft. I must say I find your diligence most impressive."

"As I'm sure yours will be, Jane."

"You can bet on it, Mr. Bancroft."

"Listen, Jane, while I have you on the phone, for what it's worth, I saw Laura Riley at Rikers today, and the woman is a mess. Hysterical. I'm telling you, some women I defend, they shoot their husbands and can't stop dancing around their cells. She's not dancing. She's a wreck. She wants him back."

"Well, then she shouldn't have murdered him in cold blood."

"Jane, listen. I'm not telling you how to do your job. I'm just asking that when you open tomorrow, keep your eyes on the jury and don't give her the finger-pointing, narrow-eyes routine. You'll have plenty of time for that later. I just want her to get used to the court, the judge and the jury first. I swear Jane, if you go for the jugular right away, she'll be in tears and I'll demand a recess."

"What is this I hear? Chip Bancroft has a soft side? You're actually worried about your client? I thought the only thing you worried about is whether the wine is chilled and your bed warm."

Chip groaned audibly. "Jane, the woman is a mess. Please. She's never been in a court before, let alone on trial for murder. All I'm asking is that you give her half a day to calm down before you start in."

Jane Spring had to say that privately she was quite impressed. No matter how tough they might be, all defendants walk into their trials like small children. It's intimidating, terrifying, hearing your name read along with the charges. And here was Chip asking for a little downtime for a client who was clearly in distress. Or was he? With Chip you never knew. He could be trying to soften her up only to body slam her in court tomorrow. There was no way she would give him an inch. None.

"Nice try, Counselor, but I suggest you read your copy of the Constitution. Everybody is equal before the law. Nobody gets special favors. See you tomorrow."

Chip Bancroft hung up the phone.

Bitch.

15

Jane Spring walked into the bathroom to shower and jumped when she caught sight of herself in the mirror. Her hair was really gone. She reached her hand around the nape of her neck; it felt strange to have it so exposed.

Onward, Jane. This is no time for getting emotional.

Showered and scrubbed, she stood back and stared at the clothes she had laid out the night before. It had taken her more than an hour to select the right combination. For her first day as Doris she would wear a pink wool pencil skirt with matching shawl-collar jacket, paired with a white silk shirt with a ribbon that tied in a bow at the neck. The shoes were white pumps, the stockings clear. In Grandma Eleanor's jewelry box she had found a pearl pin in the shape of a flower. She had chosen pearl studs for her ears and a chunky gold bracelet with a huge dangling gold coin for her wrist.

But the pièce de résistance was the bra.

Jane stared at her grandmother's pink cross-stitched satin brassiere with five rows of hooks in back and cups that pointed like torpedoes in front, and wondered if she would able to (a) do it up and (b) do it justice. Up until now she had donned spandex sports bras exclusively, which had the effect of containing rather than enhancing what nature had given her. Grandma Eleanor's bras, however, were not about containment. They were about creating a pair of breasts that filled out both a cashmere sweater and a grown man's pants in equal measure.

Jane stared at everything for a full five minutes before retying the belt on her grandmother's blue Chinese silk robe and heading back to the bathroom. It was the first time in the history of her career as a prosecutor that she was not going to swim two miles the morning before a new trial. In the past she could always comfortably allocate forty minutes to the pool because she only needed ten to get dressed. But in the dress rehearsal the night before, she had found it took a full thirty minutes to get ready (so many zips and buttons!) and that didn't include makeup and hair. She knew she would get faster with practice, but she had resolved that the pool would have to do without her for a day in the interest of fashion.

On the Internet the night before, Jane had downloaded three color movie stills of Doris Day. They were now tacked to the wall next to the bathroom mirror. Starting with foundation, she painted her face a light honey tan. She then checked against the photos of Doris, looked back in the mirror and, decidedly pleased, she moved on to the mascara, which she applied just as Alice had instructed all those years ago. Top lids first, then bottom. Not bad. Then eyeliner, which required the utmost concentration. This Alice had not schooled her in, and she had made such a botch of it while practicing the night before that she was tempted to do without it entirely, but, determined, she took a deep breath, steadied herself and forged ahead. It looked half decent, with just a few smudges she could fix with cold cream and a Q-tip. She finished the second eyelid, then smothered them both in blue eyeshadow. Jane Spring outlined her lips slowly in the pink frosted lipstick, then colored them in. Finished, she stood back from the mirror and stared at the pictures of Doris once more. Then to the mirror. Then back to Doris. She had to admit that the comparison was pretty darn close.

In her bedroom Jane slipped her arms through the straps of her grandmother's enormous brassiere. Her sports bras didn't have hooks; how would she know a woman works a bra back to front? But she would learn. After struggling and failing to fasten it, she slipped it off and spun it around so the cups rested in the crook of her back, the hooks at her waist. Methodically she clasped them together, spun it around again and lifted herself in. Then she opened her sock drawer and pulled out two pairs of white sports socks and loaded them into the cups. No, too big. She raced to the bathroom to try with tissues, stopping at five sheets per cup. Perfect! And if I get a bloody nose, I'm all set.

She put on the white silk shirt, tying the bow at her neck. She thought the bow was lame, but look what it had landed Doris. Rock and Cary. Exactly.

Face it, she told herself. You can't argue with results.

Jane was slightly taller than her grandmother, so the pencil skirt, which was designed to hit two inches below the knee, skimmed Jane's knee bone. The pink jacket buttoned up neatly over the shirt, and Jane silently thanked Grandma Eleanor for having her clothes custom made. Every piece from the ground up was designed to fit together like magic, meaning even a woman as sartorially clueless as Jane Spring would actually look like she knew how to coordinate separates.

Jane checked herself in the mirror, fascinated by her own reflection. The skirt gave her curves; the bra gave her contours. As a little girl, Jane had never been allowed to dress up. Frocks and ribbons for a girl growing up on an army base? Her father would never hear of it. The general decreed that little girls who paraded in dresses and bows were self-centered and lacked discipline. And so her father would never hear of it. A party frock from Grandma Eleanor when Jane was eight was immediately relegated to the back of the closet. As was the Halloween princess costume. Jane loyally followed his commands, and instead she had worn her brothers' hand-me-down jeans and T-shirts. Even as an adult she never ventured to wear anything but pants. So as Jane slipped into Grandma Eleanor's ensemble, she had no idea the hold her new look would have on her emotions. As far she had been concerned, dressing was simply something one had to do. But here she was, admiring herself in the mirror, turning sideways, turning back, surprised by the sensations she was feeling.

Ah, the power of a tight skirt! Contrary to the general's dictums, the outfit didn't make her feel selfish or undisciplined. But it did make her stand confidently, walk softly and feel, what was it? *Desirable.* That's it. *Sensual.* No wonder women dressed like this!

She slipped on the white pumps, which pinched because they were half a size too small, then snapped the bracelet, pin and earrings in place. Then it was back to the bathroom to comb her hair and tease it so it framed her face like a giant bubble. Doris firmly believed in the Texas adage "The higher the hair, the closer to God," and Jane obediently followed her cue.

Contact lenses came next. Normally she only wore them in the pool; now they would become a constant presence. Everyone loved to see Doris's eyes sparkle. The glasses had to go.

Dressed and coiffed, Jane guzzled a glass of orange juice and ate a piece of toast (yet to learn you put lipstick on after food, not before), then transferred her case files from her black briefcase to Grandma Eleanor's white beauty case with the two gold-tone push-snap closures. She knew the beauty case was really for rollers and cosmetics, but all the other bags Grandma Eleanor had bequeathed her were too small for the briefs Jane needed to haul into court.

At the front door she slipped on Grandma Eleanor's white double-faced wool coat with oversized buttons and fox-trim collar. She wriggled her fingers one by one into a pair of white kidskin gloves, then carefully placed a white wool pillbox hat, also with fox trim, atop her hair.

The transformation complete, Jane Spring ran back to the mirror.

Oh. My. God.

What have I done? They are going to cart me away and put me in a rubber room.

I will lose my law license.

Oh. My. God.

No, chin up, Jane. You are not crazy. In fact, if the general walked in right now, he would be very proud. This is how he raised you, did he not? "He who dares, wins, Jane."

Jane stared at herself carefully, then suddenly broke out in a huge grin. She knew what they'd say about her, but at that instant she didn't care. She felt lighter, the way she did when she was under water.

And happier, because being all dolled up in lipstick and pearls somehow made you smile. You just wanted to.

She checked her watch. It was time. She reached for her beauty case, grabbed the doorknob, turned it, then suddenly stopped in her tracks. For the first time in her professional career, Jane Spring felt sick to her stomach.

Do I walk out this door? Am I really going to do this? Think, Jane, think!

And then Jane Spring realized she already knew where to find the answer to her dilemma. What would *Doris* do?

Doris would go get herself a man, that's what. Doris would hold her head up and smile; she would never let fear or ridicule keep her from her goals. Doris would seize the day because Doris had spunk. And Doris would triumph because nice girls really do finish first.

Satisfied, Jane Spring adjusted her hat, opened the door, summoned her brightest smile and walked toward the elevator.

Small steps, Jane. Remember, small steps.

16

For the first time in her legal career, Jane bypassed the subway and took a cab to court. For one thing, Doris would; she lived in yellow cabs. And for another, there was no way she could walk more than ten steps in those heels, let alone down the broken stairs into the subway. When a cab finally pulled up, Jane didn't so much walk over, as trot, like a horse, lifting each foot carefully before putting it down again, terrified she would fall. Making it onto the backseat of a cab with both ankles still unbroken and her makeup unsmudged was her first triumph of the day.

"Where to?" asked the cabbie.

This is it, Jane! She was now and would be Doris 24/7 until her mission was complete. Only then, man in hand, would she retire the pink suits and pearls and return to the world as the old Jane Spring.

She took a deep breath and purred, "Centre Street Criminal Courts Building. Thank you, driver."

Sitting in the backseat of the cab, Jane

warmed up one last time, like an opera singer. "Good Morning, Jesse!" she said brightly. "How are you today?" Jane paused. "I look forward to sparring with you, Mr. Bancroft," she said, smiling. "Because as you know, there's nothing this girl loves more than a challenge!"

The cabbie looked at her in his rearview mirror and rolled his eyes. Just his luck the first fare he picks up after the blizzard is a nut job. Why does he always get the ones who talk to themselves?

Because of the piles of plowed snow, negotiating the city streets took forever. By the time Jane arrived at court, it was 8:55. The trial was starting in five minutes, and the lead counsel for the prosecution was nowhere to be seen.

So when Jane Spring arrived, at first there was relief on the face of Jesse Beauclaire, Chip Bancroft and the court clerks, all of whom were more than a bit concerned. Jane Spring, they knew, was usually the first person there.

The relief didn't last long. It was superseded by absolute shock. Multiple heads doing double takes. Raised eyebrows. Wrenched necks. Dislocated jaws.

Jane Spring ignored it all, walked breezily over to the prosecution table and put her beauty case down. "Morning, Jesse!" She hummed and smiled as she peeled off her coat and hung it over the back of her chair. The hat she rested to one side of the prosecution table. She then pulled off her gloves, loosening the fingers one by one, with deliberate measured elegance.

Jesse Beauclaire was incapable of responding to Jane's greeting. Instead, he just stared at her, making note of the colors more than anything. White shoes. Pink suit. Gold bracelet. Then he wondered where the long hair had gone, where the black suit had gone, where her sanity had gone. Finally, he spoke.

"Jane, is that you?"

"Yes, Jesse, of course it's me," she purred.

Jane snapped open her beauty case and began pulling out her case files.

"What I mean is, you don't look like you." Jesse leaned in and whispered, "Jane, are you all right? Because if you're not, I can handle this. I'm fully prepared."

"Jesse, I'm completely ready to try this case, and I will. I'm just trying out a new look, that's all. So what do you think?"

"I think it's very, ah, pink. That's it, pink," he stammered. Oh, my Lord, he thought. I have to get help. Spring has flipped out.

Jane sat down, crossing her legs at the ankles just as she had rehearsed.

Jesse looked frantically over at Chip Bancroft, throwing his hands into the air. Chip's eyes had dilated to the size of beach balls. The veins on the back of his neck bulged. Where did the Jane Spring he had gone to law school with go? The flat-chested girl with the personality of a drill sergeant? Where did the Jane Spring of last night's phone call go? The bitch on heels who wouldn't give his client a break?

He was about to find out. Jane walked daintily over to the defense table. In her absence Jesse grabbed his cell phone and frantically called Graham at the office.

"Morning, Mr. Bancroft," Jane said, dazzling him with a killer smile.

"Morning, Jane," Chip said, trying to remain calm. And then it hit him. He was on to her. He realized exactly what was going on, and smiled confidently to himself.

Spring hasn't lost her mind. She's too smart and in control to do that. No, this is a trick. An elaborate stunt. She's pulling this sixties ladies-who-lunch thing because there's something in it for her. And there she was on the phone last night acting as right as rain, and all the while she was planning this. Well, I've heard of prosecutors bribing judges, flirting with juries and pulling rabbits out of hats to win cases, but this takes the cake.

And then Chip Bancroft had another epiphany, which cheered him even more. If Spring was so confident about her case, she wouldn't be resorting to dressing up in her Halloween costume to bamboozle the jury.

No. Spring's nervous. Spring's scared of me. Chip Bancroft ran his fingers through his hair, adjusted his tie and sat down. He turned to face Laura Riley, who was shaking behind the defense table, and told her consolingly that everything would be just fine. See that prosecutor over there? he told her, the one in the pink skirt (God, she has nice legs. I've never seen them before, and how about those breasts?), she has no case. You have nothing to worry about, Mrs. Riley. Absolutely nothing.

Within the space of five minutes, everyone present in court (except for Mrs. Riley) had completely forgotten why they were there. All eyes, all thoughts were focused on Jane Spring. Is that really her?

Only the judge, the Honorable Ronald E. Shepherd, didn't blink. The father of three teenage daughters, Judge Shepherd was used to arriving at the kitchen table every morning to find one daughter with her fingernails painted black and her lips painted purple, a second wearing clothes even the homeless would reject and a third dressed like a successful porn star. So now a prosecutor was playing dress up. Well, so what? He saw it all the time, and it had stopped worrying him an age ago. He just put it down to hormones.

Graham had run the two city blocks from his office to the courthouse, so by the time he arrived he was sweating and doubled over with a cramp. Spotting him, Jesse ran from the defense table to corral him in the back.

"So where's the fire?" Graham panted.

Jesse helped him stand up straight, then pointed to Jane Spring.

"Am I on crack, or is she?"

"Holy fuck. Is that her?" Graham said loud enough to turn heads, including Jane's.

When Jane saw Graham, she waved, then threw him a huge smile. Graham waved back, incredulous.

Jesse spoke out of the side of his mouth. "Yep, that's her. And it's not just the clothes. She's changed her voice too. It's all soft . . . and she's humming this song:" Jesse hummed a few bars of "Que Sera, Sera."

"What the fuck is she doing?" Graham said out of the side of his mouth. "Should we call a mental hospital and have her taken away?"

And then, just like Chip, the truth about what was happening hit Jesse too.

"She says it's a new look, but I saw her yesterday and she didn't mention a thing about coming to court today like that. And the voice, that friendly attitude — some seriously weird shit is going on here, Graham. You know what I think? This just didn't happen overnight. This is definitely a trick. I don't know what her strategy is, but this is some kind of ploy to secure a conviction. Would have been nice for her to have tipped me off beforehand —"

"She's got nice legs, you know," said Graham.

"Yeah, I noticed."

"And a chest. Look, Jess, she's got a chest. A nice chest. A girl chest."

Jesse nodded in agreement.

"And she looks cute with the short hair."

"Graham."

The bailiff called for order.

"I've got to go."

"Call me later," said Graham. "Tell me if she turns up in a ball gown after lunch."

On the way back to the office Graham started humming a bar from "Que Sera, Sera." It stopped him dead in his tracks. Oh, Christ. I know what's going on. I know who she is. Spring is Doris Day.

When Graham was in law school he skipped the waiter route, making his money working three nights and Sundays in a musty used records and books store. There may not have been any tips, but for Graham what the place lacked in salary, it made up for in perks. On slow nights the owner let him sit in the storeroom and study; he prepped for more than one law school final back there. Better yet, he met more than his share of cute female freshmen, mostly art history majors hunting for rare art books. That was the plus side.

The minus was that the owner played a selection of albums Graham had no stomach for in heavy rotation to provide "ambience" for the store. *Judy at Carnegie Hall*, *Man of La Mancha*, *Doris Day's Greatest Hits*. How many times had Graham sung along to "Que Sera, Sera" while climbing the ladder to shelve books? How often had he stared at her picture on the album cover displayed at the front desk? Why was Jane Spring pretending to be Doris Day? Was she having a nervous breakdown?

Then again, let's say Jesse was right, he thought, and Jane hasn't flipped her lid. But how would playing a virginal sixties movie icon help her win the murder trial? She lost the Markham trial playing Jane Spring to the max. Maybe the acquittal hit her harder than she let on. Maybe she thinks burying *that* Jane in favor of a kinder, gentler Jane will guarantee that that won't happen again. It was the only rational explanation.

Why, that calculated little minx! She was full of surprises.

17

When Graham returned to work, he raced straight into Jane's office, and was relieved to find everything exactly as before. She hadn't covered the windows with pink gingham curtains; she hadn't painted the walls baby blue. So Jesse was right. This was a trick reserved for courtroom purposes only. No need then to warn Lazy Susan that the sergeant major had lost her mind. Clearly, once Jane returned to the comfort and security of the DA's office, she would drop the act, explain everything and resume being the drill sergeant they all knew and tolerated.

In court, Jesse sat behind the prosecution table watching Jane Spring deliver her opening statement, but he didn't hear a word of it. He was too busy preparing his own, the one he would deliver to her at the first recess. Jane, can you explain this, ahem, interesting new strategy to me in legal terms? How long do you plan to keep this up exactly? Is there going to be a new outfit every day? Do you expect me to don white tie and tails tomorrow?

In the jury box, the eight women and four men who had been carefully selected by Jane Spring also watched her deliver her opening statement.

Good morning. My name is Jane Spring, and I am representing the People of New York in this case. I am going to give you an overview of the People's case against Laura Riley. But first I want to thank you for your willingness to serve on the jury of this trial. This tells me exactly how much you care about your civic duty and your passion for justice. I wish all citizens were as committed as you.

She might as well have been talking in tongues. They also didn't hear a word of it. The men were too busy taking in her legs, the soft voice, that big smile she threw them at the end of every point she made. The women were too busy admiring the cut of her suit, the fox-trim hat perched silently on the prosecution table, the way the gold coin dangled on the end of her bracelet every time she gestured toward them.

Jane also barely heard a word of what

174

she was saying; she was so busy concentrating on her walk, her talk, her body language. Remember, Jane, she whispered to herself, you are a sweet, spunky virgin who would never steal another woman's husband, let alone shoot him. So show them what you've got.

You will hear how she stormed into the apartment of the victim's mistress (purse lips; look outraged at the mention of cheating) *in an agitated state* (point disapprovingly at her; smile at them), *then threatened to kill her husband.*

You will also hear forensic evidence that the bullet that killed Thomas Riley was not fired accidentally, but intentionally (serious face, wide eyes). *Ladies and gentlemen, in the end you will see that Laura Riley had motive, opportunity and means to premeditatively plan and commit the murder of her husband.* (Fold hands; bow head.)

Thank you. (Smile, Jane, smile.)

For the first time in Jane Spring's prosecutorial career, there was no difference of opinion among the jury as to who they thought she was or wanted her to be.

Nobody fantasized the shy schoolgirl or sexy secretary. Jane's facial expressions were so open and clear, her persona so sunny, there was no mystery, no room for interpretation. Now they all saw the same woman, that sixties movie star whose movies you see all the time on classic cable networks. She's that sweet, spunky working girl in white heels and pink suits who always ends up landing the man of her dreams.

What the woman from those classic movies was doing in a New York courtroom at nine-fifteen in the morning delivering an opening statement in a murder trial they weren't quite sure. Where did that other prosecutor go? The stern one in the black suit from jury selection? Oh, who cared? They loved this one. She was darling! Soft and sweet and what a lovely voice. And look at her! She's adorable.

Not that Jane Spring cared how they reacted to her new persona, although the approving looks were nice. This wasn't for them, no matter what Chip Bancroft or Graham or Jesse might think. This wasn't for justice, although it would be gratifying if the jury delivered a conviction. This was for *him*, the man who would, once he met her, be swept off his feet by the very sight and sound of her.

Now where was he?

At three o'clock, after Jane Spring and Chip Bancroft had completed their opening statements, court recessed for the day. Jane was pleased to note that the jury had been much more attentive to her than her adversary. Chip normally had juries eating out of his hand. But today they seemed to like the taste of Jane's. Well, isn't that enough to put a girl in a good mood?

Walking back to the office, Jesse couldn't hold it in anymore. Jane had bolted for the bathroom during the lunch break to fix her makeup, so he lost his chance to conduct a cross-examination of his own. Now with Jane Spring carefully tiptoeing through the slush as her beauty case swung by her side, Jesse started in.

"Jane, don't you think we need to talk about something?"

Jane knew Jesse Beauclaire was expecting her to turn back into Jane Spring once court was out of session. This was her chance to show him that she would never snap out of character until her own personal trial was won. She smiled at him sweetly.

"Sure. What would you like to talk about? The weather? I hope the snow melts soon. When the streets are like this, it's so hard to walk in heels."

"Look, Jane. I don't know what you're up to, and I wish you had told me so we could have discussed this, but I'm sure, given it's you, it's some cunning and brilliant plan, but do you want to tell me exactly what the *fuck* is going on?"

The one thing Jesse Beauclaire always liked about Jane Spring was that you could swear in front of her, and she didn't bat an eyelid. Growing up in the military, Jane was pretty familiar with the preferred language of soldiers. Even though it was considered conduct unbecoming to an officer, soldiers swore like it might go out of fashion. She never had any trouble dropping a few F-bombs after a bad day at the office.

"Oh, my goodness!" Jane squealed. "Well, let's just pretend I didn't hear *that,* shall we?"

"What? Oh, Jane, okay. I get it. Fine. You're still playing whoever you are. Well, can you drop the act for five minutes so we can talk?"

"What act? Can't a girl work on her image?"

Jesse let out a huge sigh and decided to let it drop for now. He would get back to the office, confer with everyone else, then confront her again, this time with backup. Enough was enough.

Lazy Susan was listening to music on her iPod and playing solitaire when Jane Spring glided past her and into her office. She put her beauty case down, but kept on her coat, hat and gloves while she quickly checked her e-mail, then, satisfied there was nothing pressing, began to undress. She had just slipped her last finger out of her left glove when Lazy Susan materialized. She was holding message slips. That was the first surprise of the day. The second was that for someone whose emotional range stretched from bored to catatonic, Lazy Susan's face was a revelation.

After the initial shock, her face became animated with surprise. "Miss Sp-Ring?" she said, handing Jane the slips and craning over her desk for a better look.

"Yes? Oh, thank you, Susan! How are you today?"

"Miss Sp-Ring. Is that you?" Susan said nervously.

"Why, who else would it be, Susan? Of course it's me!" Jane said.

"But you, you look different . . . I mean, don't you think so?"

"Do you like it?"

"It's pink. Very pink."

"I know. But I just felt with the holidays coming, it might be nice to start looking more festive."

"Oh my God," Susan muttered as she walked back to her desk. "We have to call an ambulance."

Lazy Susan wasn't the only one who was astounded. Jane Spring was pleasantly surprised by how much she was enjoying the first afternoon with her secretary. Having Lazy Susan acknowledge her with something, anything, other than boredom and disdain, felt wonderful.

"I'm running down to the kitchen for some coffee, Miss Sp-Ring; can I get you anything?"

Jane thanked her but said she was fine and pulled a copy of *Family Circle* magazine out of her beauty case.

"There is a wonderful recipe for meat loaf in here, Susan," she said, pointing to the magazine. "I'll make a copy of it for you if you like."

A clicking sound filled the room as Lazy Susan's lower jaw disconnected from her upper.

"Meat loaf? Okay. Sure . . . I love meat loaf," she stammered, then retreated outside. Instead of going to the kitchen, Lazy Susan ran down the corridor to Supervisor Lawrence Park, breaking the land-speed record for secretaries in tight pants and high heels.

Graham and Jesse were already in his office looking bewildered, and seeing Susan panting in his doorway, Lawrence Park waved her in.

"Have you seen her?"

"We've seen her," they said in unison.

Lazy Susan turned desperately to Graham. "What is going on? The clothes! And her hair! Mr. Van Outen, she's even talking about making meat loaf! She wants to give me the recipe! She's gone crazy!"

"Don't worry, Susan, your boss hasn't lost her mind," Graham answered, moving closer to her and planting a comforting arm around her shoulder. Lazy Susan was delirious. This was the first time he had touched her, the first time there had been any physical contact between them. Oh, thank you, Miss Sp-Ring. Please come to work crazy tomorrow too.

"None of us know the specifics of her plan, but she's pulling this stunt to woo the jury on the Riley case."

He withdrew his arm from her shoulder. Lazy Susan wanted to pick it up and put it back. The other one too. Then she wanted him to kiss her.

"I don't get it," she said. "Everyone talks about her like she's this hot-shit lawyer, you know. So why does she hafta dress up like Marilyn Monroe to win a case?"

"Marilyn Monroe?" said Lawrence Park, confused. "I thought she was trying to be Angie Dickinson."

"Angie Dickinson? Does she look like she's going to dinner with the Rat Pack? Can't you see? She's Doris Day," said Graham.

"Ohhh," said everyone.

"How do you know? Did she tell you?" asked Lawrence Park.

Graham proceeded to tell them about his law school job in the used books and records store.

"You're positive?" said Lawrence Park. "Beyond a reasonable doubt?"

Graham pushed his supervisor aside and starting typing commands into his computer. In ten seconds he had downloaded a page of Doris Day movie stills. They gathered around the screen and stared wide-eyed as Graham clicked through them.

"Well I just hope she doesn't expect me to start acting like Rock Hudson."

"Rock who?" asked Lazy Susan, whose dramatic tastes ran strictly from soaps to MTV and back again.

"Her boyfriend," said Graham.

"Miss Sp-Ring has a boyfriend?" she asked, startled.

"No, Doris Day does. Or did. In the movies. Rock Hudson."

"Well, sometimes it was Cary Grant," said Lawrence Park.

"Oh, right."

"So maybe she's acting all crazy because she wants to steal this Doris's boyfriend, and it's got nothing to do with the trial," she said.

"Forget it," said Jesse. "This is all about this case. That woman wants nothing more in life than to win in court. There's no way she would make a complete fool of herself in public just over a man."

But then Graham wondered. Had he told her she needed to change if she wanted men to fall in love with her? But from that conversation to this?

Impossible.

Or was it?

Marcie Blumenthal charged into Jane Spring's office, clutching a copy of *Modern Bride*. It was open to a picture of a cluster of bridesmaids in burgundy velvet Empire gowns. She slammed the magazine down in front of Jane, who turned away from her

183

computer when she heard the thud.

"We had a bridesmaids' meeting last night, and this is what won the vote," Marcie said, presenting the picture like a TV game-show hostess showcasing the prizes. "I'm still not sure. What do you think? Too *Masterpiece Theater?*"

Jane studied the photograph. "I think they're absolutely darling," she squealed with excitement.

"The thing is, I've got six bridesmaids, okay? All those burgundy dresses in a row — you don't think it's going to look like a crime scene? From a distance the color looks a lot like blood."

"Oh, Marcie, I would never think that, and I can't imagine anyone who would! These dresses are divine. Really. Like a bouquet of roses."

"I've got to tell you, Jane, I wanted something more, hmm, actually, more like the color your suit is." She reached out to touch Jane's sleeve. "Sort of this pink."

"Well, Marcie, sometimes just as a prosecutor must strike a deal with a defendant, a bride has to compromise with her bridesmaids."

Marcie nodded. Jane was right. She gathered up her magazine and left. Not a word about why Jane was wearing pink instead of black. Not a thought given to why Jane Spring was speaking in that soft, cuddly voice. What a relief, Jane thought, gathering up her papers and loading them into the beauty case. For once Marcie's self-absorption was giving her a break instead of a headache.

Which was not to be the case when Cocounsel Jesse Beauclaire marched into her office.

"Jane."

"Yes, Jesse."

He shut the door.

"Jane, I'm here to tell you we had a meeting, and we all know who you are, okay? I mean, we all know who you are pretending to be. And I'm sure once the trial is over, you will explain to me exactly why, even with all the evidence we have, you felt our case wasn't strong enough, and you had to play dress up to put the verdict in the bag. I have to say, Jane, that even for you this is off the charts. I've had calls from half the lawyers in this building asking me if it's true you showed in court today looking like a refugee from *The Donna Reed Show*."

Jesse folded his arms. Jane looked up at him and smiled. And smiled.

"You looked very nice in court today,

Jesse. Is that a new suit?"

Jesse leaned over the desk, putting his face right into hers. "I am on to you, Jane," he said, his eyes narrowing. Jesse Beauclaire was no fool, which was one of the reasons Jane Spring liked him.

"I see." Jane widened her eyes and summoned her best face of concern. She pulled all the Christmas cards she had received out of her drawer and began stringing them up across her window.

"It took me all day, but I've figured out your little plan. You think coming to court like this will send the jury a message. The one about how women in the fifties and sixties, women like those characters Doris Day used to play, didn't have any choices. The world was different then.

"If your husband was being a bad boy, if you discovered him cheating, you just put on your best pink suit and your brightest smile and you sucked it up. Right? I'm right, aren't I? And then you're going to tell the jury that today there is no stigma about divorce, and the defendant had options besides killing her husband, which is why it makes her actions all the more criminal."

Jane smiled, then nodded silently. Fine, you've got me, her eyes said. What a brilliant explanation, she thought; I can't believe I didn't think of it myself.

Finished with the Christmas cards, Jane put on her hat and coat and checked herself in the mirror. She was still adjusting to seeing a bustline where none had existed, but she was already a fan of how her newly enhanced chest made her feel. Seductive. Feminine. She'd seen how Chip, Jesse and Graham had stared at her that morning, how they admired her new contours while simultaneously absorbing the shock. She had to admit it: She liked getting those looks.

"I'll see you tomorrow in court, Jesse. Have a good evening."

18

Jane Spring knew *he* could be anywhere. Letting down her guard, even under water, meant she could miss finding him. Which is why when she dove into the pool at the Y at seven a.m. on day two of the trial, she was wearing a white rubber bathing cap covered in bouncing blue rubber flowers, and a baby-blue bathing suit that had more pleats than an accordion.

At first the regulars who lapped the pool at that hour thought the woman in the retro suit, cap and goggles was a new senior who had joined the Y. But when this senior dove into the pool, the regulars all gasped. That was some dive for a seventy-year-old. And did you see her legs? Smooth as silk and not a vein to be seen. She swam like someone half her age, fast and fluid, and the identity of this stranger had them all baffled.

They were not the only ones surprised. Jane felt something had shifted in the pool too. Was she imagining it, or did it feel as if she didn't have to stroke so hard, that the water was offering less resistance? It did. Cruising down the lanes, Jane rehashed the previous day in all its Technicolor glory. Graham's and Jesse's surprise at her new persona, Chip's obvious frustration, a jury who couldn't take their eyes off her. And Lazy Susan's face! Oh, she wished she'd had a camera. She didn't know the girl was capable of such emotion. But the biggest prize was the explanation her coworkers seized on to rationalize her transformation. Truly brilliant, if off the wall. Thanks, boys!

After Jane completed her two miles, she sat on the bleachers and scrutinized the swimmers carefully to see if *he* might be among them. Indeed, there were a number of good-looking, star-quality men in the pool, but Jane knew them, and they were all married. She would never move in on another woman's husband. That would not be right, or very Doris.

She headed for the ladies' locker room unperturbed. She was here every day, and *he* might show up tomorrow.

The entire locker room watched carefully as Jane stripped off her suit and cap. Suddenly they saw that this woman was no septuagenarian, but the prosecutor with the long blond hair who, they had to admit, they had all usually found rather curt. But today she was beaming, throwing warm smiles at anyone who happened to be staring at her. Which meant everyone.

"Jane?"

"Morning, Cynthia," Jane said in a voice that sounded just like spun sugar.

Cynthia was an early morning regular and the owner of more Speedo racing suits than an Olympic swim team. Jane never saw her wear the same one twice.

"Jane, wow, I see you cut your hair," said Cynthia.

"Oh, do you like it? Thank you," she purred.

This was the longest conversation Cynthia could remember having with the prosecutor.

Jane wrapped herself in a towel. Cynthia threw everyone a smirk that said: *What's with the voice? Has she gone nuts?*

"I like your bathing suit," said Anne, picking up where Cynthia left off. Anne was once a junior swimming champion; Jane Spring always envied her powerful backstroke. "Very retro."

"Why thank you, Anne! I like yours, too!"

Anne threw everyone a smirk that said, *Yes-she-has-gone-nuts.* Then she twirled her index finger around her ear.

But as Jane Spring headed to the showers and everyone else got themselves dressed, interestingly, nobody had a critical word to say about what they'd just witnessed. First off, this was New York City. Who didn't just snap one day and go a little crazy? God knows the woman worked hard enough, she'd earned her mental breakdown.

Indeed, as Jane walked to the showers, a number of the other women noticed that it wasn't just her hair, or her funky new swimsuit, that was fundamentally different about Jane Spring. She was kind.

19

Jane Spring's feet were killing her. She was amazed that one day in high heels after thirty-four years in flats could inflict so much pain. It wasn't just that she had blisters, her blisters had blisters. Even after swimming two miles and warming up her muscles, the balls of her feet and her arches still throbbed. So as she dressed the morning of day two of the trial, she went through Grandma Eleanor's collection of shoes looking for a pair that might not give her as much trouble as the white pumps.

But it seemed Grandma Eleanor was a glutton for punishment. All her shoes were high-heeled with narrow, pointy toes. After trying on every pair left to her, Jane settled for a pair in black patent leather. They were a touch wider across the toes, and she knew that just like a criminal who goes free on the smallest technicality, her feet would feel liberated with even the slightest bit of extra room.

On Sunday night, after taking inventory of the clothing in the cedar trunk (there was an entire set of Wedgwood china in there too), Jane Spring saw that she had one fur stole, four evening dresses, two winter coats, six pairs of shoes, five hats, three day suits, and an assortment of skirts, silk shirts, cashmere twinsets and mohair sweaters to play with. While she was deeply grateful to have anything at all, the fact was it really wasn't a lot if Jane had to keep this up indefinitely. Which was yet another reason she needed to find a man sooner rather than later. Eventually she would run out of clothes.

She realized if she split the suits up and mixed and matched the bottoms with the tops, she could get more mileage out of each outfit. Even though Doris never wore the same ensemble twice in her movies, Jane Spring, regrettably, didn't have a costume designer on her daily staff. Only Lazy Susan. And Jane doubted she could sew. For God's sake, the poor girl could hardly spell.

So on day two, after she had covered her toes in Band-Aids and stuffed fresh tissues into her torpedo bra, Jane slipped into the pale-blue pencil skirt from a two-piece suit and a white mohair sweater whose collar tied in a bow at the shoulder. She abandoned the long white coat with the fox trim (everyone had seen it) for her only other option, a pale blue cashmere overcoat with satin trim on the cuffs and collar. She selected a pair of black gloves to match the shoes and a black felt hat with a diamante hatpin.

She applied her makeup (this was kind of fun!), grabbed her beauty case bursting with law briefs and voilà!, she was ready for her second day in court.

Standing on the street corner waiting for a taxi, Jane Spring watched as Mrs. Kearns emerged from the subway, then walked right past her. It wasn't that Mrs. Kearns didn't notice Jane; she did see a woman in a blue coat with satin trim holding a beauty case. But she kept going, as you do when passing someone you don't know. Jane smiled to herself. She thought about calling out to Mrs. Kearns, but a cab rolled up and Jane climbed in.

It was probably just as well, given Colleen Kearns's face when she opened the door to Jane's apartment. Two shocks in one day might have killed the woman, and then Jane would be an accessory to murder, not exactly a rule in the Doris Day handbook.

"Holy Mary, Mother of God."

Colleen Kearns walked into chez Spring,

then walked back out again to check the number on the door. No, she was in the right place. She put her bag down and rubbed her eyes. No, the room still looked yellow. Mrs. Kearns walked around the apartment touching everything. The blue curtains. The yellow walls. The white coffee table. The silk daisies. There was a small silver Christmas tree in the corner bedecked with gold ribbons and balls. In the bedroom she saw the yellow blankets on the single bed. In the closet she noted that all of Jane Spring's black suits had gone missing; in their place were Grandma Eleanor's vibrant pastel ensembles.

"Holy Mary, Mother of God," she repeated. And then she made the sign of the cross.

Mrs. Kearns went to the fridge and poured herself a glass of wine. Yes, it was early, but if she ever needed some liquid refreshment, now was the time. She sat herself down on the yellow sofa and while sipping slowly, tried to make sense of what had happened.

Theory one: Miss Spring moved out and didn't tell me. The new owner is a woman who wears vintage clothes while running a day care center out of the living room. Well, I like children. This shouldn't be a problem.

Theory two: A renovating team from one of those surprise TV home-makeover shows did this without her knowledge, and when Miss Spring sees everything, she will have a coronary too. Except hers will be on national television.

Theory three: A complete mental breakdown.

No matter which, Mrs. Kearns still had to clean the place. And if it was going to be on television, she'd better make it sparkle.

In court, Jane called her first witness to the stand, to set the scene. He was a rookie police officer, the first to arrive after neighbors had called 911. His job had been threefold: ensure nobody touched the dead body, hold the defendant and witnesses in place, secure the crime scene. He was young and nervous, but Jane Spring led him through his testimony like a preschool teacher helping her charge make a macaroni ashtray. Verrry good, Officer! Big smile. That's right, Officer! Big smile. Excellent, Officer! Nothing further, Your Honor. Big Smile.

Even though Chip Bancroft was confident he was on to Spring's game, that didn't mean he wasn't simultaneously rattled by it. If only men kept their brains in their heads instead of their pants, Jane thought, watching him watching her. All through her questioning of the first witness, Chip Bancroft hadn't once stopped staring at her legs, the tilt of her hip as she walked, the curve of her bust beneath the white mohair sweater. When it came time for him to cross-examine the young police officer, Chip Bancroft rose from his seat, said Nothing at this time, Your Honor, and sat back down.

And that was when Jane Spring realized Jesse Beauclaire's declaration in her office the day before had been, in fact, genius. No, she hadn't done this intentionally to bolster their case. But yes, incredibly, it was doing exactly that. If going Doris has brought the defense counsel to his knees, she thought, imagine how easy it's going to be when I meet *him!*

Jane called her second witness to the stand.

Meanwhile, in her apartment, Colleen Kearns was hard at work. She dusted, she polished, she mopped the bathroom floor without complaint. If those TV people were coming, the apartment had better be ready. And then she felt it. That feeling that came whenever she was in an apartment that inspired her.

Mrs. Kearns was inspired. And now for the first time in Jane Spring's apartment, Colleen Kearns slipped off her blue uniform and started to play as she cleaned. The place made her feel like one of those characters in an old Technicolor movie. You know the kind, where the apartments are always sunny and yellow, and everyone is always falling in love.

In Jane Spring's bedroom, Mrs. Kearns squeezed herself into Grandma Eleanor's apple-green suit. Given that she had at least forty pounds on Grandma Eleanor, rolls of fat fell over the waistband. Next, she pushed her plump feet into the white pumps and her chubby fingers into the white gloves. On her head she perched a green pillbox hat. Around her neck she clasped a triple strand of pearls. Then she looked in the mirror. And how do you do? she said to herself.

By four p.m. she had scrubbed the entire place to perfection and by rights could have taken her leave. But Mrs. Kearns wanted to wait for Jane Spring. She had questions for her that despite the joy the day became, remained unanswered. Heck, she wanted to make sure it was Jane Spring who walked through the door. What if she really did have a new boss? It would be just like Jane Spring, that haughty prima donna, not to tell her she was moving on. She changed back into her blue uniform and waited. When she heard the elevator doors open in the corridor, she smoothed out her hair. When she heard the key in the lock, she stood to attention.

"Mrs. Kearns, I'm so pleased you're still here. It's always so nice to see you," Jane purred, walking in.

Mrs. Kearns was rendered speechless. She stood there taking in Jane Spring: the blue skirt and white mohair sweater, the frosted hair and frosted lips. And the voice! What was with her voice? Did she just say she was pleased to see me? "Miss Spring . . . is that you?"

"Yes, of course, Mrs. Kearns; who do you think it is?"

This conversation was starting to sound familiar.

"It's just that you look so . . . the apartment looks so . . . different."

"Do you like it? I love it!" Jane giggled. "I felt it was time for a change. You know what they say, change your look, change your life!"

"I do like it. It's very sunny. But it's very different; don't you agree? Like from another era. But pretty as a picture."

"Why, thank you, Mrs. Kearns. And you have done a simply wonderful job today. I can see my reflection in this tabletop!" Jane said, throwing her cleaning lady a smile as wide as a Mack truck. Mrs. Kearns returned the gesture; but in her head she had begun taking inventory of the day's events, and suddenly didn't like what they added up to.

Colleen, something suspicious is going on here, she thought. Very suspicious. Because she knew Jane Spring, and that woman wouldn't live in a yellow house, wear a blue skirt, talk like powdered sugar or thank you for a day's work if you gave her the Medal of Honor. And she doubted Jane Spring had temporarily lost her mind; she was too smart for that.

No, something was definitely happening here. And just as Jane Spring's colleagues had created an explanation to make sense of the nonsensical, Colleen Kearns hit upon an answer that provided all the satisfaction she needed.

Suddenly Colleen Kearns smiled at Jane Spring and let out a huge sigh of relief.

She knew.

She was on *Candid Camera*.

20

Jane Spring walked into the NYPD precinct house on West Tenth Street for her eight a.m. meeting with Detective Mike Millbank. They were to rehearse the testimony he was to give in court the following week, and given that their last meeting had not been a resounding success, Jane wanted to get this one over pronto.

She dialed Detective Millbank from the front desk and waited. As she did, the precinct clerk gave her the once-over. Jane smiled sweetly at him. Oh, what a difference a week makes! If he had done the same thing last Friday, she would have threatened him with a sexual harassment suit.

"Jane."

She put down her beauty case.

"Detective," she said, extending a gloved hand. "How lovely to see you."

Jane was surprised the detective didn't look as shocked as she had assumed he might, then realized that word about her new persona had obviously reached the

NYPD. Indeed, Mike Millbank had been apprised of the fact that Jane Spring, the one person he blamed for losing an important trial for him, had, to put it nicely, lost her marbles. He'd heard she was playing that 1960s movie star Doris Day in court, part of some ingenious strategy to secure a conviction. Apparently, her black suits weren't the only things she'd left at home.

He had heard she'd left her fangs there too.

From his own eyes, now he knew it to be true.

"Come this way."

Detective Millbank guided Jane through the main precinct room, and a huge space that only minutes before had buzzed with a thousand voices went deathly quiet.

Police officers rose up from their cubicles or leaned way, way back in their chairs to get a better look at Jane Spring. Criminals handcuffed to wooden chairs started whistling. Some called out Hey, baby, Hey, baby, as she walked by. Jane held her head high and ignored it all, marching into Detective Millbank's office and slipping off her coat like it was any other day.

"Coffee, Jane?"

"Yes, thank you, Detective. Cream and sugar, please, if you have it."

The detective headed for the kitchen, and Jane sat and looked around his office. He had moved since the last time they had come together to prepare testimony, and in his new digs pictures of a golden retriever were displayed prominently around the room. But no wife. Well, that figures, she thought. Who would marry a man with his attitude?

Detective Millbank came back down the hall with two mugs of coffee. Before reentering his office, he stopped quietly in the doorway and stared hard at the rear view of Jane Spring. Suddenly all his detective instincts kicked in. Something doesn't jell here, Mike, he thought. She wants to pull this stunt to win a trial? Fine. Well, she wouldn't be the first attorney to try to tap dance her way to a verdict. Extreme? No question, but then subtlety was never Jane Spring's strong suit.

But why doesn't she drop the act between court appearances?

Detective Mike Millbank started to ponder an alternate theory, that there was something else at work here. But what? He planned to give it some further thought, but first he had this meeting to get through.

"We didn't have cream, but I gave you

extra milk. Hope that's okay."

"Oh, it will be just fine. Thank you, Detective," Jane said, throwing him her brightest smile.

She was dying to know what Mike Millbank was thinking right then, right there. Here she was in his office in a pink suit and white pumps, a blue coat in satin trim hanging off the chair behind her. Surely he was going to say something? He was a detective, for heaven's sake and, Jane had to admit, a good one at that. He noticed specks of blood on a dirty carpet; surely he would notice a perky woman with platinum blond hair and pink lipstick in his office.

But he said nothing. Jane opened her beauty case and took out the Riley file. "Now, Detective, I suggest we go through this in Q-and-A style, just like in court."

"Fine with me," he said, perched behind his desk. He cleared his throat and sat up, ready to face the Spring firing squad.

"Obviously, we don't need to practice the preliminaries. I am sure you could recite them in your sleep. Let's go to your direct testimony. Detective Millbank, can you tell the court who was present when you arrived on the scene?"

"The defendant, the deceased's girlfriend and the deceased."

"And did the defendant say anything to you, anything specific to the crime?"

"She said, 'I killed him, I killed him,' over and over."

"But she didn't say, 'I didn't mean to kill him. It was a mistake.' Did you ever hear her say that, Detective?"

"No."

Jane smiled at Mike Millbank.

"You're doing very well, Detective."

Jane glanced down at her notes, cleared her throat and continued.

"Detective, in your interview with Mrs. Riley at the police precinct later, did she tell you why she went to see her husband?"

"She said she knew he was having an affair, and she went there to demand that he stop it."

Jane Spring shook her fluffy head and made tsk, tsk noises.

"What's wrong?"

"His having an affair!" Jane folded her arms. "Of course, I know how you feel on this subject Detective; you made that quite clear last time we met, but I —"

"Hey, whoa, let's back up here, Jane. I never said I thought adultery was acceptable. Not by a long shot. What I said was, while it might be immoral, it isn't a crime punishable by death. Christ, you can't just murder someone."

"Well, what a spirited reply, Detective. I assume, then, you've never cheated on anyone?"

The detective now folded his arms. "Never. I'm strictly a one-woman man, Ms. Spring. I think lying to someone you love is low. The lowest. Cheating is not in my playbook. When I'm with a woman, I'm hers exclusively; and when I don't want to be with her anymore, I get out gracefully. I personally don't have any respect for what my fellow officer was up to. But nobody deserves to get killed over it."

Mike Millbank couldn't believe he was talking so candidly in front of Jane Spring. What happened? She had disarmed him with that cute suit and that soft sweet voice. He had to remind himself the real Jane Spring was underneath.

"Well, Detective," said Jane, beaming. "I apologize. And I have to tell you how impressed I am with your attitude. A man like you — so honorable, so decent — I have to say I am surprised you're not married."

Jane Spring blushed. She couldn't believe she had let herself say that out loud. She had actually wondered about it as he was speaking — why, if he is as good as he says, is *he* single? — but to say it? Oh, Jane. What had happened? He had disarmed her with his candor.

The Detective blushed too. At least now they were even.

"I work too hard. I've yet to meet a woman who can stand the hours I put in. You have no idea the number of phone calls I get at three a.m. to go pick up a dead body. I go on a date straight from work — there can be blood, sometimes brains on my shoes. What am I supposed to do? This is my life. In the beginning women find it exciting, then they can't stand it. They want a normal boyfriend, and I don't blame them."

Jane knew they should go back to rehearsing his testimony but couldn't. Not now.

"If you don't mind me asking, Detective, why work so hard then?"

"Can't help it. I love my job."

"That's very commendable."

"When I was a kid, I loved doing puzzles. This job . . . for me it's like doing a puzzle. But it's real. Then after you've solved the puzzle, you help people get closure from a tragedy. I find it very satisfying."

Mike Millbank was suddenly so flustered by how open he had just been with Jane

Spring that he couldn't face her and excused himself to go to the bathroom.

In his absence Jane rehashed their conversation in her head. Wouldn't cheat on any woman. Committed to his job. Wants to help people get past their pain. She had misjudged him. He was decent, he was dedicated, he was angry at her over the last trial because he cared. He cared so much he didn't worry if his suit sleeve was missing a button (it was). He had honor, the type that would fit in anywhere in the military. What a pity he'd never enlisted.

Then she thought about Chip Bancroft. Chip, whose ego alone could qualify for a separate birth certificate, couldn't hold a candle to this guy when it came to decency and honor. So why did she get palpitations when she saw Chip in court on Tuesday? Why did her mind turn to mush when his forelock fell into his eyes?

Oh, Jane, get over him already!

When Detective Millbank returned, they resumed their Q-and-A, pretending the previous conversation had never happened. But the awkwardness hovered. When they were done, Jane rose and slipped on her coat. Out of the corner of her eye she saw Detective Millbank lean sideways to check out her legs.

"Well, thank you for your time, Detective," she said, snapping her beauty case shut. "I feel we are prepared."

He nodded. He offered to walk Jane out, but she protested.

"Oh, you're much too busy, Detective; I can show myself out," she said graciously.

Jane Spring had her hand on the doorknob when Detective Mike Millbank called out, "Jane."

"Yes," she said turning to him, eyes wide.

"Like I told you the other day, this guy was one of the family. Don't screw this up."

Jane tried to disguise her hurt. She thought they were friends now.

"Oh, Detective," she said, putting on her perkiest face. "I wouldn't dream of it."

21

Jane Spring was eager to conclude the Riley trial before Christmas. It was a week away, and she knew the break for the holiday, complete with resultant hangovers and festive spirit, all but guaranteed the jury would be unable to concentrate on their return. She had worked a trial once before that had been broken up by the holiday, and it had been agony getting the jury to refocus. It was clear that all they had wanted to do was wrap things up so they could return the presents they didn't like, or more to the point, didn't fit.

So by day three, Jane had politely but efficiently moved through three law enforcement witnesses and the private detective, and was ready to call her first big fish to the stand.

The girlfriend.

Wearing Mrs. Kearns's favorite, the apple-green skirt with matching jacket, paired with brown crocodile pumps and a triple strand of pearls, Jane Spring asked Patty Dunlap to tell the court her name and occupation, then smiled sweetly at the jury.

After the preliminaries were dispensed with: how she had met the deceased, how long they had been having an affair (at which she had shaken her head disapprovingly), Jane came out from behind the prosecution table and approached her witness.

Now, Miss Dunlap, Jane purred, would you tell the court, please, exactly what happened the night of Officer Riley's murder?

Patty Dunlap ran her left hand through her long dark hair; it fell softly to one side. Doe-eyed and busty, Patty was more *Playboy* centerfold than New York court clerk, the perfect solution — or distraction — for any man having a midlife crisis. Just looking at her made everyone's heart break for Laura Riley even more. How was a PTA mom with graying hair and twenty pounds to lose supposed to compete with that?

"Tom came over to my place around six, after he finished his shift," she began.

"I see. And then?"

"And then we talked for a bit, we went out for a drink, and then well . . . we had sex in an alleyway . . ."

"My goodness," said Jane, bowing her

head and shaking it softly. Though still facing the floor, Jane's peripheral vision could see the women on the jury nodding in agreement. That witness on the stand was a hussy, stealing someone's husband. Jesse was also lapping up Jane's performance, her mock horror at learning her witness had tangled with a married man against the side of a Dumpster. My God, he thought, I could sell tickets to this.

"Now, Miss Dunlap, after your, ahem, evening escapade, you returned to your apartment, is that correct? And can you tell the court what happened when the defendant, Mrs. Riley, arrived there?"

As Patty Dunlap described answering the door in her T-shirt and panties, Jane looked at the jury and pursed her lips. How *unladylike!* When Patty Dunlap described her lover throwing on a towel when he heard his wife at the door, Jane blushed and looked away. And when Patty Dunlap testified about hearing threats of murder, followed by gunshots and the discovery of her dead lover, Jane Spring widened her eyes like a Kewpie doll, took a deep breath, put her hand across her heart and stood at attention.

Jesse wondered if she was going to sing the national anthem. What else was left?

On cross, it seemed Chip Bancroft had regained the cockiness he appeared to have lost when Jane Spring first unveiled herself to the world. He'd had three days to acclimate, and although he still liked to stare at her ass whenever the opportunity presented, he was back in form. He realized he let Spring win too many points using the sheer element of surprise, and vowed it wouldn't happen again.

"Miss Dunlap," started Chip Bancroft formally. "You testified you heard Laura Riley say to her husband, 'I'm so mad I could kill you.'"

"Yes."

Jane made notes on her yellow legal pad.

"Miss Dunlap, haven't you ever said out loud, I'm so angry I could kill that person?"

"Oh, sure, but I didn't mean it. It's just something you say when you get mad."

"Exactly my point," said Chip.

"But Tommy's wife had a gun."

"But you didn't see her point it at Officer Riley, did you?" he asked, spinning around to face the jury.

"No."

"Because you weren't in the room, were you? At this stage Mrs. Riley had thrown you out into the corridor and closed the door."

"Yes."

213

Some jurors picked up pens and noted this testimony on the pads they had been provided. This annoyed Jane Spring. Clearly, they were biting at Chip's theory that the case, given there were no eyewitnesses, was purely circumstantial. But she wouldn't let the jury see her ruffled. Doris never would. When they glanced at her, she smiled softly and fluffed her hair. Oh, isn't she just the sweetest, they thought.

"Miss Dunlap, you and the deceased met three times a week for sexual encounters, is that correct?"

"Two or three, yes."

"A private detective previously testified that he presented photographic evidence of these encounters to Mrs. Riley."

Patty Dunlap stared at the ceiling. Chip moved closer to the witness box.

"So it's understandable Mrs. Riley would be angry and upset when she arrived at your home after seeing them, yes?"

"Maybe."

"Maybe?" said Chip, outraged. "You're not sure if she would be upset? Well, Miss Dunlap, I know I would be. And we certainly know Ms. Spring would be," he said pointing squarely at Jane. Her eyes widened. "She's made it quite clear what she thinks of your adultery, Miss Dunlap. But as angry as either of us would be if we discovered our spouses cheating, that doesn't make either of us murderers, does it? If anything, it makes us human."

"Objection! Leading," said Jane. "And Counsel has no right to suggest to the jury what I think."

"Sustained."

Oh, she wanted to kill him. To impale him on her kitten heel. How dare he use her reactions earlier, her patent disapproval of Miss Dunlap's morality, to bolster his defense?

But Jane wouldn't show anger. Breathe Jane, breathe. In. Out. In. Out. In. Out. That's right.

"Your Honor, may I approach?" Chip asked.

"Very well," he intoned, waving Jane forward too. Jane walked daintily to the bench, but all she could think about was decking Chip when she got there.

"Your Honor, my question goes to state of mind. I'm trying to show that Miss Dunlap had no empathy for the defendant," he whispered. "If you don't understand how hurtful adultery can be, you would misinterpret a natural reaction of anger as something more sinister. Like intent to kill."

"I'll allow it. But rephrase your question, Counselor. Keep it narrow."

Both lawyers retreated. Chip grinned because he had won that round. Jane beamed because she didn't want the jury to think anything was wrong.

"Miss Dunlap, suppose you have been married for twenty-three years."

"Okay."

"Now suppose your husband, whom you love very much, has an affair with another woman, let's say, for argument's sake, the lovely Ms. Spring here."

Chip walked over to Jane's table and tapped it before heading back to the witness box. The jury turned to admire her. Jane thought smoke would come out of her ears. Again! He's using her again to make his case. Oh, Mr. Bancroft!

"Wouldn't you feel anger toward Ms. Spring?"

Patty Dunlap cleared her throat. "Listen, I think if a man cheats, it's 'cause he's not getting what he needs at home," she said, looking at Laura Riley. "How can you be mad about something that's your fault?"

The jury looked at Laura Riley, now on the verge of tears. Their hearts broke for her.

"Nothing further," Chip announced, practically skipping back to his table. Jane

Spring thought she would pass out. Tomorrow she would pack smelling salts.

Ooooohhh! she squealed, staring directly at Chip and narrowing her eyes. The jury all turned to watch her seethe. They didn't like seeing Mr. Bancroft upset the lovely prosecutor, even if they weren't quite sure what he had done. But Jane knew. Chip Bancroft had used her witness and *her* to make his client look sympathetic.

Jane Spring looked at Jesse Beauclaire and said the only thing one could say under the circumstances. "Well, I never."

In the jury room, lunch had been served. By the third day of any trial, jurors have already formed cliques and alliances, and this one was no different. It ran along gender and color lines, as often is the case. At one table the four men sat together, while the eight women had split themselves into two groups, one black and one white. But among each group the topic of conversation was identical, and it didn't include complaints about their hotel, or their inability to watch *Survivor*, or how much they missed their families. It was all about Jane.

"She looked upset," said one woman. "I hope that lawyer didn't upset her. I would be very angry if he did."

"Me too. She's so lovely."

"I just love that green suit. I wish I could ask her where she got it."

"I adore her hair. After the trial I'm going to ask her who styles it for her."

"I wish my son would date women like her. All he brings home are girls with dirty hair and tattoos."

"She has lovely manners. Always saying please, and thank you, and I beg your pardon. You don't see many young women today with such nice manners."

"And morals. You saw how appalled she was when the girlfriend admitted she was dating a married man."

"Such class, don't you think? Always put together beautifully. Every outfit matches, right down to the shoes."

"I think she must have gone to some sort of deportment school, don't you?"

"I bet she has a lovely apartment."

And from the men:

"She has nice legs."

"Fabulous legs."

"Nice curves up top."

"Good curves."

"What a honey."

"A total sweetheart."

"Definitely the kind of girl you bring home to Mother."

"I would love to bring her home to meet my mother."

"I didn't see a wedding ring on her finger. Do you think she's allowed to go out with jurors?"

22

Jane Spring sat down at a table in the criminal court cafeteria and bowed her head to say grace. It was one p.m. and the room was full of loudmouth lawyers, tired cops and jittery witnesses waiting to be called. Only jurors and defendants ate lunch in separate quarters. Jane Spring crossed her ankles under the table, picked up her spoon and started in on a bowl of soup. She was eating alone, Jesse having abandoned her in favor of returning to the office to check his e-mail. It would not be an overstatement to say most people in the room were staring at Jane Spring. It would also not be an overstatement to suggest Jane Spring was rather enjoying the attention.

It had only been three days, but Jane hadn't regretted her decision to morph into Doris Day for a minute. To think she had been worried she wouldn't survive day one! She hadn't imagined then how she would be able to muffle her "Janeness" even if she knew intellectually going Doris was the right move. How was she going to hold her tongue when surrounded by everyday civilian insubordination. But her tongue, she found, was holding itself. The simple act of inhabiting Doris's sunny persona, her feline body, pretty clothes, frosted lipstick and painted nails had the one effect on Jane Spring she had never anticipated. It made her feel calm. More accepting.

Not all the time, of course. Just that morning she had wanted to wring Chip's neck the "old Jane" way. (Though, funny, the three deep breaths did help.) But more and more the burning need to chew out civilians military style was falling by the wayside. She found she was developing more patience for them and they, curiously, were returning it in kind. She couldn't deny it; she liked the way men stared and admired her face, her body. She liked the way women said, "Hi, Jane, nice to see you, today." It all made her feel beautiful, included, appreciated.

So when Chip Bancroft appeared in front of her clutching a tray bearing a sandwich and coffee, it took her a few seconds to wipe the grin off her face and put on a scowl.

"Jane, may I sit?" asked Chip.

"It's a free country, Mr. Bancroft."

"Jane, I want to apologize."

"I see."

Rock was always apologizing and trying to weasel his way back into Doris's good graces after some typical bad-boy behavior, so she should have seen this coming.

"Yes, really. My behavior in the courtroom this morning was, well, dishonorable. I know it was unethical to use you to make my client look good. I hope you will accept my apology."

Jane paused. Now what was he up to? What he had done in court today was standard operating procedure for a defense lawyer, and quite brilliant at that. Jane resolved to play along.

"Apology accepted." She took another sip of her soup.

"You've been looking very nice in court this week, Jane. I like your hair."

Jane patted her hair. "Why, thank you, Mr. Bancroft. I just had it cut in this style."

"Well, it's very becoming."

Jane smiled and continued with her soup.

"I also found your opening argument and subsequent examination of witnesses very compelling, Jane."

Oh, Lord, that lying dog was really

laying it on thick now, she thought. "Why thank you. Coming from my opponent I find that quite the compliment."

Chip Bancroft threw her his own movie-star smile, and then a forelock of hair fell into his eyes. He brushed it back, just as Jane had seen him do hundreds of times in law school. Back then, that grin, combined with the falling hair and the confidence, had made her knees buckle. Now she could see right through it. And yet, here she was having lunch with him, after all the years of waiting, and secretly loving every minute.

"Not that I don't intend to beat you, Jane; it's just that a gentleman can't help giving compliments even in the most competitive of circumstances."

"Well, how lovely to hear you say that, Mr. Bancroft."

Oh, please. Could he be any more transparent? Does he really think playing along with my game, apologizing the way a real gentleman would, will actually give him any leverage?

Actually, that's exactly what he was hoping. Chip knew he had won some big points with the jury that morning. He also sensed that he had lost all of them when they saw that Jane was angry at him.

Normally juries adored Chip, women in particular lapped up that all-American-boy persona. But not now. Now they were falling in step behind Jane; he felt their solidarity with her like a force field. But he couldn't believe they weren't growing tired of her routine. Couldn't they see it for the amateur theatrics it was? It alarmed him greatly that they were drinking it up. Placating her, he hoped, would put things back on an even keel between them when they resumed after lunch.

That was the short-term plan.

Long term, Chip had to find a way to stop the blood from hemorrhaging out of his case. He had to throw her for a loop and deliver a blow so hard Jane Spring would curse the day she'd cut her hair and zipped herself into that cute pink suit.

Chip Bancroft ran his fingers through his hair and threw Jane his best golden-boy grin. He scrutinized her carefully as she reapplied her lipstick and fluffed her hair, then, suddenly, his shoulders relaxed and his eyes lit up. Of course. There was no other way.

In the afternoon session Jane called a forensics expert to the stand and led him through the grisly evidence of bullet entry and blood splatter. She passed horrific pictures of a dead Officer Riley among the jury, and winced along with them, just like a lady would. Jesse especially loved that part. The old Jane Spring wouldn't have batted an eyelid if they had wheeled the corpse into the room.

Thanks to the U.S. Army, she had a stronger stomach for blood and guts than most men. So watching her close her eyes, purse her lips and shake her head softly as the expert provided narration for the photographs was too fantastic for words. The only thing missing was the popcorn.

Taking the floor on cross, Chip's behavior was markedly changed. The aggressive showman from the morning session had been replaced by the contrite man from lunch crossed with an English butler. He referred to Jane as "the learned counsel for the prosecution," instead of Ms. Spring. He never objected. He smiled constantly at the jury. At the recess he held the doors open for Jane; at the end of the day he flagged a taxi for her.

She could see exactly what he was doing: giving her a dose of her own medicine. Though she doubted he could keep it up for very long, she was amused by it and planned to savor it while it lasted.

"That was excellent work in court today, Jane," Chip said while holding the cab door open. "There was a lot of evidence to get through, and you laid it out clearly for the jury. I'll have my work cut out for me; that's for sure."

"Thank you, Mr. Bancroft."

In the cab home Jane Spring stared out the window. In the last three days she had gotten more attention, and downright doting, from Chip Bancroft than in the last ten years, and it felt *wonderful.* Yes, perhaps his attention was fake, but what she found herself feeling for him was real. Attraction. Lust. Desire. Again. Just like ten years ago.

Jane punched her beauty case. She didn't understand it. Now she knew exactly who Chip Bancroft was. She had forgiven herself her earlier infatuation; she had been young, unfamiliar with civilians, easily taken by their charm. Now she knew him like the back of her own hand. Chip Bancroft was a self-absorbed playboy, not to mention a dirty, up-to-no-good defense lawyer whose courtroom antics would not look out of place at a snake farm. And yet she still craved him.

Oooohhhhhh!

Jane Spring wanted to ask the cab driver

if it had ever happened to him: falling for people you know are bad for you, yet you can't help it. There was no question Chip had Rock- and Carylike qualities, but the rotten qualities: the kind only falling in love with Doris would erase.

So the question was, now that she was Doris, could she dare dream?

23

Friday, the judge called in sick with flu and court was canceled. Jane was upset; this delay almost guaranteed a Christmas interruption. But on the bright side, a day off would allow her to finish up some paperwork and then go shopping, since she needed a number of things Grandma Eleanor had been unable to provide.

So for the first full morning in a week Jane Spring remained in her office, but found herself unable to complete even one task. She was too busy receiving guests like a visiting dignitary. A number of colleagues in other departments had heard court was not in session, and they wanted to see her in the flesh to judge for themselves what they had heard all week: that Spring was taking this trial ploy so seriously she never stepped out of character. (One rumor suggested she had to maintain it lest she be sighted by the judge or a juror in public; another claimed it was to acclimate her own witnesses during last-minute prep.)

All morning the hordes came to inspect

Jane, and with each new arrival Lazy Susan would announce, "Mr. Evans is here to see you from Civil, Miss Sp-Ring." Or "Mr. Parker is here to see you from Major Case." And Jane would say, "Thank you, Susan! Please do show him in."

And then the men (they were always men; women were much more clandestine when it came to checking out Jane) would make some excuse about needing her advice on a thorny legal issue while inspecting her head to toe. As they were leaving, they would pause, clear their throats, and then, as if struck by Cupid's arrow, propose dinner or a concert.

One of the men, it should be noted, had already taken her out and ended the evening most unpleasantly. A second she had just recently dined with! Hadn't he, too, told her in no uncertain terms he never wanted to see her again? Now they were both here looking for second helpings. My, my.

But the thing that had really made Jane's morning was the surprise appearance of defense lawyer John Gillespie. The man who once called her a psychopath, then suggested he'd lower his standards and sleep with her anyway. That dirty rat.

"Hey, Jane. Just in the neighborhood to

work out a plea deal with Graham. Thought I'd say hello," he said, taking her in, and after absorbing the initial shock, liking what he saw.

"Well, hello to you too, Mr. Gillespie!" she said warmly. "My, that's a lovely tie."

This exchange was followed by some perfunctory chitchat about the weather and upcoming cases, then he laid out his offer.

"Jane, you know, once I'm done here, maybe we could, well, would you like to have a bite? My treat, of course. It's not every day I get to take a lady to lunch."

"Thank you so much for your offer," Jane said, pursing her lips. "But I'm in the middle of a trial, and have so much work to get through. Another time, perhaps?"

"Of course, Jane."

Ooooh, she never thought she'd live to see the day that heel would ask her out and mean it. Or any of the morning's parade of suitors, for that matter. Yet Jane harbored no anger toward them. As much as it hurt, she was starting to understand why they might have once rejected her. She still believed she had always been an excellent, attentive date, but a week as Doris had shown her that it wasn't just how you handled yourself that mattered — duty, honor and self-discipline were, of course, still essential — but how you handled other people. That was the key!

If you differed with someone's opinion gracefully, not derisively; if you asked rather than ordered; if you graded people on their performance constructively, not negatively (she assumed this went for the bedroom too, not that she would allow herself to find out); people responded to you differently. They wanted to be around you. They sought out your opinions. They wanted second dates! They didn't discount your intelligence because you were kind; if anything, they paid more attention to everything you said.

Incredible, she thought, what you can learn from movies. The general would never believe it.

The last guest of the morning was Marcie, who waltzed in to get an opinion on wedding invitations, and promptly laid out a selection on Jane's desk.

"Too much silver around the border in this one, don't you think?"

"No, Marcie, I think that one is just darling."

"Really? I'm going more toward this one with antiqued gold edge myself, but Howard likes the silver."

"Oh, then I'd do what my future husband wanted," said Jane. "Don't you want to make him happy and feel like he contributed? I would."

Marcie heard her phone ring in her office and gathered up the invitations. "You're right, Jane. Later."

"My pleasure, Marcie."

Jane emerged from her office to talk to Lazy Susan.

"What a busy morning, Susan! All these people dropping by!"

"Yes, Miss Sp-Ring."

As crazy as this whole thing had seemed at first, Lazy Susan loved the new and improved Jane Spring, and hoped against hope she would stick around once the trial was over. For a woman who had loathed any communication with her boss, Lazy Susan now relished every exchange.

"Oh, Susan, I was so worried when you were running late, this morning. I know it's not like you. No need to apologize, I'm just relieved you are all right!"

"What a lovely shirt, Susan. You should wear that color more often."

"Susan, thank you for taking all my messages today. Honestly, I don't know how I'd survive here without you!"

But more than how Jane spoke, it was how people now spoke to Jane that really galvanized Lazy Susan. Good morning, Jane. Good night, Jane. You look great today, Jane. Can I ask your advice, Jane? Can I take you to dinner, Jane?

No one had addressed her lord and master like that before; nobody sought out Jane just to shoot the breeze. And who was ever disappointed if she was in court all day in the past? Now they missed her.

Even Lazy Susan's morning ritual with Graham had been amended. Instead of "How's the sergeant major this morning?" she was greeted with "Is the lovely Ms. Spring in residence, or is she out picking daisies?"

Graham still rolled his eyes, elbowed Susan and laughed, but his tone wasn't like before. It was clear he also preferred this version of Jane. In fact, the biggest shift Lazy Susan had noted was how men reacted to Jane. The attention. The compliments. And they couldn't keep their eyes off her. It certainly had her thinking.

When she wasn't working, that is. Lazy Susan had found that since Miss Spring had flipped her lid, she didn't actually groan anymore when hearing her footsteps approach. Opening the mail no longer seemed such a chore, and the compliments Jane handed out somehow compensated for the drudgery of typing up case files. Even answering the phone had become something of a pleasure.

Though Lazy Susan had replaced her standard "Miss Sp-Ring's Awfice" with "Good Morning/Afternoon! Miss Sp-Ring's Awfice!" per Jane's sunny request, she found that it actually worked better for her too. Strangely, the voices at the other end proved more amenable to deal with.

Then again, Lazy Susan would have promised to answer the phone standing on her head singing "Yankee Doodle" if it meant the old Jane Spring would never come back.

Since that Spring chick had finally taken that stick out of her ass, she thought, this job actually hasn't been half bad.

24

Jane Spring learned it was easy to play dress up in New York City. It was the kind of place where people either considered you a fashion junkie or a total nut, either of which was perfectly acceptable. So walking the streets of Midtown Manhattan with her pink suit peeking out from underneath the blue coat with satin trim, with her white beauty case swinging from her gloved hands, a few people glanced at her sideways, but nobody called the police to have her arrested. Some men even whistled. A Santa standing outside Saint Patrick's Cathedral smiled and tipped his red cap to her. Jane chirped Merry Christmas! in return. It was the first time in her life Jane Spring hadn't snarled at a Santa.

Jane was heading for Bergdorf Goodman, Doris's favorite store. Once inside she found out why Doris loved it so. The store was so elegant. The staff so beautifully dressed and attentive. And their manners! How many people in New York City called you ma'am anymore?

Jane smiled sweetly at everyone as she made her way to the ground-floor cosmetics department. She was startled to see so much on offer. Duane Reade had given over a wall to lipstick and mascara. This was a whole room!

She made her way to the Elizabeth Arden counter. An elegant woman dressed in a white uniform asked if she could be of assistance.

"Yes, I'm looking to replace this," Jane said, handing the sales assistant an empty gold lipstick tube now rusted with age.

"My, this looks as if it's been lying around someone's bathroom drawer a long time," she said.

"More than forty years, I think," Jane said proudly. "It was my grandmother's. 'Coral Lustre.' I'm hoping you're still making it."

Doris wore Coral Lustre in all her films; clearly, Grandma Eleanor had followed her lead. Jane was becoming bored with frosted pink and hoped to start the next week off with a new lip color.

The saleswoman put on her bifocals, turned the tube upside down to read the label, then opened it to check if any lipstick remained inside. There was, she saw, a speck left.

"Well, we did stop making Coral Lustre in the sixties, but I'm sure we can match it."

The saleswoman pulled a number of lipsticks out of a display case and opened them all for Jane to inspect. Then she drew a line with each across the back of Jane's hand. It was clear the tube labeled "Pumpkin Patch" was a near match. And yet Jane was disappointed. Wearing a lipstick called Pumpkin Patch didn't have quite the same cachet as Coral Lustre, did it? Hardly as romantic or sensual. But just as soon as she thought this, Jane checked herself and her attitude. No, she would keep smiling and wear Pumpkin Patch without complaint. Doris would have.

She purchased two tubes, then headed up to the men's department to buy Christmas presents for the general and her brothers.

Riding the escalator, Jane made a note to return to Bergdorf's as often as her schedule and wallet allowed. The soft carpeting, the chandelier lighting, the courtly atmosphere and those delicious lilac shopping bags — they made her feel more Doris than ever. It was like taking a bath in eau de Doris. Plus, it was exactly the place the man she was looking for would shop.

In fact, she hoped he might be there today. Maybe he's buying a smart new suit for work or perfume for his mother for the holiday. Whatever it was, being a man of high standards, he would want the best quality.

On the men's floor Jane examined a number of gift options, carefully examining seams, fabrics, style and cut. She ran sweaters along her cheeks to check for softness, petted gloves to test for smoothness. She surreptitiously looked around the room, hoping her eyes might land on a hardy male specimen she might speak with.

"Excuse me, do you mind if I ask your advice? My brother is your size; could you just slip this jacket on and let me see how it fits?"

Getting a conversation going would be the easiest thing in the world. Except that finding any single men among the sea of women shopping for their husbands, brothers and fathers proved harder than she thought. The place was a madhouse.

"Can you please charge it to my husband's account?" Jane overheard the woman ahead of her in line ask the sales clerk. "I like the way you operate," the clerk chuckled, winking. "Getting your husband to pay for his own Christmas presents. You're a *genius.*"

"One of the best perks of marriage." The woman laughed.

Jane stared at the woman, then cocked her head to one side the way Doris did when she was displeased. That's what she considers one of the best perks of marriage? Jane couldn't disagree more. She would never treat her husband like a cash machine! She would respect his hard work and let him know it, always paying her fair share. Jane might be inhabiting a sixties' body, but once she found her soul mate, she intended to be an equal partner in her marriage.

She and Mr. Right would be a couple who would share the housework and the cooking (Jane noted that she would have to learn to cook; opening a can of soup wouldn't qualify) while holding down jobs they were dedicated to, reveling in each other's success.

She paid for her purchases and headed upstairs for her last pit stop, ladies' lingerie. In "Intimates," as they liked to call it, Jane was approached by a saleswoman whose name tag read Irma.

Irma had a tape measure around her neck.

"May I help you, madam? Looking for a gift for someone?"

"No, actually. I'm looking for me."

"Lovely."

"Yes. I want a robe in pink chiffon with a frill on the bottom, and it has to button up to the chin."

Irma looked Jane Spring up and down. She had seen everything in her time on the sales floor, from drag queens to drama queens, so this little blonde in the sixties' outfit didn't phase her a bit. Just another fruitcake stuck in a time warp, Irma thought. Well, New York has plenty of those too. Just play along and keep smiling. "Ma'am, I'm sorry, but we might have a small problem. We do have a few robes in chiffon, but nothing buttoned to the chin."

"You don't! Is there a reason why?"

"Well, ma'am, there isn't a lot of demand for robes like that anymore. Women today, you know, they like things cut a little more modern. Seductive," Irma said with a knowing smile. Seductive! In Bergdorf's! I am shocked to hear it.

"Thank you, anyway."

Jane began to move around the floor, and Irma tailed her. "May I show you something else, ma'am? We have a very wide selection."

Jane stopped at a rack full of lace teddies that were virtually see-through. She picked one up by its hanger and shook her head.

"I can't believe a lady would ever wear anything like this. Can you, Irma? It's positively indecent!"

Two miniskirted teenage girls on a buying spree with Daddy's credit card looked up, giggled and rolled their eyes. Jane didn't care when the odd civilian found her new incarnation amusing; she brushed it off without a thought. She was fully committed to being Doris every minute; staying in character would ensure that Mr. Right could always find her.

But there was something else. Jane Spring was getting more joy out of being Doris Day than she ever could have imagined. Every minute she played her, she felt her femininity quotient multiply. And the more woman she became, the more the world loved her for it (two catty schoolgirls notwithstanding). The approving looks, the kindnesses, the eagerness to be near her — she couldn't have felt any happier if drugs were involved.

Jane thanked Irma for her assistance and announced she hoped they would stock a wider selection in the future. Bergdorf's was her favorite store, you see. She prayed they would see the error of their ways and start to accommodate the *modest* woman.

25

Jane Spring emerged from Bergdorf's with her favorite new lilac shopping bags swinging from both arms. Because it was the last Friday before Christmas, catching a cab required both patience and strong arches. Jane was developing the former exponentially; the latter were already ruined after a week traipsing through the snow and slush in high heels. So sitting in the back of the cab surrounded by her purchases, Jane started dreaming of the bubble bath she would draw when she got home.

"Traffic's insane, miss. Can I let you off at the corner?" the cabbie asked, pulling up at the far end of Jane's street.

"Of course," Jane purred, opening her wallet and pulling out a twenty-dollar bill. The fare was $5.50. "And you have yourself a Merry Christmas."

"Thank you very much, miss. Seasons Greetings to you too."

Jane opened the cab door and stepped gingerly onto the sidewalk. Half of the snow from the blizzard had melted, turning walkways into obstacle courses. Jane stood on the corner of Third Avenue and Seventy-third Street and contemplated whether to cross the street to shop at the supermarket or to order dinner in. Chinese?

It was in that moment of indecision that Jane first saw him. A male figure walking toward her with a dog on a long leash. It was getting dark; she couldn't quite make him out, but sensed she knew him. She recognized the brown coat. The dog also seemed familiar. Must be one of the neighbors. Well, I'll wait here till they pass by and wish them a happy holiday. It wouldn't be polite to disappear now.

As the man came into view, Jane nearly fell off her heels. "Detective? Detective Millbank? My goodness! What brings you to this part of town?"

Mike Millbank tried to act cool, but Jane could see he was uncomfortable running into her. "Jane, hi. Well, isn't this something? Bumping into you like this."

"I live around here."

"Do you? I had no idea. I was walking Bishop in Central Park and once we were done, we decided to take a tour of the nearby neighborhood."

"If you don't mind my saying it, you

seem to be a long way from home, Detective," Jane remarked, smiling softly. She knew Mike Millbank lived downtown. During the previous trial they'd worked together, she had once had documents delivered to him after hours.

"You have a good memory, Jane. But occasionally I bring Bishop up to the park. For him it's like going to Disneyland. So much room to run around, all those dogs to play with and he loves charging through snow."

Bishop sat silently by Detective Millbank's side, wagging his tail. Jane leaned down to pet him. "He's a beautiful dog."

"Man's best friend," he said proudly.

Jane noted how tenderly he treated his dog. The man clearly has a heart, she thought.

"Well," said Jane.

"Well," said the Detective.

"Well," she repeated.

There it was again. The same awkwardness she'd felt at his office when they had been so open with each other.

"Jane, you know what I said last week when you left? I didn't mean to be rude," he said, shifting his weight on his feet. "I'm sure you're doing a great job in court. It's just that this case means so much to all the men —"

"I know, Detective," she said graciously. "I completely understand."

"Fine. Then I guess I'll be off," he said, gently tugging at Bishop's leash.

"Me too. I have to get these tired feet home!"

"You don't . . ." the Detective said tentatively.

"I don't what?" Jane answered.

"You don't want to grab a quick cup of coffee, do you?"

Jane smiled at the detective. "Sure, that would be lovely." She was impressed that he had apologized for his prior bad behavior. She wanted to let him know it.

"This is your neighborhood, you lead the way."

"I know just the place," Jane said giddily.

She took the detective to the local diner. Doris loved diners; she ate lunch in them in all her movies. They sat in the window so they could keep an eye on Bishop, who was tethered to a pole outside. Jane's collection of lilac shopping bags were lined up beside her on the floor.

Jane ordered hot chocolate, the detective black coffee, and if it wasn't too much trouble, did they have any bones in the kitchen for his dog? Two minutes later the waitress returned with two mugs and a bowl of soup bones. Detective Millbank excused himself, then raced outside to deliver a snack to his charge.

"People tell me I baby him too much," he said, returning to his seat, then knocking on the window to let Bishop know he was nearby. Bishop looked up from his meal and wagged his tail wildly.

"Oh no, Detective," said Jane. "I don't think you can ever be too kind to anyone, even pets."

"My brother says I should get married and have kids of my own instead of pretending Bishop's my son," he said sheepishly.

Oh, Jesus, Mike, shut up, he scolded himself. What are you doing? Don't talk marriage and family again with her, you idiot. It was weird enough last time.

"Well, I'm sure that will happen one day, Detective," Jane said. "And when the time comes, it's clear you'll make a wonderful father."

Oh, Jane, stop it, she chided herself. Don't step on this land mine of marriage and family again with him. Wasn't it uncomfortable enough last time?

They sipped their drinks in silence for a moment.

"So, how do you think the trial's going?"

Detective Millbank said, firmly changing the subject. Jane was relieved.

"Well," she said taking a breath, "apart from the fact that the reprehensible Mr. Bancroft is up to his usual tricks, I think we're doing very well."

"Usual tricks?"

"Oh, he intimated to the jury that I disapproved of my own witness! Miss Dunlap. He tried to use me to build sympathy for her. That man is a total scoundrel."

Mike Millbank stared at Jane Spring. The man was a scoundrel? Who spoke like that in the twenty-first century? What was she up to?

"But you do disapprove of Patty Dunlap, don't you?"

"That's besides the point. What I think is immaterial to the case. As is her morality, even if it is despicable. Stealing another woman's husband! Why, Detective, can you think of anything worse?"

Mike Millbank now fixed his eyes on Jane's hair. It was one thing to put on a new dress, but to cut your hair? Whatever she was up to, it was serious. Could this really be all about the Riley trial?

"Sorry?" he asked.

"Do you think there is anything worse than breaking up someone's marriage?

247

Which, might I remind you, in this case has led to murder."

"Sounds like you're prosecuting the wrong woman, Jane. Sounds to me you'd prefer to be putting Patty Dunlap away," he teased her.

"You're right. I'd like to put them both away." She smiled. "Unfortunately, I will have to settle for one conviction."

"Incredible, huh?" Mike said, shaking his head.

"What's incredible?"

"What looking for love, being in love, does to people. I see it all the time. Turns them into a person they wouldn't recognize."

"Really?" said Jane, her eyes wide.

"Patty Dunlap? I know her from Central Booking. She was a sweet kid. Never pegged her as a home wrecker. And Laura Riley? I met her once or twice around. Never in a million years did she strike me as a killer."

"She is now."

"Exactly my point."

Bishop started to bark.

"I better go rescue him. He's probably getting cold out there."

Jane finished her hot chocolate. The detective drained his coffee mug, then waved over the waitress with the check. Jane sat quietly as Mike Millbank paid. Before he put on his coat, he helped her with hers. At the front door he opened it for her.

Jane was impressed.

"Detective, thank you. That was lovely."

"You're welcome, Jane," he said, untying Bishop.

"I'll see you in court on Tuesday, then."

"I'll be there."

Jane extended a gloved hand. He shook it. They both turned in opposite directions and went home.

At her apartment building the superintendent stopped Jane in the lobby.

"Oh, Miss Spring, a man stopped by here about an hour ago asking about you. Wouldn't give his name. Asked me not to mention it to you, but I thought you should know. Might be a stalker related to your work or something."

"You were right to tell me, thank you," Jane said brightly, mentally flipping through a list of suspects. The last six people she had prosecuted were in prison, and although Gloria Markham had reason to hate her, the woman couldn't walk let alone stalk. Who was left? Chip Bancroft. That sneak.

"What did he look like?"

"About six feet. Dark hair. Brown coat. He had a dog."

Jane put down her shopping. "A dog?"

"Yeah, a big golden retriever."

Jane was shocked. Mike Millbank stopped by? Asking questions? So he wasn't just walking his dog in the park. She knew that story had holes in it. No wonder he nearly fainted when she said hello.

"What did he ask?"

"Nothing special. If you lived here. I said yes. Do you dress like this, all pink and pearls all the time, or just to go to work?"

"And what did you say?"

"I said, no, you seem to have turned over a new leaf and looked like this all the time now. That I hadn't seen you in a black suit or in your army sweats for over a week."

"And?'

"And then he left."

"Thank you. I appreciate your letting me know."

"You're welcome, Miss Spring."

Jane stepped into the elevator, her hands wrapped around her lilac shopping bags, looking the picture of calm. She was still smiling at the super when the doors closed. Then panic spread across her face.

Detective Millbank, just what are you up to?

26

Saturday morning, exhausted by the rush and excitement of being Doris for a week, Jane Spring slept in, which for her meant seven a.m. At eight she was at the pool at the Y, and by now the regulars were so used to seeing the blue-pleated bathing suit and the pretty flowered cap nobody even stared.

Stroking up and down the lanes, Jane reviewed the events of the past week in her mind. After the initial shock of her appearance had worn off, people adjusted famously to her new persona. That was the advantage of working among civilians. They have no sense of commitment, and can adapt to new situations in a minute. But she was more surprised by how easy it had been for her to adjust to being Doris. Now, in her surroundings, when she put on the clothes, the shoes and the voice, the rest flowed so naturally, it was as if Doris had always been inside her, just waiting to be uncorked. The urge to yell at her secretary, curse out inconsiderate civilians, badger witnesses — things that had come as involuntarily as her own breath — they all seemed to disappear.

Even more shocking, she adored being Doris. She was positively having the time of her life. Having Chip court her with his genteel (albeit faux) manners, having taxi drivers call her ma'am, having Lazy Susan say Good morning, Miss Sp-Ring! instead of grunting. And was she wrong in thinking the girl was actually working harder? There did seem to be more finished documents on her desk awaiting her signature every day. Well, well, miracles never cease.

Of course, she hadn't exactly met the man of her dreams yet, but it was only the first week. And she could always use the time to break in her act, so to speak. But having passed the week with flying colors, she felt she was now completely ready for *him.* What great timing then: She had plans for that evening.

At ten a.m. Jane was busy setting her hair in rollers when the phone rang. She assumed it was Jesse; they were meeting later to finalize their strategy for when Chip put Laura Riley on the stand. *If* he put on her stand. If he didn't, in a nutshell, they were home free. If he did, they were in trouble. Putting a betrayed, weeping wife in the witness box, even if she had killed her husband, usually worked like magic with the jury. Punching holes in her story required a gingerly touch: she couldn't risk alienating them as she had in the Markham trial.

She picked up the handset and answered perkily. It wasn't Jesse. It was Alice.

Although she missed her company terribly, Jane was now glad her best friend was safely across the country. If she were in New York, and walked into Jane's yellow apartment with the blue curtains and the single bed, she would have had Jane committed. Immediately. Then again, Jane thought, what makes me think she won't do it long-distance after we hang up?

"Hey, Springie. How's the trial going?" Jane could hear the racket of the nurses' station in the background. "No, tell me about that in a minute. First, how's that other stuff coming along?" she whispered. "Have you had your big meeting with Doris yet?"

"Alice. How lovely of you to call!" Jane replied, in a voice dripping of Doris, all honey and syrup.

Jane had made a pact with herself at the outset that she would never step out of character. More than a matter of practice, it was a matter of principle.

"Soldiers never go off duty just because the shelling has stopped, Jane."

But say it might be tactically smarter to go off duty on occasion — say if your best friend called from another city and you wanted to spare yourself some pointed questions about your sanity — Jane just couldn't. She didn't want to. Being Doris had turned her into a better Jane, happier, looser, and she wasn't ready yet to return to the old one.

"Oh, Alice, the meeting with Doris couldn't have gone better. She's quite incredible, really. Told me things about men that I never knew. Then we worked out a game plan — you know, things I might try to do differently. Tonight I'm going out for the first time to put it in action. I can't tell you how excited I am, Alice!"

In San Francisco, Alice Carpenter furrowed her brow, pulled the phone from her ear and stared into the telephone receiver for a second.

"Springie, what's wrong with you? You sound weird."

"Weird? Alice, I don't know what you're talking about."

Alice tapped her phone to check that it wasn't the line.

"Your voice. It's like you're on helium or something."

"Well, you sound fine to me at this end."

Alice then realized her best friend didn't just sound different, she *was* different. Upbeat. Happy. Excited. Oh, Lord.

"Springie, have you been drinking?"

"Heavens, no."

"Then what is going on over there?"

Jane looked around her apartment. Oh, nothing, she thought, other than a full-tilt sixties revival and a bloodthirsty, no-holds-barred hunt for a man.

"Nothing."

Alice didn't buy it. She had handled enough drunks in the ER first thing in the morning to know what she was dealing with here. Poor Jane, she thought. This must be one killer trial. She never drank before six p.m., and here she was plastered by ten in the morning.

"Listen, Springie. You're hammered. Now don't argue. Just listen," she said, moving into nurse mode. "After I hang up, I want you to drink lots of water. Follow that with two aspirin, then eat something light. And go to sleep for the rest of the day. I'll call later to check to see if you're doing okay."

"No, Alice, I'm fine really," Jane gushed. "In fact, I've never felt better."

Alice called again at six p.m., but Jane let it go through to the answering machine. For one, she didn't think Alice could stand two encounters with the new and improved Jane Spring in one day. And for another, she was too busy getting ready for the evening. She had high hopes for it and wanted to look perfect. This meant taking extra time with her hair and makeup as well as changing the polish on her nails. Jane had never realized how much time women took getting ready until she'd decided to impersonate one.

Tonight she was going dancing. She'd realized that in order to meet *him,* the man with impeccable manners, integrity and honor, the man who wanted a woman with spunk, she had to go places a man like that might be found. Cary and Rock *always* took Doris dancing. Cary and Rock were fantastic dancers.

And so she had signed up for an introductory class at the Fred Astaire Dance Studio on Broadway. In their ad in the Yellow Pages, the folks at the Astaire studio promised that in just one class you could learn the tango and the waltz, which Jane was more than keen to do. She knew they were both in Doris's repertoire.

Jane ran herself a bubble bath and

stepped in. She stayed there humming "Happy Birthday to Me" till the bubbles went flat, then dried off and dressed herself in a red silk cocktail dress with a V-neck and nipped waist. She covered her feet in fresh Band-Aids before slipping into a pair of red satin pumps and put two red bows into her hair, one on each side.

She put on a pair of pearl-drop earrings, then slipped into white leather gloves and her white fox-trim coat and matching hat.

Jane Spring felt like a million bucks walking out the door. Whoever *he* was, he'd better watch out.

As Jane walked into the Fred Astaire Dance Studio, her expression went blank with disappointment. Even if her future husband was there, how would he recognize her? Standing in front of her were twelve other women who had signed up for the class, all of whom looked exactly like *her.* The older ones, eager to relive the glory of their youth, had zipped their overweight and wrinkled selves into cocktail dresses that must have been hanging in their closets for forty years. The younger ones were also decked out in an array of sixties' party frocks they'd picked up at vintage shops — floral, silk, V-neck, boatneck — and all nipped at the waist.

"What a pretty dress," Jane commented to a twentysomething woman standing next to her.

"Thanks, I was afraid I'd be the only person here in costume," she joked.

So was I, thought Jane.

"But it looks like great minds think alike!" she continued.

"Yes, brilliant," muttered Jane.

There were only eight men, so some of the women had to partner up. This was not a good sign. Of the men in the room, Jane soon realized that half of them were gay. It wasn't just the leather pants, but the fact that they wanted to take turns leading. The other half did not constitute what Jane considered husband material. Three of them were geriatrics in tan pants and white shoes who called anyone under sixty-five, girlie. The only other prospect was a skinny guy called Marcel, who slicked his hair into a ponytail and wore his pants a little too high. Jane even suspected he may have slipped a sock in them. Turns out the skinny guy was also a pincher. When his hands got to your rear end, he sampled it, so to speak. When Jane protested, "Please, sir, keep your hands above my waist," he told her to loosen up and enjoy it, baby.

As if she would even have coffee with a pincher, let alone marry him.

Two hours later a dejected Jane Spring kicked off her red pumps, rubbed her feet and fell back on her single bed. The night had not gone quite as planned, but it was only her first evening out as Doris in full; and just like her first time in the court-room, she couldn't expect a conviction here either. Her theory about finding *him* outside of work was correct, she told her-self. She had just chosen the wrong venue. She sat up and unzipped her dress.

"A good soldier learns from defeat; it doesn't defeat him, Jane."

The general was right. She had not tasted victory this time out, but she would ultimately. She would get back into the battle, and she would march, head high, until she returned a winner. Slipping into her Chinese pajamas, Jane heard the Tates starting to do what they did best. And yet this time she wasn't bothered; there was no rush to the living room to turn up the TV.

Jane rolled under the covers, nestled the satin trim of the blanket under her chin and let the Tates cooing lull her to sleep. In a matter of time her own prince was coming, and confident of that, she was unflappable.

27

When the construction workers whistled on Monday as she made her way into court, Jane Spring knew she was right to dismiss Saturday night as a freak disaster, sort of like a blizzard, really. Not that she was bothered by the evening's failure; there was no way this good soldier would flee the battle.

In court, once again in her apple-green suit, with crocodile pumps, Jane sat back and let Jesse conduct the questioning of that day's witness, the medical examiner. She let him take the floor because he needed the practice, and she knew the medical examiner would be a routine question and answer sans drama: Please describe the time of death. Please describe your findings on the cause of death. Please describe the wounds. You just couldn't mess it up.

But although she was happy to help him hone his legal skills, there was another reason Jane Spring let Jesse Beauclaire take over that day. Her feet were killing her.

One whole week in high heels and the pain was now shooting like fire into her calves. She simply couldn't stand it, or even *stand* anymore. The longer she could sit, she discovered, the better off she would be. Once seated, she could slip off the back end of her vicelike crocodile pumps, giving her feet room to breathe. How the heck Doris Day smiled so much with her feet killing her the way they must have, Jane Spring could not conceive.

Jesse carried himself well in court, and when they broke for lunch, Jane piled on the compliments.

"Jesse, you were wonderful. Jesse, your questions were excellent. Jesse, I was very much impressed by the way you handled the jury. Good eye contact. You'll make a fine lead prosecutor one day."

Jesse often received feedback from Jane Spring if she let him take the floor, but nothing that ever sounded like this. More like, Jesse, what were you thinking asking that ridiculous question?

Jesse Beauclaire may have thought Jane was certifiably deranged for doing what she was doing, but he was also getting the best reviews of his career, so why complain? He accepted her compliments graciously, just the way she gave them.

After Chip Bancroft had wrapped up his cross-examination of the medical examiner and court was adjourned for the day, he approached Jane at the prosecution table and asked if he might speak with her privately.

"Mr. Bancroft, there is nothing you can say to me about this case that my cocounsel can't hear," she said pointing to Jesse.

"Jane, this is private."

Jane looked at Chip Bancroft and her heart started to race. Stop it. Stop. It. She tried to will herself to stop it. This man was the biggest cad, the slickest lawyer she knew. Just look at the way he was buttering up the jury. The witnesses. Her. She knew it all, and still her pulse wouldn't slow down. Jane Spring was disgusted with herself.

"Fine, Mr. Bancroft."

She walked toward the jury box, now empty, and waited for Chip to join her.

"Jane. Are you busy tonight?"

"Excuse me?"

"Would you like to meet for a drink at The White Lion after you're done in your office? Say, seven o'clock?"

The White Lion was the only decent bar in the neighborhood, equidistant from the courthouse and the police precinct. A lot of detectives and lawyers drank there at night, and it wasn't all fun and games either. They were doing business, comparing notes, trading information.

"Mr. Bancroft? You want to have a drink with me in the middle of a trial?"

Although prosecution and defense lawyers sometimes took liquid refreshment together after a day in court (a fact that never ceased to stun their clients), Jane always believed the practice unethical, poor judgment. But this was Chip. And it sounded like it could be a *date.*

"Yes, Jane," he said, donning his best puppy dog face. "I have some procedural questions I need to go over with you."

Darn it. It wasn't a date.

Jane smiled as she stalled for time, desperately trying to figure out what to do. Ethics aside, this might be her first and last chance to have a drink with Chip Bancroft. That was reason enough to say yes. But it could also be an opportunity to find out if he planned to put Laura Riley on the stand after Christmas.

Sure, she was on his witness list, but that meant nothing. Defense attorneys routinely kept their defendant cards close to their chests, making the final decision about letting their clients testify only after seeing how their trials were shaping up.

"What a lovely invitation. I would be pleased to meet you for a drink, Mr. Bancroft. I will see you at The White Lion at seven."

Jane returned to the prosecution table and snapped her beauty case shut. Jesse was waiting for her, and once she was dressed in her hat and coat, they headed out together. But as Jane reached for the doorknob, Jesse cut in front of her and opened the door. Then he stood back.

"After you, Jane."

After you, Jane? Since when did he step aside for her? Jesse was of the opinion that if women wanted equality in the workplace, they could open their own damn doors.

My, my, this is getting better all the time.

28

Jane Spring returned to the office at five p.m. to find that in the span of one week Lazy Susan had grown into a model of efficiency. She might even have to rethink her nickname. Busy Susan? The shortcut icon to her poker game was no longer on her computer screen. The case files had been reorganized, last month's backlog of documents were on her desk awaiting her signature, all her message slips were now organized neatly and by importance next to the telephone. Better yet, if her eyes weren't deceiving her, Lazy Susan had undergone something of a transformation herself.

The unruly hair was now dyed one shade of brown; the streaks and highlights were gone. It had been brushed straight, parted in the middle and pulled back into a pony-tail tied with a bow. The hipster pants and black lace bra were gone, the belly ring silenced. Susan was now wearing a brown tweed pencil skirt and brown suede boots. She'd paired this with a green turtleneck sweater, the same color as the suit Jane was wearing. She looked great and, well, a bit like Jane, now that she'd thought about it.

"You look very nice today, Susan," Jane said, and for the first time, she meant it.

"Thank you, Miss Spring."

Even her diction had improved.

Jane sat down and smiled. This must mean she was a good influence on the girl. She was flattered. Until it hit her that she had been of no influence as her old self. It was being Doris that did it. Now if only she could have that kind of impact on a man . . .

"I need to leave, Miss Spring," Lazy Susan announced, fanning papers out on her desk. "The first pile is for you to sign, the second pile is for you to approve and the third pile is expense reports."

"Thank you, Susan. I am very much impressed with how hard you are working."

"No problem," Lazy Susan said casually. But her smile was a mile wide.

Jane watched her secretary pack up and leave, then turned her attention to the mound of paperwork in front of her. She decided that at six-thirty she would fix her makeup and hair, and arrive at The White Lion a little after seven. Even though a soldier is always punctual, a lady has to make a man wait if she wants to make an entrance.

★ ★ ★

At 7:10, Jane walked into The White Lion to see Chip Bancroft sitting at a table for two. It had a candle in a bottle dripping wax down the neck and a bowl of mixed nuts to one side. Chip jumped up.

"Let me help you with your coat, Jane."

"Thank you, Mr. Bancroft."

Removing her coat, Chip Bancroft brushed Jane's neck with his hand, and she couldn't deny that she felt a charge. Oh, Jane, you're pathetic, she told herself. Chip Bancroft is not *him.* At least it better not be him.

Chip waited for Jane to sit, then signaled for a waiter. He ordered a double vodka, Jane a martini. She had her back to him, so Jane couldn't see that Detective Mike Millbank was also at The White Lion that night. He and his partner, Detective Cruz, had just come off shift and were having a beer before heading home.

When Chip Bancroft arrived, he and the detective had exchanged hellos. They knew they would be facing each other in court shortly. But when Jane appeared, the detective ducked quietly behind his partner, refusing to acknowledge her. He wasn't in the mood for any Jane Spring–style interrogations, old Jane or new. He had told her he just happened to be walking his dog in Central Park on Friday night. But what if she had learned he was at her apartment asking questions? How would he explain himself?

Mike Millbank stared down into his beer as Jane breezed past him toward the other end of the bar. When he looked up and saw she had taken a seat with Chip, you could have called an ambulance. She hated Bancroft; she had said as much at the diner. Why was she having a drink with him?

Jane smiled at Chip Bancroft and patted her hair. She told herself to stay cool and act disinterested, be stoic and businesslike. Doris would never throw herself at a man, and neither would she. Even if a tiny part of her was dying to get up right at that minute and go sit in his lap.

Chip Bancroft grinned at Jane. His forelock fell into his eyes. Jane felt her knees go weak. If only the women Chip dated in law school could see them now. Chip Bancroft was here with *her!* Jane Spring.

"Jane, I know I asked you here to talk shop, but before we get down to that, there's something I want to ask you."

"Why certainly, Chip."

"Jane I . . . I'm just going to come out

and say this. I like you. I mean, I really like you. You're making me crazy, Jane. I haven't looked at another woman this entire week."

For Chip Bancroft that was probably a record. He should call a press conference.

"I'd like to see you, Jane. Dinner, dancing, whatever you like. I just want to spend time with you."

He said dancing! So she was on the right track. Good thing she'd taken the lesson.

"But I thought . . . what about that model you were —"

"Bjorgia? We're done. Over. I want to be with you. Besides, she couldn't speak English. I was getting tired of asking her everything in pantomime."

Jane Spring thought she would die of joy right then, right there. Chip Bancroft was asking her out. Of course, this could all just be a trick, and most likely it was. She certainly wouldn't put it past him. She tried to hold herself together but thought she would burst at any moment, throw Chip across the table and tear his clothes off.

"So?"

"So what?"

"Will you go out with me?"

Jane wanted to believe him, wanted to

believe that her playing Doris had actually snared a real-life Cary Grant, but this was Chip Bancroft. He had already adopted her manner in court as his own; was he now upping the ante? Was this some kind of ruse designed to humiliate her later? She decided to hedge her bets and remain mysteriously indecisive. This is what Doris would do. Besides, if she took him up on his offer immediately, he would think she was *easy.* And Doris would never be easy.

"Well, Chip, I hope you understand I really can't answer that now. I'm going to think it over before I give you my decision."

"I understand, Jane. But I hope you know I'm very serious about my offer."

Oh, please, Lord, make it be so.

Drinking his beer, Mike Millbank kept his ears on the conversation at his table, but his eyes on Chip and Jane Spring. What were they talking about? They were smiling too much to be discussing work. It bothered him, their meeting like this. And it bothered him that it bothered him — in ways he didn't understand and couldn't explain.

Jane refused another drink, but Chip was already into his third double vodka and rather buzzed. Even without the aid of alcohol, Jane Spring was positively giddy.

She had, or hoped she had, Chip Bancroft in her pocket. He had just confessed to falling for her, hadn't he? If he was being honest about his feelings for her, then *he* was *him* after all.

A declaration of infatuation was one thing, but Jane needed something else from Chip Bancroft right then and wouldn't leave without getting that too.

"Now, Mr. Bancroft. Are you going to tell me if you are putting Laura Riley on the stand, or are you going to keep me in agony?"

Chip sat back, sipped, and one eyebrow went up.

"I'm undecided at the moment, Counselor."

"Really? That's not like you."

"I know. But thing is, you're not like you either, and that's my problem," he slurred. Jane opened her eyes wide and kept smiling.

"Why, Chip. I don't understand."

"See, if I could be guaranteed the other Jane Spring would be in court that day, I'd put Laura Riley in the box in a flash. That other Jane Spring, the one who had long hair and wore black, she was one mean motherfucker. She would have attacked Laura Riley's testimony like a shark. She would have made her cry or faint — she's good at doing that — and the jury would take pity on my client, which is all I need for reasonable doubt.

"But if the current Jane Spring turns up that day — *that's you* — I'm screwed. You'll flutter your eyes and sweet-talk Laura Riley, and she'll be putty in your hands. Do you see my problem, Counselor? I need to know *who* you're going to be after Christmas."

Jane Spring wanted to slap him. How dare he call her a mean motherfucker? A shark who liked to make defendants cry! Faint! The nerve. But she would stay calm. Breathe Jane. In. Out. In. Out. Just like you practiced. Like Doris.

Chip Bancroft leaned forward until his face was two inches from hers. She could smell the alcohol on his breath. "I know what you're up to, Jane, with all this," he said, touching her suit and hair. "It's not often you see prosecutors go out on a limb for a trial, so I give you a lot of credit."

"I don't know what you're talking about," said Jane, seething, but still smiling. Keep smiling, Jane.

Chip leaned back. "Sure you do. You don't really think I believe a woman as bright as you are woke up one day and decided to turn into Doris Day?"

Actually, Chip, that's exactly what happened.

"I see what's going on. This is some strategy you cooked up to help you win the trial. Well, it's working, Jane. You've got the jury eating out of your hand. You've got the judge sustaining every objection you raise. You could get Mother Teresa convicted if you wanted."

"Well, I'm shocked you would suggest I resorted to some stunt, Mr. Bancroft. That's the craziest thing I've heard today."

"Oh, it's not crazy, Jane, and neither are you. The thing is, I don't care. I love the new you. Even though I know it's not you. You were a real bitch on wheels before."

Now Jane wanted to slap him. Doris slapped all paramours who offended her.

"But now you're cute and sexy as hell."

Now Jane did slap him. Then she threw the rest of her drink in his face, picked up her coat and stormed out. The whole bar, including Detective Millbank, watched the exchange. Chip wiped his face as Mike Millbank wondered what the hell had just happened. Professional differences? Lovers' quarrel? He would have continued to wonder if Chip Bancroft had not grabbed his coat and run after Jane.

Mike Millbank pulled a ten-dollar bill out of his pocket, dropped it on the table and bid his partner good night. Then he grabbed his coat and ran frantically into the cold night air.

29

Jane Spring flagged a cab and sped away. Chip Bancroft jumped into another and ordered it to follow the one in front. And bringing up the rear, Mike Millbank trolled not far behind, hoping Chip wouldn't make him in his unmarked police car. Slowly the convoy of cars negotiated the traffic and made their way to Jane's apartment.

Inside the second cab, Chip Bancroft was kicking and cursing himself. My God, why did I set her off? I was doing so well in the beginning.

It was those damn vodkas that had caused him to go off the script. Well, now he'd better make it up to her, and good; otherwise his entire plan would crash before it even got airborne.

On Third Avenue and Seventy-third Street, Chip Bancroft watched Jane emerge from her cab and walk to her apartment building. Clearly, she looked upset. He waited until she was safely inside, then he jumped out of his cab and headed into an all-night deli. Mike Millbank idled his vehicle nearby and waited. Two minutes later, Chip emerged with a bunch of roses and started walking down Seventy-third Street. Mike Millbank waited a minute, then turned the corner to tail him. He parked across the street from Jane's apartment, then watched as Chip approached the front door of the building he himself had visited not days before. The doorman had gone off duty at 8 p.m., leaving Chip at the mercy of the intercom.

Chip buzzed; Jane did not respond. He buzzed three more times; she continued to ignore him. Chip held the intercom button down and began making his case.

"Jane, it's me, Chip. Please let me up. I want to apologize."

Nothing.

"Jane, please."

Nothing.

Chip Bancroft backed away from the front door and positioned himself on the sidewalk in front of the building.

"Jane," he screamed, looking up to the fourth floor. "Jane, I'm *sorry.* Let me *in.* I want to explain."

Jane peeked through her blue curtains, then quickly drew them shut again.

"Jane, please."

Jane stood in her living room and took

three deep breaths. In. Out. In. Out. In. Out. Good, Jane.

Chip was clearly plastered; it was doubtful at this stage of the game that he would go away. More likely he would stand in her street all night screaming, which on the one hand rather appealed to her. A man declaring his love from outside her window — now that would show the Tates she wasn't a person with a "disability," wouldn't it? On the other hand, it would wake all the neighbors who weren't dialing the police already, a situation Doris would never tolerate.

Jane buzzed Chip in, but would not, she told herself, let him past the front door. He could deliver his mea culpas from the hallway and take his leave.

She heard the elevator approaching her floor. Seconds later Chip Bancroft was in the hall, pressing his face against the chained door.

"I'm listening, Mr. Bancroft."

"Jane, please let me come in and apologize. I'll stay just five minutes. I promise."

She had never imagined Chip Bancroft's face squooshed between the doorjamb and the door, with the chain pressed across his forehead like that. He looked so . . . adorable.

Against her better judgment, Jane Spring

unchained the door and let him enter.

"Ooooohhhh!" she muttered.

Chip strolled into Jane's bright yellow living room with blue silk curtains and couldn't contain himself. He handed her the flowers, which she promptly tossed onto the coffee table.

"Jesus, Jane. You really are taking this seriously. I mean I thought this was just for court but . . ." He started moving excitedly through her apartment, Jane alongside him trying to turn him back.

"Wow, look at this bathroom," he said, surveying all the makeup lined up on the vanity shelf.

"Chip, please. You have no business coming in here. I allowed you into my building so you would stop making a scene on the street. Now if you would like to say whatever it is you came to say and leave, we can call it a night."

Chip wasn't listening. He was too buzzed with alcohol, buzzed with excitement. The apartment intrigued him. He couldn't believe how far she was going with this stunt. Chip charged into her bedroom. Jane nearly fainted with shock.

"Out, Mr. Bancroft! Now."

Chip, for chrissakes, don't antagonize her any more, he reproached himself. Remember why you came.

He sheepishly marched back to the living room. Jane stood in front of him, arms folded.

"Jane, I'm so sorry. I didn't mean to invade your home. I came here to apologize. What I said before at The White Lion, I take it back. It was rude, thoughtless and insensitive."

Jane pursed her lips. "I should say so."

The fact was, Chip Bancroft needed to apologize to Jane Spring for many reasons. One being that he could hardly afford to alienate her. The jury adored her; he could see it. She put Jesse on the floor, but they didn't stop looking in her direction, pining for her. It was embarrassing. If he let Jane finish their fight at The White Lion in court instead of now, Laura Riley could kiss her freedom good-bye. And then there was, of course, that other thing . . .

"Jane, I will understand if you never speak to me again. But I want you to know how deeply sorry I am that I've offended you. My offer still stands. I really would like to see you."

"Oh, really?" she snapped.

"I'm not joking, Jane. And I'm not lying when I say you have absolutely turned my life upside down. I haven't been this crazy about a woman in years. You've seen me in court. I can barely concentrate on the trial. Is that the Chip Bancroft you know?"

Jane had to admit that he had a point. Chip hung his head and looked really pained. He did care for her; she could see it now. She wanted to kiss him. And then she wanted to kill him. How dare he hurt her like that? What had he called her? A bitch on wheels!

"I think what I'd like right now is for you to leave my apartment, Mr. Bancroft."

"Oh, Jane," he said holding his head. "I feel dizzy."

Chip sat down on the sofa and did his best to look woozy.

"Well, that will happen if you consume half a bottle of vodka in less than an hour, Mr. Bancroft."

"Ohhhhh," he wailed.

"I'll go and get you some aspirin," she said, shaking her head. "And then you're going right out that door."

In the bathroom Jane grabbed two pills and a glass of water. When she returned to the living room, Chip was passed out on the sofa. Asleep.

"Oh, God," she groaned. "There's nothing worse than a man who can't hold his liquor."

Jane marched into her bedroom, lifted one yellow blanket off her bed, returned to Chip and draped it over him. She stood and watched him sleep. He was so . . . adorable. Yes, there was no other way to put it.

Jane turned out the lights in the living room and closed the door. In the bathroom she took off her makeup with cold cream, brushed her teeth and put one roller in her hair at the crown. Five minutes later she had slipped into her Chinese pajamas and was lying underneath the remaining yellow blanket.

On the sofa, Chip Bancroft opened his eyes. He grabbed the aspirin, downed them with water and looked at his watch. He would wait some time before leaving, to make it convincing.

In bed, Jane stared at the ceiling. What a night. He confesses his love for her, insults her, now he's asleep in her living room. Then again, why is she surprised? This always happened to Doris in the movies.

One hour later, Chip Bancroft slipped off the sofa, quietly unlocked the door and left the apartment.

Downstairs, Detective Mike Millbank was still sitting in his police car. He quickly slid down his seat and peered over the steering wheel to watch Chip exit the premises.

Standing on the street corner waiting for a cab, Chip Bancroft wore a self-satisfied smile and an odd glint in his eye.

What it added up to, the detective didn't know. But of this he was sure; it was a number he didn't like.

30

Jane Spring had no idea what time Chip Bancroft left her apartment, but she was plenty relieved he was gone when she woke in the morning. Finding defense counsel hungover on her sofa was not exactly how she planned to start the day. Not to mention it was probably grounds for an appearance before the bar association's ethics committee.

She swam, then arrived at her office at eight to answer e-mail and do general housekeeping before court started at nine. Lazy Susan had left two piles of documents on her desk for her to check and sign, and Jane suddenly realized that even if she failed to find a man, her Doris metamorphosis had still been a success: Her secretary had finally turned into a secretary.

Housekeeping completed, Jane turned to her trial notes and glanced over them. Today she would finally call Mike Millbank to testify. Today was also Christmas Eve, and she was not happy putting such a crucial witness on the stand when the jury would barely be paying attention. They were sitting only half a day, and she was sure most of them would be mentally cooking their turkeys and wrapping their presents.

And she really couldn't blame them. After court was over, she, too, would be going home to wrap her gifts for the general, Charlie and Eddie Junior. The boys, stationed in California, were flying in for the holiday; she would see them and her father for Christmas lunch. Jane hadn't allowed herself even to think about how that encounter was going to play out.

Jane walked out of her office clutching a vase of daisies. She was heading to the kitchen to fill it with fresh water when she heard footsteps, turned and saw Detective Mike Millbank coming toward her. He was wearing a navy blue suit, and Jane took note that it fit. It must be his court suit, she thought. His shoes were shined and his tie matched his shirt. My, he looked sharp.

"Detective. Good morning. What a surprise to see you here."

Jane wondered if guilt had overtaken him, if he was coming to confess to interrogating her doorman and snooping around her neighborhood. She sure was curious about what he was up to.

Mike Millbank stopped short for a second to take in Jane Spring. She was wearing a yellow pencil skirt with matching jacket, a white-pearl-buttoned shirt and white pumps. If you threw in the platinum hair and the big smile, she looked like a ray of sunshine.

"I'd like to speak with you in your office for a minute, Jane."

Jane panicked. His tone was ominous — it certainly didn't suggest he was here to fess up to digging into her personal life. This sounded more like bad news. Oh, Lord, he was going to tell her evidence had been lost or mishandled. He was going to change his testimony. She couldn't stand it. Breathe, Jane. In. Out. In. Out. Once again. That's good.

"Is there something wrong, Detective?" she asked calmly.

"You tell me, Counselor."

"Excuse me?"

"Jane, I was at The White Lion last night."

"Oh?"

"I was sitting with my partner in back. You didn't see me, but I saw you."

Jane could only stare at him.

"I saw what happened, Jane. Now I don't know what Chip Bancroft said or did, but it was clear that he really upset you."

"I see."

"Is he giving you trouble, Jane?"

Jane looked out the window.

"Because if he is, you tell me and I'll organize some protection."

Mike Millbank wants to protect me? Now isn't this a nice way to start the day. "That is very kind of you, Detective, but I will be fine. I have dealt with the reprehensible Mr. Bancroft, and I consider the matter closed. He knows not to bother me again."

"Well, if he gives you any more lip during the trial, you come and see me."

"Thank you, Detective."

Suddenly Mike Millbank felt uncomfortable and wanted to bolt. Just like the last time, he had shared a moment of closeness with Jane Spring and then wanted to take it back. He didn't know exactly what it was that had taken him to her office early that morning with an offer to watch over her, but he'd been unable to stop it.

He was just doing his job, he told himself in the elevator on the way down.

That's what I do as a police officer.

Protect and Serve.

It's not like I like her or anything.

When Jane Spring saw Mike Millbank in

court an hour later, they both acted as if it was the first time they had seen each other that day, as if their earlier conversation had never happened. This suited Detective Millbank perfectly. He was the first witness, which also suited him perfectly. He wanted to get it over with. After he had placed his hand on the Bible and sworn to tell the whole truth and nothing but, Jane put him through his paces just as they had rehearsed.

Only this time it was different.

This time as Jane asked him questions, he thought about what it might be like to kiss those frosted coral lips, to peel off that happy yellow suit.

This time as Jane heard him respond to her questions, she kept thinking about how sweet and concerned he had looked earlier. He thought she was in trouble. He wanted to protect her. He really was the most uncommon civilian. Not like Chip Bancroft at all.

Detective Millbank not only understood the army credo of duty, honor, loyalty; he also lived it. He was so dedicated to his job that he had no time for love. He was so dedicated to his career, he offered to protect a woman he blamed for losing his last big case. And Jane Spring couldn't believe how handsome he looked in that blue suit.

"When you arrived on the scene, did the defendant say anything to you, anything specific to the crime?"

Mike Millbank imagined holding Jane's hands across a table. They were in a restaurant. It was snowing outside; a huge log fire burned inside.

"She said, 'I killed him, I killed him,' over and over," he answered.

Jane, who had been behind the prosecution table, walked over to the witness box and leaned on it, looking Detective Millbank directly in the eye.

"But she didn't say, 'I didn't mean to kill him. It was a mistake.' Did you ever hear her say that, Detective?"

"No."

Mike Millbank couldn't understand what was happening. Was it her legs? He was a legs man. Was it the curve of her bust underneath the white pearl buttons of her shirt? Was it the voice? He had always been a pushover for sweet, soft women. No question Jane was soft and sweet. Or at least pretending to be. What the hell was going on here?

Mike Millbank hated himself for feeling something for this Jane Spring. He knew it defied logic, but since when did the brain ever rule attraction? He told himself not to panic, that it would surely pass. Jane, he knew, would return to her previous incarnation after the trial, and he could go back to disliking her as usual. What a relief that would be.

"Detective, in your interview with Mrs. Riley at the police precinct later that evening, did she tell you why she had gone to see her husband?"

Jane Spring noted that the detective was staring at her intensely. She also noted that when she approached him, there was a certain frisson between them. Nor was she the only one to note this. Chip Bancroft did too. Were they flirting?

The detective eagerly answered all her questions. She thanked him profusely after every response. He combed his fingers through his hair. She brushed hers behind her ears.

They *were* flirting!

When Jane's cross-examination of the detective finally concluded and court broke for the day, Chip ran over to her table.

"I feel sick about last night, Jane. I want to apologize again. But properly. Now that I'm sober, so you know I really mean it. Have lunch with me? I've booked a table for us at '21.'"

Jane could see the detective waiting off to one side. She signaled that she would be over to speak with him shortly. Jane stalled. Should she go with Chip to prove what a lady she was or maintain her rage?

What would Doris do?

She folded her arms and assumed an angry stance. Her eyes narrowed, and she pursed her frosted lips. "Mr. Bancroft, your behavior at The White Lion last night —"

"My God, you're gorgeous when you're angry," he whispered.

Jane looked down and tried not to smile, but it crept out along the edges of her mouth. Then she looked up at Chip. Big, blond, blue-eyed Chip Bancroft. It was Christmas Eve. She really should, in the spirit of giving, cut him some slack. Doris would. And at "21"! Nice to see Chip was thinking on his feet. That place was positively swellegant, as Doris would say.

"Mr. Bancroft. As a lady, I am duty-bound to accept your apology, and in the spirit of the season, I would be pleased to join you for lunch."

"Thank you, Jane."

Detective Mike Millbank watched as a beaming Chip Bancroft placed his hand on the small of Jane's back and escorted her out. He stood aside at the door so Jane could leave first, then turned to the detective and locked his eyes onto him. Merry Christmas, Detective, he mouthed, looking smug, then turned on his heel and followed his prey.

Suddenly Mike Millbank's face lost all its form. Stunned wouldn't even begin to describe him.

31

At lunch Chip did not drink a lick of alcohol. He ordered wine for both of them, but never touched his glass. The night at The White Lion had nearly derailed everything, and he would never let that situation occur again.

Over a meal of crab cakes and Christmas pudding, Chip was nothing but the perfect gentleman. He pulled out Jane's chair for her; he rose when she went to powder her nose. They avoided talking about the trial, but instead swapped stories about their respective childhoods. He gazed into her eyes, giving her his undivided attention. He actually felt sorry for her when he heard how she had lost her mother. But it was only for a moment. Then it was back to business.

"You know Jane, I have to be honest. I've always had a crush on you, going way back to law school. I never asked you out before because . . . well . . . I thought you would never date guys like me."

"Chip, I don't understand."

"I just knew I wasn't smart enough for you. I mean, yes, I studied hard and kept my grades up, but you, you were the school genius. I just wasn't in your league and I knew it."

"Oh, Chip, you're crazy. You were very bright in school. I remember you in some of those law review meetings; I couldn't keep up with you."

Jane finished her wine, and a waiter materialized to fill up her glass. Chip didn't really mean that, did he? That he wasn't good enough for her? No. Then again, he did seem serious when he said it. Maybe there was a bit of truth to it. Maybe behind the sharp suit and the bedroom eyes and beneath that mop of movie-star hair, he was a little insecure.

Maybe. Jane Spring should have known better, but when you're blinded by love, when the man you have been pining over for ten years is sitting right there gazing into your eyes, reason is the first thing that goes right out the window. And never climbs back in. "Jane, I have a surprise for you," Chip said when they were done and standing on the street outside the restaurant.

"Surprise?"

"You'll see."

Chip hailed a cab, and once inside, he whispered something to the driver and covered Jane's eyes with his hands as the car started moving. Jane tried to peel his hands off her face playfully, but she let him win. She understood now why so many women fell under his spell. When he liked you, Chip Bancroft made you feel like the only woman in the world. The taxi stopped and Chip pulled away his hands.

"Look up."

Jane peered up and out of the window to see that they were in front of the Empire State Building. In all her years in New York she had never been there. She thought it was a cheesy tourist attraction; now it seemed to be the most romantic place in the world. Chip, she thought, you really are something.

"You afraid of heights?"

They didn't have to wait in line; Chip had already bought tickets. The elevator ride made Jane's eardrums pop, but she forgot how much they hurt when she stepped out on the roof deck. Jane and Chip stood against the railing, and he put his arm around her to protect her from the cold. New York stretched out before them in every direction. Every inch of the city was strung with Christmas lights. Even the Brooklyn Bridge sparkled. "Merry Christmas, Jane," Chip said giving her a peck on the cheek.

Jane was so delirious she thought she would fall over the railing. "You too, Chip," she said.

If this were a movie, Jane knew, Doris would burst into song right now. She felt like she could too, but she would spare Chip the horror.

"Jane, you know how I feel about you," Chip said facing her. Jane beamed. "And I'd like to know how you feel about me. I understand you don't want to get involved in anything serious during the trial; we are, understandably, working opponents. But if you can just give me a sign, so I can know if we have a future, I'd be very grateful."

Breathe, Jane. Breathe, she told herself. In. Out. In. Out. Don't do anything rash.

"Well, Chip, I'll have to think about that," she said. "But I am very much flattered by your interest. As we lawyers say, I'll take it under advisement."

"Of course, Jane."

Later, in the bathroom at home, drawing herself a bubble bath, Jane couldn't stop thinking about Chip's request.

"If you can just give me a sign, so I can know if we have a future, I'd be very grateful, Jane."

With cold cream all over her nose and chin, Jane marched out of the bathroom and grabbed the box of Christmas cards she'd purchased the week before. She had already mailed a number to colleagues; surely it wouldn't hurt to send one to Chip? And maybe that would be the place, along with her Christmas wishes, to tell him that she did see a future for them, and that she cared for him too. She always had. In the movies, Doris always told her suitors she was interested. Heck, the day she met Cary Grant in *That Touch of Mink*, she proposed to him!

Jane opened a card and picked up a pen.

Dear Chip,
  Wishing you all the best of the season . . .
  Chip, you've already made it very clear how you feel about me, but now I must be honest about how I feel about you . . .

Jane filled the card on both sides and signed it "Love, Jane." She had never written a card like that to a man before. Her heart was racing. She fixed a stamp to the envelope and looked up his address. She would mail it first thing the next morning.

  She couldn't wait to see his response when he got it.

32

Jane Spring rented a car to drive to West Point for Christmas lunch. One of the perks of living in New York, once you adapted to the reality of living among civilians, was that it was a city of instant gratification. You want to rent a white 1960s Corvette Roadster in mint condition with a soft top? No problem. You just needed to know which vintage car dealer gave the best deals.

Jane discovered New York had not one, but two rental companies that specialized in renting vintage cars. Film studios were their biggest customers, followed by automobile enthusiasts, followed by pretentious high school seniors looking for a unique way to arrive at the prom. An assistant district attorney impersonating a sixties movie star for the sole purpose of finding her soul mate? They had never had one of those.

Lunch was at one p.m., and Jane left the city at eleven-thirty, giving herself plenty of time to make the short one-hour trip north. She tuned the radio station to Christmas carols, but was barely paying attention to the music. She was thinking about Chip Bancroft . . . and at odd times, Mike Millbank. Chip she understood. But Mike? How had he entered her thoughts? She didn't know.

As Jane neared West Point, she started thinking about her father. There was so much she wanted to tell him. So much she had learned these last ten days.

Did you know, Sir, that if you smile all the time, people want to be your friends? They bring you coffee, and flowers, and volunteer to carry your groceries home from the supermarket. (And they flirt with you. They take you to "21".)

And did you know, Sir, that when you compliment people for their efforts instead of pointing out their flaws, they actually work harder for you?

And, Sir, can you believe that if you never raise your voice, if you never issue an order, it actually brings out the best in people? They open doors for you, they hail cabs for you, they willingly type up their work for you.

It's incredible, Sir!

But Jane knew she would probably never voice any of this. To criticize the way he had raised her would be tantamount to betrayal. Instead, she focused on how the general would handle his daughter once he'd laid eyes on her. Dear Lord, if you exist, now is a good time to show yourself and protect me.

Jane Spring knew that if there was ever a time to drop the routine, this was it. But she had made a pact with herself never to resume her old persona until her mission was accomplished. To abort now, even for an hour, might break the spell forever. The general, in truth, should have nothing to complain about. It was he who had drilled her in the finer points of warfare, on the importance of staying the course to secure victory.

Well, Sir, you asked for it.

At the security check at West Point, Jane stopped the car and smiled at the guard. He stepped out and studied her base pass for a long time before waving her through. (You would too if you were on security detail at a military facility and a blond woman in a pink suit and a white Corvette drove up to your gate.)

Jane drove around the military campus twice to pull herself together before parking outside her father's house. West Point was eerily quiet with most everyone gone. The drill grounds, her father's favorite place to be, were covered in snow. Jane stepped out of the car, gathered up her presents and her courage, then rang the doorbell, her stomach churning.

"Chin up, Jane."

Eddie Junior answered the door.

"Jane?" He looked at his sister — up and down, up and down. His sister, unless his eyes had suddenly failed, had pink bows in her hair, which, incidentally, she had cut short and blown dry. She was wearing pink lipstick and blush, a pink skirt and jacket, white high heels and white gloves. She held a clutch purse in one hand, three silver boxes wrapped in purple ribbon balanced on the other.

Eddie thought he was going to pass out.

"Jane? What are you doing? Is this some kind of joke?"

"Close the door, son, you're letting in the cold."

"Yes, Sir."

Eddie ushered his sister into their father's house. The general had set up a plastic green Christmas tree in one corner, hung with the same decorations as last year, and the year before that . . . and the year before that — three rounds of silver tinsel and a collection of colored balls and strings of fairy lights.

In the dining room the general had laid the table with the china Jane knew her mother had picked out when they married. It hurt to look at it. She walked over to the plastic tree and put her presents down.

Charlie was in the kitchen with his father. He was leaning against the fridge flipping through a gun magazine while the general pulled the ham out of the oven and began to carve it. For the past thirty years in the Spring home, Christmas had been baked ham, green bean casserole (made with frozen beans and a can of cream of mushroom soup), followed by Christmas pudding (store bought), brandy sauce (from a packet) and eggnog (from the carton). The boys liked a beer with their meal, the general poured himself a scotch, and that was Christmas.

Eddie Junior ran into the kitchen. "Jane's here." The general nodded. Charlie kept flipping through his gun magazine. Eddie lowered his voice. "Sir, I think I should warn you —" Jane walked calmly into the kitchen and put down her purse. "Merry Christmas, everybody!"

Then she pulled off her gloves, one finger at a time. Charlie dropped his magazine. The general nearly sliced off his finger. Charlie looked at the general, waiting for instructions on how to proceed. Eddie looked at Charlie. The general looked at his daughter.

"I can't believe you've already set the table, Sir. You should have allowed me," said Jane.

Eddie walked over to the general and gently took the knife out of his hand, laying it on the carving board.

"Jane?"

"Yes, Sir."

"You're wearing a dress, Jane."

"Yes, Sir."

"A pink dress."

"Yes, Sir. Do you like it? I've revamped my wardrobe."

The general now waited before he spoke again. He was thinking. When he finally continued, it was not what Eddie and Charlie were expecting.

"Jane. How was the trip up here?"

"Oh, fine, Sir. The roads were a little wet but other than that, it was uneventful."

Eddie's and Charlie's eyes were fixed on the general. Why wasn't he losing it? Demanding an explanation for that silly costume, insisting she take it off? They knew the general had no patience for crazy behavior like this.

"And tell me, Jane, how's the trial going?"

"Very well, Sir. I believe we'll have a conviction by early next week."

"Excellent. Good work, Jane."

"Thank you, Sir."

The general retrieved the green bean casserole from the oven, and Jane immediately went to help him. Charlie and Eddie looked as if they'd been electrocuted. Their sister, the one who wouldn't wear a skirt if you paid her, was standing there in a pink one. Their sister, who hated to cook, was volunteering to help. Their sister, the hell-raising prosecutor whose voice could snap a window shut, was speaking as if she'd swallowed a helium balloon.

And what was their father doing?

Nothing. Just kept her talking as if it were any other day.

"Got a lot of work coming up after this trial, Jane?" he asked, his eyes scanning her carefully. She looked ridiculous in that outfit, he thought, nothing like the daughter he'd drilled and raised. But he had to admit that she also looked sort of . . . pretty. Like her mother when he first met her. His daughter was actually quite a beautiful woman.

"Work? Same amount as always, Sir."

The general looked at the clock.

"We'll be eating soon. Jane, why don't you go to the bathroom and uh, you know, freshen up?"

"Yes, Sir."

Jane picked up her purse and headed down the corridor. Now, that didn't go too badly, she thought. She guessed the general was playing it cool because

a. He was in shock.
b. He was saving the tongue-lashing and push-ups for after lunch.

While Jane reapplied her lipstick, General Spring huddled with his sons in the kitchen.

"Now, boys, you've obviously noticed there is something different about your sister."

"Permission to speak, Sir," said Charlie.

"Granted."

"She's nuts, that's what's wrong, Sir!"

"I don't understand," Eddie jumped in. "Why is she talking like that? Why is she wearing that outfit? It's like one of those movies where the aliens kidnap you and return you to earth with a different personality."

"Yeah, and from a different decade."

"Dad, she cut her hair!"

"I know. Now, boys, I want you to quiet down and listen to me. You haven't seen this before, but I have."

"What?"

"This is a . . . mental break. It happens to troops after a lot of pressure under fire. I saw it in Vietnam; I saw it in the Persian Gulf. The stress builds and builds, and one day, they snap."

The general snapped his fingers.

"They think they're someone else. I had a guy in my unit in 'Nam who fought sixty days straight, then woke up and thought he was Elvis. Still does. There are guys who think they're Jesus. I heard about a pilot who came back from the Gulf; he thinks he's Eleanor Roosevelt."

"You're saying Jane's had a mental break?"

"Yes, son."

"But she's not fighting in a war."

"Oh yes, she is, son. Every day down there, living with all those *civilians,* your sister fights her own war. You don't know what her life is like. Those New York bohemians and criminals have no discipline, no order, no respect for authority. You should go down there sometime, son. I swear it's worse than dealing with the Viet Cong. You have drug dealers on street corners, kids with guns on the subways. This is my fault, boys. Sending her to live with civilians. I knew this was a possibility. But what could I do? There was no alternative."

"God," said Charlie.

"Yeah," said Eddie, jealous that his sister had contracted a militarily recognized condition before he had.

"Sir, do you know who Jane thinks she is?" asked Charlie.

The general nodded.

"I think I do. Now, boys, I want you to stay calm when I tell you this."

The boys agreed.

"Your sister."

The boys leaned in.

"Your sister thinks she's the Avon Lady."

There was silence as the boys took it all in.

"Boys, when we sit down to eat, you just play along with her. Act natural; don't mention the other Jane. I remember the army psychiatrist telling us to call the crazy soldier Elvis because that was who he thought he was, and to suggest anything different might set him off."

"Yes, Sir."

"Yes, Sir."

The boys both saluted their father. It was at that moment that Jane walked back in.

"Right on time, Jane. We're starting," said the general.

At lunch the general paid Jane more attention in one hour than he had in her entire lifetime. He ignored Eddie and Charlie's request to debate the new design on the Uzi machine gun in favor of asking Jane a series of questions designed to reveal just how bad her break was.

Did she still work every day at the district attorney's office? Yes, Sir.

Was she still living in her apartment on Seventy-third Street? Why, yes, Sir.

Had she purchased any new makeup? Oh yes, quite a bit, Sir, to go with my new look.

Had she entertained anyone in her apartment recently? Yes, a number of people had been to visit in the last month. Technically that wasn't a lie if you included the moving men, Mrs. Kearns and Chip Bancroft.

Upon learning that she was still very much employed and residing in her apartment, the general was — to a degree — relieved. She had not taken on extra work, which meant she wasn't yet going to door to door. But she had entertained in her apartment, which indicated she was hosting makeup parties at home. He remembered once when his late wife, Carol, had hosted an Avon party in their house at Fort Benning. He had come home after a day of drilling cadets in 95-degree heat to find fifteen women in his living room painting their nails and trying on blush.

The general smiled at his daughter and began to devise a battle plan as he ate. First he would call the base psychiatrist about getting help. Then he would go down to New York City, move her out of her apartment, get her away from the poisonous influence of civilians and bring her back to live with him at West Point.

To her brothers' irritation, Jane Spring was enjoying herself immensely. For once she had their father's undivided attention. And how sweet it was!

After lunch Jane did the dishes while her brothers watched, incredulous. Normally, the four of them washed and dried mess-tent style; that day Jane wouldn't hear of it. They could stay and keep her company if they wished, but they weren't to get their hands dirty. Which was fine by them.

Traditionally, once the dishes were put away and the leftovers in the fridge, Jane and her brothers headed outside for a game of touch football. Charlie looked nervously at Eddie Junior, who signaled not to worry. Their sister might be cuckoo, he mimed, but their Christmas football toss was sacrosanct.

Eddie Junior grabbed the family football. "Hey Jane, meet you outside in five minutes," he said, tossing it to her in the corridor. But Jane didn't reach for it. Instead she let it fly right by her, crashing into the telephone table.

"Jane. Football. C'mon," said Charlie.

"Football? In these shoes? I'll break my legs. And you know all that running will muss up my hair. I'll pass. I'm sure you understand."

The boys smiled at her as the general had instructed, then corralled him in the kitchen, where he was pouring himself another scotch. Jane went to rearrange the presents under the tree.

"Sir, she's not even playing football anymore!"

"I know, son. I told you. Right now she's not your sister. But she will be again. I'm going to call mental health services in the morning. You just leave everything to me."

"There's really no need, Sir," Jane said, walking into the kitchen, startling everyone. "No need to call anyone about me. I'm fine. Really. And do you know something, Sir? I don't think I've ever felt better."

The general examined his daughter top to toe. She did seem brighter, he had to admit. And she was still Jane in all the ways that mattered: dutiful, obedient, self-disciplined. All the values he'd instilled in her remained present and accounted for. Just the presentation and packaging were different. She was softer, prettier. That's what was so jarring — Jane was acting like a woman now.

The general changed the subject by ordering everyone to sit around the tree and open their presents.

The boys gave Jane a Swiss Army knife.

"It's the latest model, Jane. Just came into the PX," said Eddie Junior.

"Why, thank you. It's lovely."

"With this one, you can skin a rabbit in half the time," said Charlie proudly. "The blades are twice as sharp."

"Wonderful," Jane said.

The general gave her the new biography of General Norman Schwarzkopf — he believed it was important always to have inspirational books about warfare on your bedside table — and the newly released anniversary edition of *Patton* on DVD.

"What a thoughtful gift. Thank you, Sir." She beamed. "I know I'll find it most exciting."

Every year Jane gave her father a subscription to *Soldier of Fortune* magazine and tickets to the National Antique Gun Show in New York. She gifted her brothers with subscriptions to *Guns & Ammo* and drugstore soap-on-a-rope, all wrapped in holly-flocked paper that came on a roll.

This year all Jane's presents came in silver boxes from Bergdorf's wrapped in purple ribbon.

"This is for you, Sir," she said, excitedly handing the general his gift. He cut the ribbon with his pocketknife, then lifted the lid off the box. Inside he found mounds of lilac tissue paper. He tried to hide his shock. A good soldier never betrays emotion. But this was certainly like no other present he had received before. He tore through the paper to uncover a rose crystal martini pitcher and two matching glasses at the bottom.

"I know you're a scotch man, but I thought you might like to experiment with mixed drinks sometime," Jane said sweetly.

"Thank you, Jane," the general said politely, thinking it wasn't the worst idea he'd heard. Why *not* mix a drink sometime?

But the boys smirked. Crystal on an army base? Their sister was ready for a rubber room.

Jane gave Eddie dove-gray cashmere socks and a matching scarf. The labels on both read "Made in Paris." As he dug through the lilac tissue paper he turned to Charlie and rolled his eyes.

"They're the best quality, Eddie. They'll keep you warm on those cold nights on patrol."

Eddie ran the socks between his fingers and noted their softness. These really will feel good inside his combat boots, he thought. He threw the scarf around his neck; it felt like heaven compared to his scratchy wool army scarf. He would have to cut off the labels so the guys on the base wouldn't call him a girl for wearing cashmere from Paris.

"Thanks, Jane," he said, surprised.

"Oh, I'm just thrilled you like them, Eddie," she purred.

And she was.

Jane gave Charlie an Italian leather fishing-tackle bag. When Charlie wasn't killing people for a living, he liked to kill big fish for sport.

"It's got separate compartments for all

your hooks and bait; and look, this is where you put your flask," she said excitedly. "It's handmade, from Florence. And it's waterproof!" Charlie ran his fingers over the bag; he couldn't believe how soft and supple it was. Even though he loved his old rotting canvas fishing bag, he had to admit this was better.

"Gee, Jane, this is really cool," he said, stunned.

Jane Spring clapped her hands. "You know, it's so wonderful when you pick out presents for people and they really do appreciate them. Merry Christmas, everyone."

"Merry Christmas, Jane," said her father and brothers in return.

And it was. A merry, merry Christmas.

33

When Jane Spring returned to the office after Christmas she had no idea the amount of money that had changed hands in her honor. Just before the break Graham had started a betting pool: five dollars a bet and you could place as many as you liked. Lazy Susan placed six. One first thing in the morning, then another five throughout the day, giving her the perfect excuse to visit Graham around the clock without arousing his suspicion.

"You're back again?" he said, laughing as she handed over yet another five-dollar bill. "What do you know that we don't?"

Graham Van Outen looked at Spring's secretary and wondered if he was going crazy. Was she dressing differently now, too? Where were those low-fitting pants and the wild hair? Was that a bow on her ponytail? *My God, the women in this place are falling under some kind of spell. Maybe we'll have to call an exorcist.* He never thought he'd say this, but thank God Marcie was still the same.

"I don't know anything," Lazy Susan

said, blushing. "I'm just praying."

The bet was whether Jane would return to work as the old version or the new. The big money was on the old. Nobody in the entire department thought she could keep the act up anymore, or needed to. Everybody assumed her plan was to deliver her closing statement as the tough, kick-ass Jane Spring to shock the jury into making their decision.

But when Jane walked into her office at eight a.m. on the Thursday morning after Christmas in pumps and the blue coat with big buttons and satin trim, you could hear the sighs of relief in Montana. Everybody loved the new Jane; they wanted her to stay forever. But they knew better than to raise their hopes, hence the betting pool. It was a way to channel their fears into something tangible.

As it turned out, Lazy Susan won the entire pot. Only she had bet that Jane would return as Doris. Whether it was an answered prayer or a stroke of genius, Graham didn't know. What he did know was that Spring's secretary was now $175 richer. And she'd been so confident Jane would be back as the new and improved version, Lazy Susan had also returned in her new and improved version.

Though she was disappointed Graham

hadn't commented on her transformation (maybe he hasn't noticed yet? Guys can be so clueless that way), let alone asked her out, Lazy Susan was supremely confident he would. Look how a sixties' makeover had worked with men for Miss Spring.

"Good morning, Susan. You look very smart today," Jane said, noting that her charge was clad in a brown tweed skirt, a camel sweater set, brown pumps and the marcasite pin Jane had given her for Christmas.

"Thank you, Miss Spring."

Jane noted that a vase of carnations was now perched on Lazy Susan's desk, and next to it a plate of freshly baked chocolate chip cookies. Behind the plate was a note that read: "Happy Holidays, Please take one." Jane reached for one and took a bite.

"Oh, these are delicious, Susan! Did you make them yourself?"

"Yes, Miss Spring," she said, smiling.

So she'd bought the cookie dough from the supermarket. So what, Susan thought. She'd baked them herself, and that was what mattered. Susan hoped Miss Spring wouldn't take another one; she wanted plenty left for whenever Graham came by.

"And thank you for finishing up those witness reports on Christmas Eve. I appreciate your staying late," Jane said, wiping crumbs from her mouth.

"Sure thing, Miss Spring."

Lazy Susan blushed. Nothing felt as good as a compliment first thing in the morning. If you didn't count staring at Graham's dimpled chin.

"Jane, I need you for a minute."

It was Marcie.

"Marcie, I'm sorry. You know how I hate to be rude, but I have to be in court."

Marcie grabbed Jane's arm and marched her into her office.

"This will take thirty seconds, I promise. That one, or that one?"

Marcie pointed to two sets of cups with matching saucers she had set out on her desk. One set was white with a gold rim. The second had a Dutch blue floral design.

"Excuse me?"

"Which pattern do you like better? Howard and I are choosing china for our registry. I've narrowed it down to these because it's easy to get replacement settings on eBay."

"Well, is this going to be your good china or everyday? If it's formal, I'd go with the white. Everyday, the blue."

"You don't think the blue is good enough for formal?"

Jane shook her head. Incredible how two weeks ago Marcie wouldn't have considered Jane an expert in taste; now she was consulting her at every step.

"Marcie, I just don't think you can make a mistake with white. And you wouldn't want to make a mistake, would you? I know I wouldn't."

"Jane, you're right. I'll tell Howard."

"Send him my regards."

As Jane had suspected, the jury members were restless. Some were probably hungover from the previous day's festivities; the sleepy ones Jane put down to too much turkey. All in all it was not a good time to put Mike Millbank back on the stand and subject him to cross-examination by Chip Bancroft.

At quarter to nine Jane walked into the witness holding room to find Detective Mike Millbank. She was looking forward to seeing him for reasons completely separate from the trial. Reasons she couldn't quite articulate, although you might be able to guess them if you saw her. She had definitely gone the extra mile getting dressed that morning. She had taken the skirt from the pink suit and paired it with a pink angora cardigan sweater. She had put two pink bows in her hair and pearl drops on her ears.

"Good morning, Detective," said Jane breezily, putting down her beauty case and slipping off her gloves.

"Ms. Spring."

There was a sharp inflection to his voice that made Jane uncomfortable.

"You did very well the other day, Detective. Your testimony was very precise. But I'm sure you know today won't be quite so easy. Mr. Bancroft will try to shred your testimony. But I don't want you to be concerned. I will be with you every step of the way, and whenever he is unreasonable, I will object."

"Well, that's very big of you," he said caustically.

"Excuse me?"

"I said it's very big of you to offer to support me today."

"Excuse me, Detective, is there something wrong?"

Mike Millbank moved closer to Jane. "Do you want to know how you can help me? How you can help this case? You can stop flirting with the defense counsel and keep your focus on your job."

"What?" screamed Jane before she could control herself. "Detective, whatever do you mean?"

"You heard me. I'm not blind, Counselor. Going for drinks at The White Lion with him. Going for lunch to '21' on Christmas Eve. Blushing every time he whispers in your ear. This is a murder trial, Counselor, not a singles' party. A police officer went down, and we're here to convict his killer. Well, that's why I'm here. I thought that was why you were here too, but clearly I was wrong."

Jane's eyes quadrupled in size. How dare he impugn her commitment, her professionalism!

"Detective," she said coldly. She folded her arms, a scowl starting to creep across her face, which looked a lot like the old Jane's. But she caught herself just in time. "I —"

"Don't 'Detective' me, Counselor," he snapped back. "If you take your eyes off the ball, we could lose this thing. I, for one, feel an obligation to the badge to make sure that doesn't happen. You clearly feel no such obligation, seeing as how you've found time in your trial schedule to romance Mr. Bancroft."

"Well!" said Jane, now hyperventilating. "I am outraged and offended you would say such a thing. For your information, Detective, I want a conviction as much as you do. And for your further information, I am not flirting with the defense counsel. I would never do anything so unethical.

Those were legal meetings. *Everything* was trial-related."

"Really? You always drink martinis at legal meetings? Funny, I don't."

The bell rang to signal court was starting. Jane picked up her beauty case and turned to leave. Her face was bright red.

"I'll see you on the witness stand."

Marching all the way to the prosecution table, Jane Spring thought steam would come out of her ears the way it did to characters in cartoons. How dare he accuse her of taking her eyes off the prize. Just because she'd had one drink and lunch with the man didn't mean she wasn't giving 100 percent to her job. Blushing around Chip? Garbage. The detective had a vivid imagination.

She would just have to show him how committed she was to this trial.

Which was just as well because when Chip Bancroft took the floor at 9:05, the sweet, contrite lawyer who had taken her to lunch, and had romantically poured his heart out to her on the observation deck of the Empire State Building, was nowhere to be seen. Instead, the cocky, obnoxious big man on campus had come to work for the day. Jane understood what was going on. From a tactical standpoint, he needed to crush and destroy this witness mano a mano. That couldn't be achieved if he was playing Cary Grant.

Charm was out. Aggression was in.

And that's what Chip Bancroft dished out for two hours straight, trying to shoot down Mike Millbank's testimony, not to mention his character. Jane could barely stand to watch. Here was the man she thought she wanted (on Monday) attacking a man she then thought she wanted (on Tuesday). Now it was Thursday and she didn't know what or whom she wanted anymore.

"Tell me, Detective, when you interviewed Mrs. Riley, was she distraught?"

"Yes. She was upset."

"Upset because she had killed her husband accidentally."

"Objection. Leading," said Jane sweetly, taking an extra second to stare back at the detective. I will prove to you I am fully committed, she said with her eyes.

"Sustained."

"Withdrawn. Detective Millbank, you testified that after your arrival at the scene, Mrs. Riley told you she had shot her husband."

"Correct."

"Yet isn't it true that when you interviewed her an hour later at the precinct, she claimed the gun fired in error?"

"Yes, but I believe by then she had had time to think about changing her story. And she did."

"You believe?"

"Yes."

"Detective, this is a court of law. We try facts. We don't care what you 'believe.' Can you imagine society if we found people guilty based on just what the police believed? Given how inept you people are, you'd probably charge Snow White with soliciting after she shared a bed with the Seven Dwarfs."

The jury laughed. Score one, Chip.

"Objection!" Jane screamed out a little louder than Doris would. She realized it immediately and reigned herself in. She repeated herself, this time softly. "Objection."

"Counselor," said Judge Shepherd. "Save the dramatics for your community theater and your opinions for your memoirs. The jury will disregard the previous statement."

Jane fumed. How dare Chip insult the detective's integrity. She had to let the jury know just how wrong Chip Bancroft was. She sighed loudly and made indignant muttering sounds. The jury noted it, but for Jane it wasn't enough. She wanted to yell. She wanted to shout out, "Ladies and gentleman of the jury, even though I am mad as hell at him right now, that man up there is as honest as the day is long. That man up there is so dedicated to the job of protecting the citizens of this city, he hasn't even found time for love." She wanted to grab each juror by the throat and say, "That man up there has so much integrity, he offered to protect me even though I let him down." Instead she patted her hair and recrossed her ankles under the table.

"Detective, this trial is personal for you, isn't it?" Chip asked smugly.

"Personal?"

"Yes. A police officer is killed — that's an attack on your tribe. Isn't it true that whether Laura Riley is guilty or not, you want to convict her because according to your unwritten code, somebody has to pay?"

"No, the right person has to pay."

"Like Rose and Arthur Steiner? Were they the right people?"

Mike Millbank flinched. He couldn't believe this viper was dragging that up. Behind the prosecution table, Jane nearly fell off her chair. She had no idea who Rose and Arthur Steiner were, but she knew she didn't like where Chip was going.

"Objection, irrelevant."

"Your Honor, permission to show cause?"

"I'll allow it."

"Detective Millbank, is it true that on the night of August twenty-fifth five years ago, you and your partner, Detective Cruz, broke down the door of an apartment belonging to retired seniors Rose and Arthur Steiner, handcuffed them, read them their rights and announced you were charging them with drug dealing?"

"Yes, but —"

"A simple yes will do, Detective. And isn't it also true that it turned out these poor confused seniors were entirely innocent, that you and your partner had stormed into the wrong apartment?"

The jury gasped collectively.

"It was a bureaucratic error," Mike said, turning to the judge. "The drugs were in apartment sixteen. The warrant we were given said sixty-one. These things happen. We apologized profusely to the Steiners, and the department installed a new door for them the next day."

"How thoughtful of you, Detective. A gift of a new door, after you arrested this innocent couple, humiliated them and terrified them."

"Objection, badgering," Jane said.

"Sustained."

Jane saw the jury taking notes and her head started to throb. It was the first time in ten days that the old Jane Spring was pushing to the fore, begging to be heard. But she couldn't lash out. Doris wouldn't. Instead, she took three deep breaths and put her hands in her lap. Mike Millbank attacking her was one thing. If she were really being honest, he might have had a point about her consorting with the defense counsel mid-trial. But Chip's attack on Mike's credibility, his sterling reputation, with a five-year-old case of bureaucratic bungling was positively infuriating.

Jesse could feel Jane's tension. Her shoulders were rigid, and anger was seeping out of her pores. He wondered what was upsetting her. Defense lawyers routinely had their police witnesses for lunch, and Jane had never blinked. She knew it was part of the game. You attack mine; I'll destroy yours.

"So, Detective, let me ask you again. Have you ever charged the wrong person or persons with a crime?"

"Yes, but —"

"And didn't it go on your departmental record that you made a false arrest?"

"Yes."

"So officially you're a rogue cop, aren't

you? You like taking the law into your own hands, don't you?"

"Objection!" Jane said, bouncing out of her chair.

"Sustained."

"Nothing further," Chip said, licking his lips.

With Mike Millbank's testimony complete, the judge announced that he had a motion hearing to attend and called a recess for the day. Chip strolled over to Jane at the prosecution table and sat down on the edge.

"No hard feelings, Jane? Sorry I had to rough up your guy a bit. But you've scored too many points off me lately."

"Mr. Bancroft, I felt those attacks on my impeccable witness were, frankly, conduct unbecoming to a gentleman. Detective Millbank's unfortunate incident five years ago, which, might I remind you, was not his fault, has no relevance to this trial, and you know that. Clearly you have a much weaker case than I assumed. Otherwise why resort to such bad behavior?"

"Bad behavior?" Chip burst out laughing. "You used to 'behave' like that all the time, Jane. My, what a short memory we have."

"People change."

Jane looked around for Detective Millbank. She wanted to compliment him on his composure. But he was gone.

She slipped on her coat.

"Have dinner with me?" said Chip.

Jane snapped her beauty case shut and put on her gloves.

"I'll see you tomorrow morning, Counselor. I have to go home and wash my hair."

"Not exactly a great day in court today," Jesse said glumly as they walked back to the office.

You have no idea, Jane wanted to say. First, Detective Millbank read me the riot act about my behavior. Then Chip Bancroft had our witness, the aforementioned detective, for lunch. "I can't believe Chip Bancroft would impugn the integrity of Mike Millbank like that," was what she did say.

"Don't worry, Jane. We still have a strong case. And your act is paying off brilliantly in there."

Was it? Now Jane wasn't so sure. Chip had really scored a home run today. Once back at work she would review all her case notes to make sure all the ducks were in a row.

In her office Jane closed the door and called Detective Millbank. She wanted to let him know how well he'd handled Chip's attack, and that she intended to restore his reputation on the stand at the first opportunity. But the detective had instructed the precinct front desk to hold all his calls. Jane left a message. He did not return it.

She thought some caffeine was in order, and rose to make her way to the kitchen. Walking past Marcie's office, she saw that Counselor Blumenthal was out, and suddenly, impulsively, she wandered in. Jane noted that the pile of wedding magazines on Marcie's desk had grown since the last time she had visited. Had Marcie left any copies on the stands for the other brides getting married this century?

She pulled one off the top and began flicking through it. Her thoughts turned to Detective Millbank, then back to the magazine. Dresses. Rings. China. Cakes. All things for weddings. She flipped through an article about honeymoons. One picture depicted a couple in a heart-shaped tub at a resort in the mountains. No, that wasn't for her. But a picture of a couple walking along a beach in Hawaii at sunset, that she liked.

Jane leaned against Marcie's desk as she

concentrated on a twenty-page spread devoted to wedding gowns. No. No. No. Oh, that's awful. Oh, that's nice. Oh, I do like that one. Jane stopped at a page displaying a fifties-style white midcalf dress with a bow at the waist and matching gloves. She spun around and quietly tore the page out of the magazine.

"Hey, Jane," Marcie said, walking into her office.

Jane was startled. Frantically she folded the page behind her back and then slipped it into her shirt.

"Marcie, hi," she said breezily, turning and carefully putting the magazine back atop the pile. "I just dropped by because I wanted to get some advice from you on a discovery issue I'm having trouble with."

"Sure, Jane."

She asked Marcie a simple question she knew the answer to, thanked her, then decamped to her office. Once there, she pulled the crumpled page out of her bra and flattened it out across her desk. And smiled. She had found the dress. She had, she knew, in these past two weeks, also begun to find her true self.

Now all that was left to find was him.

34

Exceptional as it was, Chip Bancroft was actually nervous. Court was starting in ten minutes and he had yet to decide whether to put Laura Riley on the stand. He would only make a final determination when Jane showed up, and she wasn't there yet. Of course she had to make an entrance, he fumed. Women. In the old days Jane was always the first person in court; it was she who would scold him for running a second late.

Jane finally breezed in at 8:55, fresh as a daisy. Chip examined her from stem to stern, and one thought immediately came to mind: Laura Riley is not testifying.

The rumor mill had been working overtime about this very moment, with the big bucks on Jane's showing up as her old self to deliver her final punch. But Jane Spring was not wearing black pants and flat shoes as Chip Bancroft had hoped. Prayed.

She was wearing a slim white pencil skirt and a fluffy white angora sweater and looked, to the outside world, like a kitten.

A snowflake. To any man with a pulse she looked like sex on a stick. And to the jury she was still the same woman they had fallen in love with. If he put Laura Riley on the stand, this Jane would not make her cry, would not bully her and would not condescend to her. She would sweet-talk her until maple syrup seeped out the sides of her mouth, and no jury would develop serious sympathy for his client that way. Only if Spring the bitch was in court would Laura Riley stand a chance.

Which she wasn't.

He told his client she would stay put, and because she was his last witness, he announced he was resting his case. The judge called a fifteen-minute recess. Jane and Jesse conferred at the prosecution's table about her closing argument. Jesse was now convinced Jane would finally reveal to the jury, to him, the grand plan behind the game of dress up.

But when Jane Spring took the floor for her closing argument, she didn't mention her appearance. Instead she focused on the forensic evidence, which her expert had interpreted as proof the gun had been fired intentionally. She emphasized motive, opportunity and the defendant's depraved indifference to her husband's plea for mercy. She reminded the jury that when a man betrays you, shooting him in cold blood might be cathartic, but it is still a crime.

"Laura Riley had choices," Jane repeated as she walked calmly, elegantly, in front of the jury box, stopping every few seconds to lock eyes with a juror, throwing him or her a slight smile.

Her eyes said, I trust you; please trust me. And when she finished making her case, she asked them, as good citizens of New York, to remember that the city had been robbed of one its finest policemen, and finding the defendant guilty would see justice served. "If Laura Riley didn't want to put up with her husband's philandering," Jane said in summation, "she should have requested a divorce, not reached for a gun." Then she slowly walked back to the prosecution table and sat down, crossing her ankles, one over the other.

Chip Bancroft put his arm around his client, then rose to his feet. Jane's closing argument was convincing. Very convincing. The jury clearly was lapping it up. Along with her. This left him no choice. He would have to do it. Well, Jane, he said to himself, you asked for it.

Chip Bancroft tightened the knot in his tie and pushed his forelock out of his eyes. He walked toward the jury box and took a deep breath, making eye contact with each juror just as Jane had done.

"Ladies and gentlemen of the jury. You have heard the evidence, and now it is time for you to decide the guilt or innocence of Laura Riley. This is, as you know, a momentous task, and I ask that you consider everything you have seen and heard in court very carefully. Your decision could alter the life of Mrs. Riley, the mother of two children who need her very much. They have already lost their father; please don't let them lose their mother too."

Chip then carefully laid out the case for his client. Laura Riley was deeply in love with her husband, yet he had lied to her, betrayed her, had broken his vows and taken another woman to his bed. Chip reasoned that Laura Riley had only gone to see her husband to demand that he honor his marriage vows. She loved him. She would never want to hurt him. When the gun went off in the struggle, it was an accident; he reminded the jury that his rebuttal witness, a second forensics expert, had said as much. And he reiterated that she was the mother of two beautiful children.

Jane Spring uncrossed her legs and folded them at the ankle. Jesse Beauclaire passed her a note that read: "What do you think?"

Jane wrote back: "We have nothing to worry about. He's using the mommy defense. He's desperate."

But just how desperate she would learn soon enough.

Chip Bancroft lowered his eyes to the floor, then looked up again. He walked over to the defense table and stood beside it.

"Ladies and gentlemen of the jury, I have laid out my case, and I believe you will, in your wisdom, see that my client is innocent of this charge. But before I finish, I would like to ask you to consider one more thing. I would like you all to look at the following photograph." Chip suddenly swiped a photograph off the defense table and held it up before the jury. He moved toward them, and they all leaned forward excitedly to get a better look, then turned their attention to Jane.

"What — ?" Jane cried out. "Objection!" There had been no mention of a defense photograph in discovery. "Permission to approach, Your Honor!"

"Approach, Counselors. With the photograph, please."

Chip and Jane approached the bench and it was then that she saw that the photograph Chip had just held up was of *her*, a black-and-white eight-by-ten of Jane from a month or two back. Long hair, black glasses, permanent scowl. Jane thought she would faint.

"Your Honor, I strenuously object. I have no idea where counsel is going with this, but showing *my* photograph to the jury is irrelevant to this case. And it was not entered into discovery. I demand a mistrial!"

The judge turned to face Chip and raised his eyebrows.

"It goes to credibility of counsel, Your Honor," Chip pleaded. "I am not entering new evidence into the record, so there was no legal requirement to list it in discovery. I am merely showing a photograph that, combined with my verbal statements, will make up my closing remarks."

Breathe, Jane, breathe. In. Out. In. Out. In. Out. "Oooooohhhhh!" she roared.

The judge stared at the photo, then turned to address Jane. "I'm not going to allow him to show it again, Counselor, so your objection is sustained. But since it isn't material evidence, your request for a mistrial is denied. Further, I will instruct the jury prior to deliberations to disregard the photo as having no relevance to the facts in evidence."

"Your Honor," Jane said, trying to keep calm. "We all know that now that the jury has seen this, asking them to ignore it in the jury room is pointless." Chip was smirking. "Which is, of course, what Mr. Bancroft here is banking on."

"Don't tell me how to do my job, Counselor, and I won't tell you how to do yours," Judge Shepherd said smartly. Then holding on to the photo, he waved them away.

Chip returned to his spot in front of the jury, Jane to her table. She thought she would burst into tears.

"Ladies and gentlemen," Chip continued. "Do you know that if you had been in court any day this year, sitting in judgment on any case but this one, Ms. Spring, the state's fine prosecutor over there, would not have been smiling at you, or fluttering her eyelashes, or appearing in front of you in pretty suits and pearls?"

The jury sat up. Jane Spring looked straight ahead, avoiding their eyes.

"No. You would have met the woman in the photograph you just saw. The woman in black. The one who appears so heartless that little old ladies could faint and she'd mock them in their moment of need. Which, you should know, has happened. But, ladies and gentleman, this is not the only reason I draw your attention to the picture. What you really must understand is that although Ms. Spring — he pointed directly at Jane — normally doesn't look like this, she doesn't act like this either. Let the record show that her Miss Goody Two-shoes performance, brilliant as it is, is also all a sham."

"Objection!" Jane shrieked.

"You can't object during closing statements, Ms. Spring. Sit down."

Jane sat dejectedly. Breathe, Jane. In. Out. In. Out. Jesse held on to the back of her chair, terrified she might fall over.

Chip licked his lips and continued. "Ladies and gentlemen, the lovely Ms. Spring here wants you to believe she was shocked, shocked! by all the talk of adultery and sex you heard during this trial. But I have something that I believe, in the interest in justice, I must tell you. The entire time she was in this court playing the virginal Miss Congeniality, she was throwing, yes, throwing herself at me. I tried to tell her I wasn't interested, but she would not be dissuaded. She invited me to drinks, then to her apartment — all supposedly to discuss 'business.' Well, I'm a man; I have moments of weakness. I admit it; I slept over. She has yellow blankets, by the way. But none of it was my doing," Chip said, lowering his face. "She seduced me."

Jane thought her head would explode.

Oh, you poisonous snake. You invited me to drinks, Chip, and the only reason I let you in my apartment was because you were making a scene on the street. You slept over? You passed out on the couch! You told me you loved me; how can you do this to me? When we leave here I am calling West Point and getting the army down here to deal with you, you traitor.

"None of this happened the way he insinuates, Your Honor!" Jane said, jumping to her feet.

"Sit down, Ms. Spring, or I will hold you in contempt. Mr. Bancroft, what is the meaning of this outburst?"

"Really, Jane? Why don't we let the jury decide," he said smartly, reaching into his jacket pocket and pulling out a Christmas card. Oh, God, it was her Christmas card. Jane felt all the veins on her forehead bulge and course with blood.

"Dear Chip," he began to read. "You've already made it very clear how you feel about me" — that's right; I did tell her to stop pursuing me — "but now I must be honest about how I feel about you. I have been in love with you since I first saw you at the law school pool . . . This week when you fell asleep in my apartment . . ." He stopped and turned to her. "This is your handwriting, isn't it, Jane? Shall I go on?"

"Your Honor!" Jane pleaded.

"Mr. Bancroft, this is neither the time nor the place to read love letters that Ms. Spring has sent you. I am sure the jury gets the drift, a drift I will, of course, be instructing them to ignore. Now wrap it up or sit down."

"Yes, Your Honor." Chip walked right up to the jury railing and folded his arms.

"Jane Spring, as you have seen and heard, is lying about who she really is, ladies and gentlemen," Chip continued. "And she has done this for your benefit, to *deceive* you. She wants you to think she is some lily-white holier-than-thou innocent who would never steal another woman's man, but let me assure you, that is not the case."

"Oh, Lord," Jane whimpered.

"And I want you to ask yourselves, if she has been lying to you for nearly two weeks about who she is, then wouldn't she also be lying to you about this case? Wouldn't it draw into question all her witnesses, not to mention the charge that Laura Riley is guilty of murder? Laura Riley was driven into a rage that night by a woman not unlike our Ms. Spring. Blinded by anger and passion, she struggled with her husband, the gun went off, and her life was changed forever. Please don't punish her any more than she has already punished herself. Think of her children. Thank you."

Chip Bancroft returned to the defense table and made a big show of putting his arm around Laura Riley. Jane Spring thought she would pass out. He had revealed her! Worse, he had suggested she was a seductress! A hussy! A woman who writes love letters and lures men over to her apartment!

Jane started to hyperventilate. Before this she had had the jury eating out of her hand. They loved her, they believed the case she had put before them. Now everything was up for grabs. What if they believed Chip? What if he had convinced them that her playing at Doris was for their benefit, to fool them because her case didn't hold water? Then they would surely vote against her. The last jury had turned on her. It could happen again.

"I'm sorry, Jane," Jesse whispered in her ear. "Don't worry, we'll appeal."

Jane Spring took a deep breath and asked herself one question. What would Doris do now? That's right, Jane, breathe. In. Out. In. Out. Smile, Jane. The stunned jury all looked in her direction. Keep smiling, Jane. Head up, Jane.

I am such a fool. The drinks after work, the visit to my apartment, the lunch at "21," the protestations of love on top of the Empire State Building, the request for a sign, was it all a ruse? Oh, Jane! Oh, Jane! He's ruined you!

Of course, as a lawyer Jane Spring understood that you pull every last trick out of your sleeve if you want to win. Goodness knows she had in the past. But he'd said he loved her!

As the jury sat expectantly waiting for Judge Shepherd to issue final instructions, Jane sat smiling and perky, intimating to the jury that she was completely unperturbed by Chip's allegations, because they were *not* true. Would I still be smiling if they were?

As the judge addressed the jurors,

demanding that they disregard the photograph and love letter as immaterial to the
facts in evidence, then adding that Ms.
Spring's dalliance with Mr. Bancroft was
no business of the jury's, Jane threw Chip
a glacial stare, her anger palpable.

He said he cared for me, and maybe he
did, she sat thinking while the judge's voice
droned on in the background. But if he
truly loved me, he would never have betrayed me to win this case. No, the only
person he loves is himself, and I see that
now.

And then another feeling overcame Jane
Spring, and this one, unlike the anger, was
shocking in what it delivered.

Relief.

Two weeks as Doris Day and Jane Spring
had finally found where she would draw
the line about love. And that was at a man
who would ruin her to save his own ego.

"Oh, thank God," she muttered, patting
her hair.

Thank God.

After ten years, she was finally over him.

35

In the jury room there was no attempt to follow the judge's instructions to disregard the photo and the letter because there wasn't one person who believed Chip Bancroft's allegations to begin with. Not one. Because here was a jury that had never fantasized that Jane Spring was anyone other than the beautiful woman in white mohair sweater and pearls they had seen right in front of them. She was neither the sexy secretary nor the gawky schoolgirl. She was that bubbly, adorable prosecutor with perfect manners and impeccable morals. They knew she would rather throw herself in front of an oncoming train than dupe them about her real identity. And having a man in her bedroom? He must be dreaming.

Love truly is blind. Even juries fall under its spell.

So after barely three minutes of discussion, the jury resolved to ignore the accusations made by the defense about the darling Ms. Spring. Desperate measures, said one.

Impossible to believe, said another. The photo was probably doctored; the love letter? surely he wrote that himself. Ms. Spring would never lie to us. Ms. Spring wasn't just a woman, she was a lady. Ladies do not lie.

What a pity Jane Spring could not have heard them. It might have stopped her stomach churning, her eyes watering. Immediately after the jury retired to deliberate, Jane returned to her office, instructing Lazy Susan that she did not wish to be disturbed. Frazzled, she opened the *Post* to Page Six and there it was: a picture of Chip Bancroft and Bjorgia with a caption that read: "Celebrity defense attorney canoodling with sizzling Swedish model."

Jane's heart started to race. That dirty rat! She scowled, pounding her fist on her desk.

If they believe Chip and we lose the trial, she thought, this will all be my fault. Mine. And all I was doing was trying to find love! Now a murderer may go free.

In the jury room, the forewoman, Mrs. Pirella, tabled all the evidence. Given that she was a second-grade teacher, she reconstructed the crime as if she were telling them all a story. By the time she had finished, the jury was more frustrated than they could have imagined. On television this looked easy. There a person's guilt or innocence was obvious. There was always one piece of damning evidence that sealed his or her fate, and then Perry Mason walked into the sunset.

Not now. Here both the prosecution and the defense had presented strong arguments for their sides. Ms. Spring had experts who swore the gun had been fired intentionally. Mr. Bancroft's swore it was an accident. There were no eyewitnesses to the crime. The only people in the room were the defendant and her victim. And she was a mother. But she did kill a police officer. What to do?

"But as the defense argued, just saying you're so angry you want to kill someone doesn't mean you will. We've all been there. Well, I know I have," said juror number eight.

After they had talked themselves hoarse for four hours, Mrs. Pirella handed out paper and pens and announced they would have a first-round vote.

The room went eerily silent. Jurors picked up their pens, but nobody wrote. Now they saw that what the judge had said in his deliberation instructions was true.

Sitting in judgment of a fellow citizen's guilt or innocence was a momentous task.

Juror number nine put down his pen for a second and looked at the ceiling. If this were a chess game, he thought, you would call it a draw. Identical conversations played out in the minds of the eleven other jurors. Was it intentional? Was it an accident? Laura Riley didn't look like a murderer, but a man is dead and her fingerprints were on the gun. But she is a mother. Betrayed by her husband. That poor woman. Can we really imprison a mother?

The jurors scratched out their responses and handed them up to Mrs. Pirella. She read each one, then knocked on the door to tell the clerk they were ready with their decision. When the call came to Jane Spring that the jury was back in, she thought she would vomit all over her beauty case.

"Has the jury reached a verdict?"

"We have, Your Honor," said Mrs. Pirella. She was loving the moment. All eyes were on her, and unlike ordering seven-year-olds to stop bickering, what she was about to say now was of real consequence.

Laura Riley was on her feet, shaking.

Jane Spring was on her feet, shaking. If she lost this case because Chip convinced the jury she had deceived them, she would have to leave town. She would move to Canada. There would be no getting over the shame. Chip Bancroft caught her eye. He was grinning from ear to ear.

"We the jury find the defendant Laura Riley . . . guilty of murder in the first degree."

Jane Spring turned to Jesse for confirmation. "Did she just say *guilty?*" she whispered. "We won?"

"Yes, we won. Jane, what's wrong with you?"

She sat down. "Nothing. It's just that I thought that after everything Chip said, the jury would . . ."

"Jane, what are you talking about? The jury loved you. I think half of them want to go home with you. There was nothing Chip Bancroft could say that would change that."

In fact, what had sealed things for the jury was Jane herself. Faced with a case where both sides have merit, the jury did what all juries do. They approached the verdict like a presidential election. There an undecided vote boils down to two things: trust and charisma. Who do you trust is telling you the truth, and whom would you prefer to have dinner with?

When the jury framed it that way, there was simply no contest. Mr. Bancroft was a rake, smearing Miss Spring's good name like that. But her they would trust with their own children. And talk about *charisma!* The women wanted to be Miss Spring; the men wanted to marry her. She was adorable! So stylish! Who can forget those fabulous pastel suits she wore? (And the legs!) It was like watching one of those Technicolor movies they show on cable.

They loved her. They would never let her down.

Jane Spring started to hyperventilate. She was so happy. She wouldn't have to move to Canada. They have blizzards all the time. Look what had happened in the last one.

"Congratulations, Jane." Chip sat down on the edge of the prosecution table. "I'm sure you know I'm going to appeal."

Jane folded her arms and said nothing. She didn't have to. Her face said it all.

Chip leaned in and whispered. Now was the time for damage control. There would surely be another trial; he had to diffuse her anger.

"Jane, you know I had to do that. You left me no choice," he said sheepishly.

"You swine. How dare you?" she said loud enough to turn heads.

Chip lowered his eyes and leaned in to Jane. His sad puppy routine always worked with women. "Come on, let me take you out for a little celebration drink," he said, putting his hand on her arm. Jane brushed it off. "Some place cozy so we can really get to know each other better."

Jane Spring slipped into her white coat with the fox trim, adjusted her hat and snapped shut her beauty case.

"That won't be necessary, Mr. Bancroft, thank you," she announced. "I already know everything I need to know about you and, frankly, that's nothing to celebrate."

36

Jesse had called Lawrence Park with the verdict, and by the time he and Jane had returned to the office, Lazy Susan had already been dispatched for supplies. Normally when an assistant district attorney won at trial, there would be beer and chips in the conference room. This was going to be different.

At Supervisor Park's instruction, Lazy Susan went by cab to a gourmet delicatessen ten blocks away and bought quiches, smoked salmon and canapés. He himself went to The White Lion and bought ten bottles of Cristal champagne, then slipped the manager a few bills to borrow a box of glass flutes.

If Jane had gone to the trouble of becoming Doris to win the trial, the least they could do would be to toast her in kind.

Graham was dispatched to buy flowers; Marcie was charged with setting up the table.

"I don't get it," Marcie told Lawrence

Park. "Why is Jane getting the special treatment?"

At six p.m. with their workday officially over, the entire Criminal Division made its way to the conference room. Expecting paper cups and bottles of beer, the sight of champagne flutes and canapés raised every eyebrow.

When Jane and Jesse arrived, the room burst into applause.

"Congratulations, Jane. Congratulations, Jesse."

Marcie put a glass of champagne in Jane's hand. "I'm having this champagne at my wedding, Jane. Tell me what you think," she said.

"Mmm, wonderful," Jane replied taking a sip. "This champagne is simply delicious."

Marcie beamed like a klieg light.

In a corner Graham had pulled Jesse off to one side. "Man, I can't believe what Bancroft pulled in court for his closing argument," said Graham.

"Listen, when he held up that photograph, I had a sudden urge to go the bathroom," Jesse whispered. "But then when he suggested some clandestine affair, I knew he was sunk."

"He really told the jury he and Jane had an affair?"

"Something sort of like that."

"Jesus, he really must have had no case."

"For the record, Jane told me that after they had had some meeting, he did show up drunk at her apartment, but she tossed him out."

"Yeah, and knowing Jane, she probably bypassed the door and threw him straight out the window."

"You know, I don't think so. I think this new Jane just used the door. And probably kept smiling the whole time."

The two lawyers laughed and high-fived each other.

"Speech. Speech. Speech," started a chorus of voices.

Everyone in the room stopped nibbling quiches and canapés and turned expectantly to Jane. They were all excited, convinced now that the trial was over that she would come clean about the Doris Day costume party.

"Thank you all for coming," Jane said, as breathy as ever. Lazy Susan edged her way over to Graham, positioning herself at his side.

"I would like to thank my cocounsel, Mr. Beauclaire, for assisting me. It was not an easy case, but the jury obviously examined the evidence carefully and did the right thing. And here we are! Thank you."

Jane bowed her head and stepped back. That was it? No, I'm dressed up like your grandmother because . . . No, the big secret behind my speaking like a sugarplum fairy is . . . No, I thought the jury needed to see me as Doris Day because . . . Nothing. Everyone exchanged looks with rolled eyes and raised eyebrows. What if this wasn't for the trial? Maybe Spring really is crazy?

"Why didn't she explain herself?" Graham asked.

"No idea," Jesse said, stunned. "Maybe she'll tell us later. Maybe she just doesn't want the whole department to know."

Lazy Susan looked desperately at Graham. "What if she never tells us? Then what's going to happen tomorrow? Is she coming to work like my old boss or my new one?"

"Oh, Jesus," said Graham. "I hadn't thought about that. I mean there's no question this Jane is nuts, but I'm in no hurry to have the sergeant major back in the office."

"*You're* in no hurry?" squealed Lazy Susan, gagging.

"Don't worry, Susan," Graham said in a deep mock superhero voice. "If the monster returns, I'll protect you," he declared, putting his arm around her. Susan's knees buckled.

"Oh, Susan, could you come help me for a minute?" Marcie beckoned. Lazy Susan, now also Helpful Susan, excused herself and decamped in the direction of Marcie's voice.

Graham watched her move across the room in a way he never had before. Lazy Susan was clad in a pale blue turtleneck and navy pencil skirt. He'd never noticed what a cute ass she had. Pretty face too, now that you could see it.

Nor had he realized before just *how* much fun they had together, even if it was all because of Jane Spring. When Susan returned, he'd ask if she wanted to have a bite on the way home. You know, to commiserate that this might be the last day of the cease-fire before the shelling begins again.

Marcie approached holding a tray of crackers topped with smoked salmon and Brie. She had ordered Lazy Susan to work the other side of the room.

"Have one, and tell me what you think. If you like them, I might add them to my wedding menu."

Jesse and Graham bit into one and

nodded approvingly. "Very good."

"It's final then. I'll tell the caterer."

"Tell the caterer what?" said Jane, approaching her colleagues.

"About these canapés."

Suddenly Marcie put down her plate and looked at Jane, casting her eyes over her slowly, starting at her feet and ending at her head.

"Something wrong, Marcie?" Jane asked, sweet as honey.

"Jane, did you cut your hair?"

Graham elbowed Jesse in the stomach.

"Why, yes, Marcie."

"Looks great, Jane. Really suits you. Who's your hairdresser? Maybe I'll do a trial run before my wedding."

With the cocktail party in full swing, Jane slipped into her office and picked up the phone to dial Mike Millbank. Officially, she wanted to thank him for his assistance with the trial. Unofficially, she wanted to hear his voice. Hear if he was still mad at her. Surely, she thought, he might take pity on her after hearing how Chip had humiliated her in court. If he wouldn't, she would have to try to broker some peace between them. Jane dialed five digits, then put the phone down. If he was still angry, an apology via telephone would hardly be as effective as contrition in person. No, she better go see him.

Jane slipped on her coat and hat and made her way quietly to the elevator. She didn't want anyone to see she was leaving her own party early. But she couldn't stay. Detective Millbank's shift finished at seven, and it was already six-thirty. If she missed him at work, that would be it.

She took a cab to the precinct. A light snow was starting to fall. At the front desk Jane made a point of sounding officious when announcing she was there to see the detective. She stood and waited, watching the second hand on the wall clock tick by. Soon she heard footsteps and frantically patted down her hair and rubbed her lips together.

"Jane?"

It was not Detective Millbank standing before her, but his partner, Detective Cruz.

"Hello," she said, extending her gloved hand.

"Congratulations. I heard you won one for the boys in blue."

"Yes, thank you."

"You're here to see Mike?"

"Yes, I did come to see Detective

Millbank. Is there a problem?"

"No. Other than the fact he's not here."

"Oh, I thought he worked until seven."

"He does. But he left early today."

Jane tried to hide her disappointment and look as chipper as possible.

"Gone to interview witnesses?"

"No. Sounded like a date. He said he was going to meet a woman."

"Oh, I see," said Jane as the color drained from her face. "Well, please tell him I stopped by. I just wanted to thank him for all his hard work on the case."

"Wow, I should call the papers. We don't get too many DAs coming round here to thank us."

"Well that's a pity."

"We think so."

Jane picked up her beauty case and turned toward the door.

"Good night."

"Good night, Jane."

Jane Spring wondered if Detective Cruz noted that she had turned white when he mentioned that Mike had left early to prepare for a date.

He did.

37

By the time the cab pulled up at Jane
Spring's apartment, the snow was starting
to thicken. A man was standing under an
umbrella in front of her building.

"Jane."

She jumped back.

"Jane, it's me. Mike Millbank."

"Oh, my goodness, Detective! You
scared me half out of my wits!"

Jane didn't have an umbrella, and the
snow was sticking to her hair and her
clothes. Mike Millbank moved forward to
cover her with his. They walked silently
into her building, stopping to shake themselves out in the lobby. Jane forced herself
not to smile. He's here! If he's here, he
can't be mad at me. Unless he's here to
yell at me in person.

Under the bright lights of the lobby, Jane
could see that Mike Millbank must have
gone home from work to change. He was
wearing his smart navy-blue suit, and just
looking at him destroyed her. He smelled
divine, all freshly showered and wearing af-

tershave. He *was* going on a date. She was just a pit stop on his way to meet the other woman.

"I," he said.

"I," she said.

"You first."

"No, you first."

The detective cleared his throat. "Jane, I came by because I wanted to thank you for winning the trial. It means a lot to me, and it means a lot to everyone in blue."

Jane was now in agony trying not to smile, and she failed all the same. A slight smirk crept across her face. He's thanking me!

"You're very welcome, Detective."

"And I wanted to apologize. I misjudged you. You gave the trial one hundred percent, and I see that now."

Jane tilted her head to one side.

"I have made reservations for dinner."

"Oh, I see. I won't keep you then."

"No, for us. To thank you properly."

Jane tilted her head again. "Dinner?"

"Yes, if you're free? You've had dinner before haven't you, Jane?"

"Why, of course, Detective. But not with you."

"Well, I hope we can change that."

"But I'm not dressed —"

"I know. You go and get changed; I'll wait here. We have time. The reservation is not until eight."

Jane looked at her watch. It was 7:10. She calculated she had half an hour to get changed. Jane Spring walked calmly to the elevator and stepped in. Once the doors were closed, she broke into a little Irish jig. When they opened on her floor, a supremely calm Jane Spring walked out.

The Tates had started early that night. They were already in full swing when Jane entered her apartment. Again it failed to bother her. If anything, she took it as a sign, a sign of things to come. Fingers crossed. Of course, she would have to be married first.

She surveyed her wardrobe and settled on a navy-blue cocktail dress (to match his suit), rhinestone dress clips, white pumps and the white fur stole.

Oh, my God, she thought. What am I thinking? He is a detective. He's probably taking me to Denny's. Cops love Denny's. Then again, he is wearing his best suit. So maybe not.

The phone rang and Jane stared at it. It was probably the general calling to say what time he would be arriving in New York that weekend. Soon after her visit, he had spun her a story about an old army buddy now living in the city whom he was meeting for a New Year's drink. But something told Jane there was no celebration planned, that most likely when she arrived at her father's hotel, his army pal — no doubt a military psychiatrist — would just happen to drop by, if he were not there already.

Yet Jane wasn't worried about this in the slightest. In fact, she was looking forward to it. She welcomed the opportunity to show the general she wasn't sick. She needed him to see once more that his daughter was no longer his good little soldier, but a real woman. Which she loved being. No psychiatrist could fix that. Who would want to?

But it wasn't her father, it was Alice, calling to see if the verdict was in yet. Jane had e-mailed her that she expected it shortly.

"Hi, Alice. We won. Isn't it delicious?"

"Excuse me? Did you just say the verdict was *delicious?* Jane, what's wrong with you? You're talking all weird again."

"Listen, Alice, I can't speak now. I'm getting dressed for dinner, and I haven't even started on my hair. Mike made reservations for eight o'clock," Jane said, loading fresh tissues into her bra and dabbing Chanel No. 5 behind her ears.

"Mike? Who's Mike?"

"My date tonight. I'll call you tomorrow."

Jane hung up, and three thousand miles away Alice stared again into the receiver. I know I said she had to do something, but I think this Doris woman is a terrible influence, she thought. She's ruining my best friend. Jane is becoming so *nice*.

Twenty-five minutes later a freshly coiffed and dressed Jane Spring reappeared in her building lobby. Detective Millbank was talking football with the doorman.

"You look beautiful."

"Thank you, Detective," Jane said, beaming.

"Please, call me Mike."

"Mike."

He opened his umbrella and walked Jane across the street to his unmarked police car.

He opened the passenger-side door for her, then walked around to slide in on the other side. His suit was now covered in snow.

"May I ask where we're going?" Jane asked sweetly, praying the answer wouldn't begin with a D.

"It's a surprise. But something tells me you'll like it."

Jane Spring and Mike Millbank drove in complete silence across town.

"There it is," he said, pointing to a restaurant at the end of the street where he had parked. That's where we're going."

Jane squinted through the windshield to see. She could make out that the first letter on the sign was a C. Well that was a relief. C.O. As they walked toward it, Jane started reading off the letters until she had assembled the whole word.

"Copacabana!" she screamed.

Mike Millbank looked very pleased with himself.

"I figured this was your sort of place."

"Oh, I've always dreamed of the Copa!" Jane screamed. In her movies, Doris went there all the time.

Inside, the maître d' led them to their table. If you blinked, Jane thought, you would think it was forty years ago. All the waiters wore cream tuxedos with black bow ties. A fourteen-piece band was playing — fifteen, if you counted maracas. Twenty tables were positioned around a huge dance floor, and all the drinks had little monkeys and umbrellas in them.

"Oooh, I love this place!" Jane squealed

as Mike pulled out her chair.

"I thought you might."

Mike and Jane ordered martinis. Jane smiled at Mike, and Mike smiled at Jane.

"Want to dance before dinner?"

"Oh, I'd love to."

Jane and Mike hit the dance floor. Thank God she'd taken that dance lesson. Mike Millbank pulled her so close she could feel his heart beating. Jane barely heard the music; she was so busy singing "Happy Birthday to Me" in her head. Jane and Mike danced two slow numbers without saying a word to each other, then sat down.

Their martinis were waiting for them. They both took a sip, then Mike Millbank leaned into Jane. A candle flickered between them.

"Jane, I really want to thank you again. And apologize. Even though I had my doubts, I see now you worked really hard on the trial."

"Thank you, Mike."

"But I do have one question about your legal strategy."

"Yes?"

Mike Millbank folded his arms the way he did when questioning a suspect.

"What's with the getup?"

"Excuse me?"

"The outfit. The shoes. The gloves. The voice. Your hair. *Why?*"

Jane Spring took another sip of her martini. And then for the first time in two weeks, she spoke in her *own* voice. Her own deep, firm, Jane voice. No froth, no bubble, no Doris.

"My God, my feet are killing me," she said, rubbing her calves. "Do you know what it is to wear high heels fifteen hours a day?"

Detective Mike Millbank broke into a huge grin. "So you're not crazy."

"No. Did you think I was?"

"Not for a second. But there are plenty of people who do."

"So I've gathered."

"Tell me why you did this."

Jane blushed. "You know why I did this. To win the trial. Everybody says so."

"Everybody but me. I don't think this had anything to do with the trial."

"Why not?" Jane was curious to see how smart the detective really was at being a detective. Nervous too.

"Jane, you're too smart a lawyer to need to resort to this kind of stunt. You could have won on the evidence alone."

"We don't know that."

"Jane. Level with me. Why?"

Jane Spring looked past Mike Millbank,

pretending to watch the band.

"I can't tell you. It's too embarrassing."

"I'm a cop, Jane. I listen to embarrassing stories for a living."

"Not like this."

"Try me."

Jane shook her head.

"Okay, if you don't want to tell me, I'll tell you."

Now Jane Spring was terrified.

"As a detective piecing together the evidence, I'd say you impersonated Doris Day because you were after something Doris had."

Jane nodded. Her eyes were still fixed on the band.

"And did you get it?"

Jane Spring turned and looked Detective Mike Millbank in the eye. "Yes, I think I did."

"I have to tell you, Jane, I really admire your resolve. I don't know too many women, barring psychopaths and serial killers, who would assume a new identity just to get something they wanted."

"A good soldier never retreats in the midst of battle. My father taught me that. He's a general. So once I started, I had to go all the way. Attack on all fronts until victory was mine."

"I see. So now that you've won your war, do you go back to the way you were?"

"I'd planned to, but now I'm not at all sure. I love being Doris. But I do miss Jane. I don't know; what do you think?"

Mike Millbank took Jane's hands in his. "I think maybe Jane and Doris in combination would be good. I like some of the Doris side of you, but I like the Jane parts too. See, Jane is smart. She's independent, she has her own mind, and she's passionate about her work. I like all those things in a woman. But Doris is patient, and kind, and Doris looks sexy in a skirt. You can be both, you know."

Jane Spring thought she would burst into tears. Yes, she could. And she would.

And best of all, he understood.

38

It had stopped snowing when they returned to Jane's building. With Christmas lights still in every window, her neighborhood looked like a winter wonderland. Jane held on to Mike for support as they crossed the street.

At the front door, she let go of his arm. "Well, thank you for a lovely evening, Mike," Jane said now in her sweetest, powder-soft Doris voice.

Mike Millbank rolled his eyes and laughed loudly. After two hours of Jane, she was back to her alter ego. As a detective, he should have seen that coming.

"Can I see you again, Jane?"

"I think that would be lovely, thank you."

"Can I kiss you good night, Jane?"

"I think that would be lovely too, thank you."

Mike wrapped his arms around Jane's waist, drew her toward him and kissed her. This feels just like when Rock kisses Doris at the end of the movie, Jane thought.

When they were done, Mike Millbank stroked her hair and softly whispered, "Can I come up?"

Jane Spring widened her eyes and a look of outrage fell across her face. Then she slapped the detective across his. Hard.

"I can't believe you asked that, Detective. I can't believe you would think a lady would allow you to come up to her apartment!"

Mike Millbank rubbed his cheek.

"I'm sorry, Jane. I don't know what came over me."

"Hmph. And you call yourself a gentleman."

Jane Spring stormed into her building and waited five seconds before turning around to see Mike Millbank still standing there.

She opened her mouth and her own voice came out.

"Just give me five minutes, Detective. I'm just going to change into something more comfortable."

About the Author

SHARON KRUM is a freelance journalist who writes for major fashion and news magazines around the world. Her first novel, *Walk of Fame*, was published in 2001. She lives in New York City.